DEADLY
FORCE

DEADLY FORCE

A LIZZIE SCOTT NOVEL

JONATHAN SHAPIRO

ANKERWYCKE

Cover design by Monica Alejo/ABA Publishing.
Interior design by Betsy Kulak/ABA Publishing.

Printed in the United States of America.

20 19 18 17 16   5 4 3 2 1

Library of Congress Cataloging-in-Publication Data

Names: Shapiro, Jonathan (Lawyer), author.
Title: Deadly force : a Lizzie Scott novel / Jonathan Shapiro.
Description: Chicago : American Bar Association, [2016]
Identifiers: LCCN 2015043294 | ISBN 9781634252751 (alk. paper)
Subjects: LCSH: Women lawyers—Fiction. | Civil rights lawyers—
    Fiction. | California—Fiction. | Legal stories.
Classification: LCC PS3619.H355976 D43 2016 | DDC 813/.6—dc23 LC
    record available at http://lccn.loc.gov/2015043294

Discounts are available for books ordered in bulk. Special consideration is given to state bars, CLE programs, and other bar-related organizations. Inquire at Book Publishing, ABA Publishing, American Bar Association, 321 N. Clark Street, Chicago, Illinois 60654-7598.

www.ShopABA.org

To my mother, who taught me to read,
and my father, who encouraged me to write.

"Police business," he said almost gently, *"is a hell of a problem. It's a good deal like politics. It asks for the highest type of men, and there's nothing in it to attract the highest type of men. So we have to work with what we get—and we get things like this."*

—RAYMOND CHANDLER, *THE LADY IN THE LAKE*

CHAPTER 1

The wind ripped down the San Bernardino Mountains.

It roared down the desert floor, kicking up dust devils, bending the mesquite and Joshua trees low, twisting their branches into weird shapes.

Under a yellow moon, the state road cut a black line into a dirty gray landscape. Two lanes in each direction, it took 30 miles off the trip from L.A. to Vegas. But it carried a bad reputation for head-on collisions.

Sleepy truckers made it a death trap. Local cops made it a speed trap. Smart drivers preferred the newer Interstate 15, a straight shot, five lanes in each direction.

Tonight the old road was almost empty.

A battered pickup was parked on the soft shoulder of the northbound lane. The letters spelling "Toyota" were scratched out so that just "YO" remained. It was rusted to the chassis. Red tape covered a busted taillight. The front bumper was tied on with rope.

A Dodge Charger blocked the lane behind the pickup. Even in park, its engine growled like a beast. Light bar flashing, siren wailing against the wind, the Charger's high beams and side swivel lit up the road in front of it like a stage.

There, in the light, Joe Rincon lay on his back in the middle of the road. Staring up at the sky, he couldn't put together how he got there or why it mattered.

Blood bubbled from his chest. He couldn't catch his breath. His guts felt like a bag of broken glass. An image flashed in his mind; his grandma was pacing up and down their small apartment, rubbing her hands together, looking worried.

He drifted into a stupor.

Now someone was bending over him, shining light in his eyes, asking something he couldn't understand. Rincon tried to move his head away, but it felt like the heaviest thing in the whole world.

Rincon's last thought was a memory. He was at his grandma's day care center, lying on a mat on the cold linoleum floor with the other kids for nap time, but he couldn't sleep.

He got up and walked into his grandma's room, the one she used as an office. She was asleep in her recliner. Her cigarette burned in the ashtray.

The little TV was on, volume low, showing a black-and-white movie. There was an old man on the screen.

He wore a work shirt, pants held up with a rope belt, and a battered hat. He stood in the desert. He looked like someone's grandpa or uncle.

But this old man was different. He wasn't worn out or sad. He was laughing, clapping his hands dancing so his boots kicked up little clouds of dirt.

That's what God looks like.

That *is* God.

Except now even that thought was dead and gone.

And so was Joe Rincon.

CHAPTER 2

John Paul Jones was not built for speed.

He had big, callused hands, and the thick body of someone used to operating heavy machinery. The impression served him well. People trusted farmers.

He lumbered up the outside concrete stairs, carrying a battered briefcase in one hand, and a bag full of grapefruits in the other. He stopped at the top of the landing to sniff the morning air.

God's waiting room, downtown Palm Springs, so quiet he could hear the timer click from a traffic light on an empty street.

He unlocked the front door.

Jones was always first to arrive. Often he was the only one. The Palm Springs satellite office was budgeted for two agents. For the last six years, his partner, Nancy Walsh, was on maternity leave four times.

Jones didn't mind. He felt good about keeping the Walsh kids in new shoes. Plus, he preferred to work alone; he could listen to his music. Not everyone loved Merle Haggard.

The FBI's office was in a strip mall above a nail salon. There was also a yogurt store. The Bank of America branch was robbed so often the tellers had Jones's number on speed dial. There was also the obligatory marijuana dispensary, the subject of much ribbing from the local DEA agents whose office was three blocks away.

Jones went through his usual morning routine; turning on the lights and coffee machine, hanging up his suit coat and studying the floor for any rat shit that accumulated over the evening. The 99-cent Chinese restaurant downstairs went out of business, but their most loyal customers remained.

He finished sweeping, put his briefcase on top of his cubicle desk, and took out case files and a gun. An ancient .38, the leather of its holster brown and cracked, it was carried by his father, himself an FBI man.

The Bureau could be sentimental. Jones wasn't the only second- or third-generation agent. Nor was he the only one who got an equipment waiver to carry a wheel gun instead of the standard semiautomatic. He locked the .38 in the top drawer of his desk and began to take the overnight messages off the phone.

It was the usual nonsense.

An elderly man said his neighbors were Islamic terrorists.

A defense lawyer talked about getting a cooperation deal for his hedge fund client.

The Personnel Office, J. Edgar Hoover Building, FBI headquarters, Washington, D.C., reminded all agents to fill out their health-care forms before the deadline passed.

His stomach rumbled. Just because he mentioned Lady—their Labrador—looked a little chubby, Jones's wife, Mary, put *him* on a diet.

He put the phone on speaker and began to peel a grapefruit. The tree put out a bumper crop which was too bad. Jones's stomach didn't tolerate grapefruit.

The tenth message sounded like a loser. The caller's voice was thick, slurry; a heavy smoker, an old drunk.

"I'm in custody."

Jones kept peeling.

Inmates used to call the FBI all the time. Back in the day, it was to threaten to kill the president. The goal was to get transferred out of a state prison and into a newer, nicer federal facility. For those serving long stretches, it was a good tactic. Judges always ran the time concurrently. So the move didn't add time to the sentence. It just improved the quality of the inmate's experience.

Congress got wise and passed a law. A prison sentence for threats against federal officials had to run *after* the state sentence was over, not at the same time; consecutively rather than concurrently.

The number of inmate calls fell. Now, if they phoned, it wasn't to confess, it was to complain. Their civil rights were being violated. They were innocent, wrongly convicted, mistreated. Most of it was hooey.

That's not why this guy was calling. "I want to make an anonymous tip," he said. "A cop murdered a kid. I saw him do it."

Jones stopped peeling.

He took the phone off the speaker to get a better listen. There was a steady electronic beep on the other end of the line, standard for inmate calls. It was there to remind them everything they said was being recorded and could be used against them. The beeps cut down on things like murder-for-hire schemes to take care of witnesses.

"The cop shot the kid for no reason, then just left him there in the road."

The caller paused, like he was trying to remember something, or maybe he was debating whether to go through with it. Jones counted. After the tenth beep, the man spoke again.

"This was six or seven months ago, I can't remember exactly. It was out on that old stretch of road by the Union 76 station."

The man covered the phone with his hand. When he came back again, his voice was a low, raspy whisper.

"This cop is going to kill me." The voice rose to a whine, a scared animal. "Oh, man, I can't handle this shit. . . ."

There was a long pause. Then the man hung up.

Jones checked the message's time stamp. The call came in at 5:38 A.M., a few minutes before Jones arrived. He just missed it.

The caller never gave his name.

CHAPTER 3

Lizzie Scott stood in the middle of the ring snapping razor-sharp leads off the face of a fighter named Frankie Duarte.

A ribbon of blood trickled out of Duarte's nose. Sweat burned his eyes. He was starting to think sparring with Lizzie was a bad idea.

The gym's owner was a former heavyweight gone to fat. He waddled over to where Jones was watching the action.

"Can I help you?"

"I can't see how," Jones said. "Somebody ought to call a cop. That poor guy is getting creamed in there."

Duarte tried to bob out of Lizzie's way. She caught him anyway. He threw a left to slow her down. She pivoted on her front leg, leveraged her weight behind a right cross, and smashed it into the side of his face. Duarte saw black stars cut shapes into a gauzy sky.

"*Time!*" the trainer yelled.

Lizzie bounced back to her corner fresh as when they began.

Duarte spat out his mouthpiece then had to fish around for it on the dirty canvas. He draped his arms over the top rope, shook his head clear, and tried to figure out how shit like this always seemed to happen to him.

He remembered. The gym owner promised to write off Duarte's overdue locker fees if he went four rounds with her.

"Is she pro?" Duarte didn't want to mess with one of those MMA fighters. The owner assured him Lizzie was an amateur. "I don't know," Duarte said. "I don't want to hit a woman."

"Then don't. Just dance around, give her a taste; otherwise, she wants her money back."

Lizzie was a tall, big-boned girl. With her ponytail and a sweat-drenched tank top, she looked like a college kid. Duarte, a natural bantamweight, was giving up height and quite a few pounds, but it wasn't like she was some kind of bodybuilder.

The owner never mentioned she was a southpaw.

"*Time!*" the trainer yelled.

Lizzie came out firing—*pop, pop, pop*—her long reach making it impossible for Duarte to punch over her right hand.

Never fight a lefty. Everything is backwards. Duarte couldn't slide toward her without stepping on her big foot, and he couldn't get out of her way. She kept cutting off his escape, using her long stride to keep him right where he was.

"*Mix it up!*" the trainer yelled.

She tossed a massive overhead behind her lead then followed it with an uppercut which caught Duarte somewhere between his neck and chin.

"Not *you*, Lizzie," the trainer yelled. "*Duarte! You mix it up!*"

Duarte no longer had any qualms about hitting a woman. He had been trying for the last four rounds. He couldn't reach her.

"*Time!* That's it."

Duarte stumbled out of the ring toward the locker room. The owner draped a dingy gray towel around his neck.

"Thank you!" Lizzie called out after him. "That was really fun!"

Duarte never looked back. The last anyone heard, he moved his training to a gym in El Monte, then quit boxing altogether to become a roofer.

"Hey, champ," Jones said. "That wasn't very nice, you beating up that guy."

Lizzie pressed a gloved hand to her nostril and blew snot onto the floor.

"Oh, sorry," she said, embarrassed.

Jones apologized for bothering her on a Sunday.

Once a month, each Assistant U.S. Attorney has to do a rotation as weekend prosecutor, on 24-hour call to handle emergencies. Jones seemed to think this was Lizzie's weekend. It wasn't. Davey Berg was the duty assistant this weekend.

"I need a warrant to spring a witness from county jail."

Lizzie squeezed her ponytail through her gloves to get the sweat out and shook it back into place. "No problem," she said. "But if you want to get an inmate out of county jail, what you need is a *writ*, not a warrant."

Jones played sheepish and smacked his forehead with his palm. "A writ, I should know that. Thanks."

Lizzie Scott told him she'd be a minute.

She headed toward the owner's office, the only room in the place with a door. The owner let her use it as a changing room.

He was afraid she'd sue him if he didn't.

She was nice about it. He liked her okay, but sometimes he wished she'd find another hobby or maybe just blow out a knee.

CHAPTER 4

Lizzie hit the street in her weekend uniform: jeans, plain white tee, beat-up sneakers, and an old-school, periwinkle blue Angels baseball cap.

Jones stood by his Crown Vic.

"So," she asked, "who's the guy we're getting out jail?"

"His name is Henry 'Hoot' Scanlon."

"Hoot?"

"No idea," Jones said, opening the passenger door for her. "You can ask him yourself when you talk to him."

She hesitated.

"I'll buy you breakfast. You got to be hungry."

Lizzie was always hungry.

"I'll follow you."

She headed down the street, gym bag over her shoulder, and disappeared around the corner. Jones thought she ditched him. She did things like that. That was part of her charm, if you found that sort of thing charming.

A few moments later, her black Pontiac G8 squealed around the corner. He jumped into his car, catching her as she made the turn onto 17th Street.

Lizzie always drove fast and alone. It gave her time to think. Right now she was thinking about Jones.

He was the best FBI agent in the Inland Empire. He acted like everyone's goofy uncle, but he was a dogged investigator and a great interrogator. He was also tough, the last man standing in an infamous gun battle years ago with a carjacking suspect.

Yet if a case file showed up with his name on it, Lizzie handed it off to someone else.

She didn't entirely trust Jones. He was sneaky smart, much smarter than he pretended to be. She didn't believe for a second he forgot the difference between a writ and a warrant, or that he really thought Berg was on duty this weekend.

All good investigators are manipulative. It wasn't fair to judge him for it. The real reason she avoided Jones was personal.

He knew things about her.

Nobody else did. She kept a strict separation between the personal and the professional. Her privacy and her past belonged to her. She shared with no one.

Except with Jones, but only because she had no other choice.

When Lizzie was hired to be a prosecutor, but before she could start the job, she had to go through a security background check.

Every prosecutor does. It is designed to be thorough. Before a lawyer is allowed to wield prosecutorial power, they must be judged themselves. It's only fair. Few people can do more justice—or cause more grief—than an Assistant U.S. Attorney.

If the background check feels invasive, it's meant to be. Before "don't ask, don't tell," when being gay was still considered a reason to deny someone a security clearance, some new prosecutors faced a choice. Tell the truth and maybe lose your job or lie. If they caught you, you could lose the job *and* maybe face prosecution for perjury. Either there were no gay federal prosecutors before the Clinton Administration or a lot of good people looked the other way.

Lizzie had to list every address she ever lived at, the names of the people she lived with, the schools she went to, the jobs she had, the drugs she took. Then she signed it under oath. FBI agents went out to check if she lied or left anything out.

For weeks, she got calls from old friends, ex-lovers, favorite professors, teammates on her high school and college basketball teams, distant relatives:

"Lizzie," they would say, worried. "The FBI was just here."

The process takes weeks if everything goes smoothly. If the FBI finds an inconsistency, they demand more information, more interviews. The new prosecutor's start date can be delayed weeks, months, a year, forever.

Jones was assigned Lizzie's background interview.

They sat alone in the office. His partner was having another kid. Lizzie stared at the wall art, exhibits from past trials, blown-up photos of bank robbers, a crate of AK-47s, a burned out PCP laboratory in an empty desert.

Jones had her application, the interviews with her family and contracts; he hated to pry but certain issues had to be addressed if she wanted the job.

"Here's the deal," Jones said. "I'm a straight shooter about this stuff. So why don't we cut out the preliminaries and get right to it."

"Tell me about your church."

Lizzie told Jones about Convocation.

It wasn't a cult, she explained. It was worse than that.

He never asked for more information, never used what he knew against her, never told anyone else about it, at least as far as she knew. For three years, he maintained her secrecy without even being asked.

She owed him for that.

She sensed he had come to collect.

She just hoped the chit wasn't too big.

CHAPTER 5

THE WAITRESS WALKED THEM TO A BOOTH. TWO SANTA ANA TRAFFIC cops were sitting on the other side of the divider. Jones smiled and nodded at them, then quietly asked the waitress for a different table.

They ordered. Jones slid a file across the table.

"You ever handle a murder case?"

He knew she hadn't. Most prosecutors never would, especially not in the U.S. Attorney's Office. Federal prosecutors drive the heaviest machinery the government owns, but they don't take it out of the garage very often. When they do, it isn't to charge murder.

Lizzie stared at the file. "Looks kind of thin."

"Yeah," Jones said, "but what's there is choice."

Lizzie took a sip of coffee. Instinct told her she didn't want this case. "What's the hook?"

Jones lowered his voice. "The killer was a cop."

Murder is mostly a local matter, crime work for cops and D.A.s. Congress has to pass a law to make a federal case out of it. Murder of the president and a long list of other officials is federal. So is murder on federal land. It happens more than you might think. Murder committed by certain groups—terrorists, drug dealers, the Mafia—can also be federal, thought it doesn't have to be.

When a cop commits murder while he's doing his job, it's a federal crime, too; the granddaddy of all civil rights violations. It takes away due process, equal protection under the law, the right to be free from cruel and unusual punishment, and every other right you can name, now and forever. Amen.

Lizzie took another sip of coffee.

She was only three years on the job. She was off Rookie Row, the offices reserved for new prosecutors, but hardly seasoned. She had 11 trials under her belt, was undefeated, but none of them had been that tough.

Murder cases against cops are poison. Controversial to bring, harder to win, and a lot of cops and agents never forgive you for going after one of their own.

Whenever a cop shooting makes the media, the talking heads on cable ask why prosecutors don't do something about it. The simple answer is that prosecutors don't like losing any more than anybody else. Unlike other lawyers, they are expected to win pretty much every case they bring. Otherwise, why bring them at all?

Jones noticed Lizzie hadn't touched the file.

"The kid was unarmed," he said. "He was minding his own business, driving home after work. He gets pulled over by a cop and the cop shoots him dead. Now, does that sound right to you?"

Jones must have a reason to bring this to her it, but she couldn't figure out what it was.

"Did I mention we have an eyewitness?" he pushed. "That's the guy I need the writ for. The guy saw the whole thing. The cop didn't even know the guy was out there."

Lizzie still didn't pick up the file.

Jones played his last card.

"You know what's wrong with your office?"

She didn't bite. Whatever complaints she had about her office stayed there. She had no respect for a player who bitched about her own teammates.

Jones noticed and liked it.

"Okay, not wrong, exactly," he walked it back a little. "Maybe it's good they're cautious. Maybe it's better they don't rush into things. But sometimes it seems like nobody has any guts over there. They're afraid to lose a case."

The waitress brought their order. Lizzie dug into her enormous stack of pancakes. Jones picked at his half grapefruit.

"Is that all you're eating?"

"My wife's decision." Jones tapped the file. "Look, it isn't like you *can't* win this thing. So long as the eyewitness holds up."

Lizzie put her fork down, dabbed at her mouth with a napkin, and crossed her arms. "I give up. Why would you bring this to me? Seriously. You should take this to somebody with more experience."

Jones laughed.

"Do you think anybody with experience would *touch* this case? Do you think Davey Berg would get anywhere *near* this case?"

Davey Berg was a senior prosecutor best known for emceeing roasts of departing prosecutors. He spent the rest of his time reading history books. On paper, Berg was Lizzie's supervisor but he let her do what she wanted. It was easier for him. The sign on his office wall read:

"Mieux vaut demander pardon que permission."

"Let me tell you something about Davey Berg," Jones said. "Back in *my* office, we say *your* office is like *The Wizard of Oz*. Everyone over there is missing something: a brain, a heart. Davey's the Cowardly Lion: nice man, no courage."

"He's not that nice," Lizzie said. "Who am I?"

"Dorothy. If Dorothy was hard to work with."

Lizzie flashed angry.

Jones held up his hands. "The word is, you have a complicated personality."

Lizzie stopped herself from asking what that meant.

"Anyhow," Jones said. "I waited to bring you something worth doing."

"Why?"

"It's time you moved up in class, handled something big. Get yourself transferred up to the L.A. office. Get out from behind the Orange Curtain."

She took the file.

"I'll call you about the writ."

Jones thanked her.

"Say hello to your folks for me," he said. "And Sarah."

He knew about Sarah?

It was like he was stalking her.

CHAPTER 6

LIZZIE SAT CROSS-LEGGED ON HER BED WITH THE FILE MATERIAL spread out in front of her.

There wasn't much there.

No crime-scene photos, no autopsy reports, no personnel file on the police officer involved in the shooting.

Until Jones was sure he had a prosecutor on board, he wouldn't ask for them. Because the day he did, the news would whip around the law enforcement community, fraying relationship between the feds and the locals, stirring up a massive shit storm.

Jones's initial FBI 302 investigation report was only half a page long. It described the anonymous tip on the FBI phone line and named Henry "Hoot" Scanlon, 45, Inland County, as the tipster.

How did Jones get the name of an anonymous tipster?

Lizzie jotted a note to remember to ask Jones about it.

There were three news articles from the *Inland County Recorder*.

The first article ran the night after Joe Rincon died.

SUSPECT IN KNIFE ATTACK KILLED BY POLICE

A man who allegedly attacked a Blanton Police Department officer with a knife during a routine traffic stop was shot and killed Thursday evening.

The victim's identity was withheld pending notification of the next of kin. By law, the media couldn't identify the officer until the department said they could. The badge carries its own bill of rights.

Bodhi jumped on the bed and curled up in her lap, wanting attention.

Lizzie yelled at Sarah: "Could you please walk the dog?" Sarah yelled from the kitchen that she would just be a minute. She was making cookies for tomorrow's Convocation service.

Lizzie was in training for a bout in two weeks and couldn't eat cookies. The smell was killing her.

"Why does she have to bake so much?" Lizzie asked the dog. The dog yawned.

The second *Recorder* article was dated a week after the first.

SUSPECT IN KNIFE ATTACK WAS EX-CON

This article identified Rincon and ran an old booking photograph. It showed the face of an awkward, confused looking boy. The article claimed Rincon had been convicted of assault with intent to kill.

Lizzie checked Rincon's file's rap sheet. He was once *arrested* for *simple* assault. He wasn't *convicted* of anything.

It no longer surprised her. Every article she read about one of her own cases contained at least one major error.

She made a note to find out the details of Rincon's arrest.

The last article was the longest of the three.

OFFICER CLEARED IN SUSPECT'S DEATH

This one carried the byline of crime reporter Lizzie knew.

"The Inland County District Attorney's Office has cleared a Blanton police officer of wrongdoing in last October's shooting death of Joe Rincon. During a routine traffic stop, Rincon became violent and attempted to stab the officer with a knife."

The article showed a copy of a crime-scene photograph. The knife lay in a chalk circle on the road next to an orange evidence cone. Its curved blade was shorter than the light wood handle. Lizzie's father had one just like it. It was small; good for cutting floor tile.

"The officer involved in the shooting was identified as senior patrolman Dwayne Wayne Lee, a five-year veteran of the Blanton Police Department."

There was no mention of Rincon's family.

There was also no mention of an eyewitness.

Bodhi, who never barked, let out a polite "urf." Meaning he needed to go out. Now.

"Sarah!" she yelled. "Walk the dog!"

Lizzie loved her privacy and hated having a roommate. But Sarah needed a place to stay. You don't say no to your best friend.

Bodhi jumped off the bed and began to scratch at the door.

"I'm coming," Sarah yelled. "Just taking out the last batch. You want some?"

"Do *not* bring cookies in here!"

Lizzie looked at Officer Dwayne Wayne Lee's DMV records and photo. He was six months older than she was. He had brown hair and light brown eyes. There was nothing interesting about his face except his mouth. Thin lips, drawn tight, they seemed to be on the verge of turning into a sneer.

Or was she projecting that?

Sarah came in holding a plate of cookies and a glass of milk. Her long curly hair was tied back with a sock. Wisps and ringlets framed her face. "Are you hungry?"

Lizzie tried not to sound mad. "Sarah, do you remember I told you I'm in training?"

"Oh, no! I'm so sorry, I totally forgot." Sarah spun back toward the kitchen to hide the cookies and milk. "I think Bodhi had an accident."

Lizzie cleaned it up.

You had to love Sarah. Lizzie tried not to. It couldn't be helped.

Sarah had a perfect figure but never worked out, the warmest heart and shortest attention span of any human being alive. She was sweet, kind, and made promises she meant to keep but then forgot. Lizzie never knew anyone with a purer character or less confidence. From the time they were 10 years old, she caused Lizzie all kinds of trouble but never wanted anything but the best for her.

There was nothing Lizzie could do. She loved Sarah. They grew up together, Convocation girls, raised to be followers, pressured to conform. Lizzie rebelled. Sarah didn't. Lizzie could never decide whether that was because Sarah wasn't strong enough or because she was too kind to hurt those around her. Not that it mattered. Lizzie would never give up trying to free Sarah from Elder Evans.

Lizzie grabbed Bodhi, a leash, a yellow legal pad and pen, and headed for the front door. While the dog ran free in the park, Lizzie made her daily to-do list.

Meet Hoot Scanlon.

Meet Rincon's family.

Meet with the Inland D.A.

FIND SARAH AN APARTMENT.

CHAPTER 7

THE U.S. ATTORNEY'S SATELLITE OFFICE WAS CHEAP OFFICE SPACE in low-rent Santa Ana. The building started life as a corrupt savings and loan. Seized by the feds, it had the same yellowing white paint, filthy carpets, and marked-up walls from the 1980s. Only the bullet-proof glass and concrete barricades were new.

Across the street, the sun shone on the newer, state-of-the-art Reagan Courthouse. Its courtrooms were empty most of the time. Nobody seemed to want to go to trial anymore.

Lizzie walked past Davey Berg's office.

"Lazard," Berg said in a Pepé Le Pew French accent. "Comment puis-je vous être utile?"

Berg was reading Simon Schama's *Citizens*, an enormous history of the French Revolution. He'd been working through it for the last few weeks instead of working on his cases. Berg enjoyed being a midlevel bureaucrat.

Lizzie asked if he would handle arraignment court for her. "I'm going to meet an eyewitness."

"What kind of a case?"

She told him. He shuddered.

"What does Jones have on you?" Berg asked, then changed his mind. "Wait, don't tell me. I don't want to know. Whatever it is, it must be appalling."

· · ·

Two hours later, Lizzie and Jones were in the middle of the desert.

Because he said she had a reputation for being hard to work with, she agreed to drive with him, and even to let him have the wheel. They'd pulled off the freeway miles back. They were now on a two-lane desert road. They hadn't seen another car in half an hour.

"You'd never find this guy on your own," Jones said.

"How'd you find him? The guy was an anonymous tip."

Jones was hoping she would ask. "First thing I did, I fired up the computer and typed in 'shooting, dead, Southern California, highway, and police.'"

Articles describing 10 police shootings over the last two years came up. They had all been deemed justified kills. None resulted in the prosecution of the police.

Jones started with the most recent one. It involved a cop from the City of Blanton and the old state highway. Jones once worked a crash on that road, helping the CHP catalog seized guns from the back of an overturned trailer. He even filled up at that gas station.

"But it hasn't been a Union 76 for a long time. It's a Valero now." Which made Jones think the tipster was a long-time local, someone who had been around back before the station changed owners.

The caller's accent was definitely local, Southern California by way of the Dust Bowl; the twang of folks whose folks came out with the Joads. Meaning he was white. Jones guessed his age as 35 to 50, maybe older, definitely not younger.

Jones called the local county inmate information lines, punching through the computer directories until he got to live deputies, putting together a list of possibilities.

He cut out the white collars. His tipster didn't sound like a banker. He also eliminated big-time dopers and gang-bangers. They would never tip the FBI under any circumstances, at least not on a recorded phone line.

Jones whittled the list down to 135 suspects.

"A pretty sorry bunch of hombres," he admitted. "But that's who calls in tips."

They were in custody for arson, murder, domestic violence, DUI, public intoxication, shoplifts, burglaries, and grand thefts.

Jones cut out the killers. The guy hadn't sounded hard enough. He also took out the child molesters. "I'm prejudiced that way," Jones said. "Plus, in county, they'd be in isolation to keep them from the other guys, which means no access to the phones in the main holding area."

Eventually, Jones worked his list down to nine guys who lived around Blanton and met all the other factors. "Hoot was the fifth one I talked to."

Jones pulled off on an unpaved road.

"I think you'll like him. He's different."

They parked near an abandoned campsite.

"We got to walk from here."

Lizzie stepped out of the car and into the broiling heat.

"Watch out for the rooster," Jones said. "Hoot says he's a rescue, but I don't know that fighting birds can retire. You might have to fight him."

CHAPTER 8

BROKEN TOILETS LINED A PATH THROUGH SCRUB TO AN OLD TRAILER. It sat at an angle on uneven concrete blocks.

Henry "Hoot" Scanlon stood in the doorway wearing filthy hospital scrubs, souvenirs from one institution or another.

"Go away," he croaked. "I'm not talking with you."

He was a sunburnt, prune of a man: a desert rat with the bad luck to see what happened to Joe Rincon and the bad judgment to send in a tip about it.

"Sorry, Henry," Jones said. "No take backs. Anyhow, I'll just testify I recognized your voice from the call. And I'm going to get the jail tape."

Jones walked toward him.

Scanlon stepped back into his trailer like a dog afraid of getting hit. "Get the hell off my land! I didn't give you consent to come on my land!"

"We've been through this, Henry," Jones said. "This is not your property, it's unincorporated county. You need a permit to be here. You don't have a permit."

Scanlon cursed under his breath.

"Mr. Scanlon?" Lizzie said, smiling. Jones was always surprised how pretty she was when she smiled.

"My name is Lizzie Scott. I'm a federal prosecutor. I work with Mr. Jones."

Scanlon jerked his head up and down and shrugged and rubbed his hand through his hair making it stand up in different directions.

"Yeah, Jones told me you'd come."

"May I ask you a question, Mr. Scanlon? Would that be okay?"

Scanlon muttered, "Okay," suddenly shy, unable to look at her.

"Why do they call you Hoot?"

Scanlon scratched his chest. "Because I don't sleep," he said. "Like an owl."

"That's good," Lizzie smiled. "I was afraid it was because you were crazy."

Scanlon shrugged and squinted and admitted some people thought he was.

Jones put his head past Scanlon to have a look inside the trailer. The reek almost made him gag. "Well, Hoot, I guess we can talk out here."

Scanlon leaned toward Jones to whisper. It came out loud. Living out there alone messed with his volume control. "You didn't tell me she looked like this."

"Like how?" she asked.

"Good," he said. "I like big women. Healthy, I mean. You could be a stripper."

He meant it as a compliment.

"Hoot," Jones leaned close to Scanlon and sniffed. "You're drunk."

Scanlon just shrugged. "I never said I wasn't."

Prosecutors don't get to choose who their eyewitnesses are going to be. Fate does. You win with what you get.

"Mr. Scanlon," Lizzie said. "Can we buy you something to eat?"

Scanlon said that would be okay. And she could call him "Henry."

They packed him into Jones's car and left the windows open. They landed at an Arby's off the 5 Freeway. Jones went to order. Lizzie snagged a table.

"Maybe you should go wash up," she suggested.

Scanlon staggered toward the men's room.

Less than a minute later, he came back, headed for the exit.

"Where're you going?"

"I can't piss in there. It's too clean. Don't want to mess it up."

She walked him to the gas station next door.

Three roast beef sandwiches and lots of coffee later, Scanlon was within sight of sober.

"I could eat about a million of these," he said. "Food doesn't usually agree with me. Must be the company."

Scanlon had *some* social skills. Clean him up, he could work out. Maybe.

Jones told Scanlon to tell Lizzie what he saw the night of the shooting.

CHAPTER 9

SCANLON SPENT THE NIGHT CAMPED UNDER A PLASTIC TARP, HARD up against a drainage abutment, right off the state highway. "Some of my shit is still there, probably."

Jones already checked. There was nothing there.

The reason Scanlon was out there was because the inside of his trailer caught fire the week before. He was letting it air out. He remembered the night was so windy he had to find extra stones to weigh the tarp down. He was almost asleep when he heard a siren.

"Not like it was moving, like it was right there in front of me."

He scrabbled up the small rise to the highway then flattened himself onto the ground. Maybe 30 yards away, he saw an old pickup and a cop car pointing north.

Scanlon grabbed a mustard packet off his tray and put it on the table. "This here is the cop car."

Scanlon put a ketchup packet in front of the cruiser and to the right of it. "This ketchup is the beaner mobile."

Jones gave him the look: We will have none of that.

"Okay, the pickup then. They were like that, right in front of me."

Lizzie asked about the light.

"It was lit up real good. The cop had his lights on."

Scanlon pointed at the ketchup packet/pickup. "The kid's here, still in the pickup, scared shitless, trying like hell to open his door. But he can't. The goddamn thing won't open. Rusted piece of shit, probably it's jammed, I don't know. The kid's got his hands on the window, pressing against it."

Lizzie asked where the officer was.

Scanlon pointed back at Rincon's pickup. "The cop is standing next to the pickup's window. He's trying to pull the door open, too, to get the kid out of there."

Lizzie drew a quick sketch of the scene on a napkin. She used Greek symbols to show where the cars were. Pi was Rincon, delta was Officer Lee: legal shorthand for plaintiff/victim and defendant.

Scanlon said he was facing the pickup and Rincon. The cop's back was to him, but angled so he could see what he was doing with his hands. Lizzie made a cross on the sketch, shorthand for witness, to show where Scanlon was.

"After awhile, I hear this sharp metal snap, loud, and the pickup door flies open. It sends the cop flying back. He lands right on his ass. You believe that?"

"I don't know yet," Lizzie said, pushing him to see how he took it. "Is any of what you're saying true?"

Scanlon jerked his head up and down, agitated. "I seen it *myself*, I swear to God!" His voice was rising. "Once the door's open, the kid steps out of the pickup with his hands right up in the air."

Without being asked, Scanlon shot out of the booth, stood next to the table, hands in the air, fingers wide. The other customers stared.

"The kid's like this, okay?" Scanlon was now yelling. "He's just like this. And he looks scared, you understand?"

"I got it," Lizzie said quietly. "Come on back to us, Henry."

Scanlon sat down and put his hands on the table to stop them from shaking. "I get wound up sometimes."

Lizzie took a beat to let him catch his breath. "Okay, then, Henry, go on. You got the kid outside the pickup, with his hands up . . ."

Scanlon nodded and kept his voice low, as if he were afraid Lee was listening.

"The cop is *pissed off.* You don't *ever* embarrass a cop like that. The cop scrambles up to his feet and yanks that big old flashlight out of his belt and POW. He whacks the kid in the head with it. But I mean *hard*. It knocks the kid a couple of feet forward."

Jones passed Lizzie an inventory report from the Inland Sheriff's investigation. It listed all the equipment Lee had on his tool belt the night of the shooting. Lee signed it under oath, swearing it was true and accurate.

There was no flashlight on the list.

"Henry, are you sure it was a flashlight? Could it have been, say, a baton?" Lizzie asked.

Scanlon got angry. "I just told you, it was flashlight! Listen to me!"

The people in the next booth scurried to another table. Scanlon didn't notice.

Lizzie put her hand on Scanlon's.

"Henry, buddy," her voice was sweet. "When we talk about this, and we're going to have to talk about this, *a lot,* you need to calm down, and you need to use your indoor voice. Can you do that?"

Scanlon stared at her hand on his and mumbled he would try.

"The thing is," he said, back to whispering, "when a cop hits you like that, what he's saying to you is, get down and *stay* down. But this kid didn't do it. He was woozy, like he was out on his feet, but he wouldn't go down."

Lizzie knew what that was like. In her first bout, the girl caught her with a shot just as the bell rang. Lizzie suddenly heard the sound of the ocean in her head and couldn't get her legs to move. The referee had to lead her back to her corner.

"Did the officer say anything? 'Get on the ground' or something?" Lizzie asked.

Scanlon thought so, maybe, he wasn't sure. He couldn't hear over the wind. "I was thinking he was going to smack the kid with the flashlight again, but he didn't. He put it back in his belt. Then he took out his gun."

"How far away were they from each other?" she asked.

Scanlon thought maybe 15 feet.

"The kid starts swaying, like he's finally going down. He tries to stop himself, keep his balance, like when you're drunk, you know? He takes a step, like to his side . . ."

Scanlon squeezed his eyes tights and shook his head, trying to get rid of the memory.

"That's when the cop shot him," Scanlon said, still unable to quite believe it himself. "When he took that step to the side. That was it." Scanlon's chin dropped to his chest. "I wish I hadn't seen it."

He was crying.

Lizzie wiped a paper napkin over the table to give him time to calm down.

* * *

SCANLON SAID THAT AFTER THE SHOOTING, HE DIDN'T SEE ANY point to sticking around. He scrambled back to his burned-out trailer and his two gallons of Stater Brothers store brand vodka.

"I got drunk, but I couldn't black out. I tried. Every time I fell asleep, I'd see the cop standing over me. I tried to tell him I didn't see anything, I've been here at the trailer the whole time. But the cop couldn't hear me, because it was so fucking windy."

The chemical and charcoal smell of burned upholstery and cheap wood paneling made him retch, but he stayed in the trailer for days, he wasn't sure how many. He only left when he'd run out of vodka and food.

"I'm kind of paranoid most of the time," Scanlon said, staring into his coffee. "Seeing that kid get killed put me right smack over the edge."

Lizzie checked her notes. "You're on probation, right? Shoplifting?" Scanlon blinked at her, confused. "You had to report to your P.O. at some point, right?"

That connected some scrambled wire in Scanlon's brain. "Yeah, that's right. That's another reason I left."

He walked the mile and half to the mini mart to use their phone, his head on a swivel, sure that at any moment a cop bullet would rip into his back.

His probation officer told him he had Cal-Trans trash road crew the next day.

Scanlon gave Lizzie a crazy grin. "He was telling me I had to go back out to the fucking highway! If I didn't report, the P.O. would violate me. I'd end up doing the whole 90-day sentence in county. How's that for fucking karma?"

Too upset to go back to his trailer, he hung around the mini mart cadging cigarettes and change from the drivers, reading the local dailies yellowing in the racks. He didn't see anything about the dead kid, but that just meant the cop covered the whole thing up.

The Korean woman who owned the place had enough. "Buy or go!" Scanlon yelled, squinting his eyes as he impersonated her.

Lizzie gave him a stare that could've burned paper.

Scanlon whined defensively. "Hey, I'm telling the truth. That Korean bitch hates me because I'm white. You should go fucking investigate her on civil rights shit—"

Jones laid a giant paw on Scanlon's skinny shoulder. "We'll have none of that, Henry." Jones gave the shoulder enough of a squeeze to make Scanlon wince.

Scanlon said he finally bought a gallon of water and a gallon of vodka. "You buy. *Now* you go!" Scanlon said in his high-pitched version of the Korean woman.

"I kind of lost it." Scanlon grabbed a handful of beef jerky and ran. He was almost home when a Blanton police cruiser pulled up next to him.

"I fucking shit my pants," Scanlon admitted. "I'm serious."

Fortunately, Lee wasn't behind the wheel.

"It was some black guy," Scanlon said. "Some big fucking black guy."

The cop didn't want to take Scanlon in any more than Scanlon wanted to be taken. The cop didn't even want to put Scanlon in his car. But neither of them had a choice. Scanlon had warrants on top of the Korean woman's shoplift complaint.

He eventually entered a guilty plea to the shoplift and drew a three-month sentence.

Two months after he got out, he failed to report to his P.O. then missed a meeting, and was picked up on a probation violation. This time, the sentence was a full year, which didn't make any sense at all to him. "Hell, I used to get less time for burglary."

Scanlon used his one call to leave the message with the FBI.

"How'd you know our number?" Jones asked.

Scanlon said it was listed on the Inland County booking room bulletin board.

"You're pretty smart, Henry," Lizzie said. "And observant."

Scanlon shrugged. "I do stupid shit, sometimes, but that doesn't mean I'm stupid."

On the drive home, Lizzie told Jones she believed Scanlon was telling the truth, but they were going to need as much physical evidence as they could find to back him up.

She gave Jones subpoenas to get Lee's personnel file.

CHAPTER 10

THE INLAND COUNTY DEPUTY D.A.'S OFFICE WAS BETTER FURNISHED than Lizzie's. His salary was bigger, too; most D.A.s were paid better than the U.S. Attorney's Office.

Dan Seave was a florid man with a beer gut and easy smile. He disliked the federal government on general principle. He didn't take it out on Lizzie and Jones, though, even if they were there to second-guess his decision on the Rincon shooting.

"I'm surprised you guys have time for this," Seave said. "It was kind of an open-and-shut deal. Officer Lee had to shoot the guy. The guy had a knife."

Were Rincon's fingerprints on the knife?

"Yes and no," Seave said. "The Blanton detective didn't check the knife for prints. We did and we got partials for Rincon and Officer Lee. Have you met Lee yet?"

They had not. He was the target of their investigation. It was too early to approach him.

"Too bad," Seave said. "He's a solid citizen, a good cop. He had a kid in the hospital when this happened. Did you know that? His boy. Hit by a car. Almost died."

It was the first they heard about it. Jones made a note to look into it. Lizzie felt sorrow for the boy and guilt over bringing more misery to the Lee family. She tried to put it out of her mind. The job didn't allow for those feelings.

It did, however, require that she consider whether or not stress at home explained what Lee did the night of the shooting. Would the

31

defense use the boy's injury to create sympathy for Lee? Of course they would. She hated to be cynical, but that was a big part of the job.

Deputy D.A. Seave handed her his two-page declination memo, explaining why he didn't charge Lee with murdering Rincon.

"... *Officer Lee effectuated a traffic stop, at which point said SUSPECT removed his vehicle to the shoulder of the road. Despite repeated verbal commands, the SUSPECT refused to exit the vehicle, thereby forcing Officer Lee to approach the vehicle and attempt to extricate the SUSPECT from the vehicle, whereupon a struggle ensued...*"

Good lord, Lizzie thought. They weren't paying him based on his writing.

"I can sum it for you real quick," Seave said. "Officer Lee was way out there all alone, in the middle of the night, in the middle of nowhere. Most cops wouldn't have the balls to pull anybody over. But Lee did. Just because the pickup had a busted taillight. I think that was pretty brave of him."

"They should have given him a medal," Jones said.

Seave stared at Jones, unsure whether he was serious or not. It wasn't always easy to tell with Jones. Seave went on:

"Rincon acted like he couldn't get out of the pickup to draw Lee close. He hit Lee with the door and went after Lee with a knife. Lee was lucky he didn't die out there."

"*After the SUSPECT was shot, Officer Lee radioed for an AMBU-LANCE, then examined the SUSPECT and attempted lifesaving emergency procedures to stem the flow of blood from the gunshot wound to the SUSPECT'S chest.*"

"You got the radio runs, backing all this up?" Jones asked.

Seave did. He handed them a box of audiotapes.

Lizzie asked if anybody noticed blood on Lee's uniform pants. "If he went down to help Rincon, it's likely he would have gotten some on him."

Seave shifted uncomfortably. If it wasn't in the report, he couldn't say. He wasn't there. Ask Detective Vern Moeller, the Blanton P.D. investigator who was first at the scene.

"Detective Moeller isn't the sharpest tool in the shed," Seave admitted.

According to the Memorandum of Understanding between Blanton and Inland County, police shootings were initially investigated by the police department and then referred for further review to the sheriff.

"That's standard procedure for pretty much every small police department in California," Seave said. "First responder is the officer's own department. The sheriffs only come into it when they're called in by the department detective."

Jones added Moeller to the interview list.

"So, basically," Lizzie said, thinking it through, "you know what happened that night from Detective Moeller. But where did Detective Moeller get the information? It sure didn't come from Rincon, we know that, so Lee had to be the source."

Except how could that be?

No cop in a shooting case gives a statement without first consulting his attorney or a union rep. And they can't be compelled to give testimony against themselves in a criminal prosecution.

Seave said Lee agreed to talk without a lawyer immediately after the event, under oath, waiving all his special cop rights, including his legal right to not give any statement at all.

"That impressed me," Seave said. "He acted like he had nothing to hide."

When they were leaving, Seave couldn't help himself. He had to ask.

"What, exactly, am I missing here? Do you guys know something I don't know? Because, honest to God, I thought this was a good shoot. I didn't even think this was a close call."

Awkward. So, so awkward.

Lizzie hated to hide things from Seave, who seemed like a decent enough guy. But she was not about to disclose Scanlon's identity. The name of an eyewitness to murder is not uttered unless absolutely necessary. She had no reason to think Seave would tell Officer Lee or that Officer Lee would go gunning for Scanlon, but she wasn't going to risk it.

Scanlon was in a tough spot. He tipped them to a possible murder, but they hadn't yet been able to corroborate his tip enough to justify the trouble and expense of protecting his life. If this ever went to trial, Scanlon was going to be the biggest part of the story.

Lizzie wanted to keep him alive long enough to play his part.

CHAPTER 11

Lizzie wrote "RINCON" on yellow legal paper and taped it to the wall of her office. Then she began to build her case the same way a writer builds a story: with an outline.

Once upon a time, in a land far away . . .

The first section of the wall was devoted to the place. The law calls this part of the story jurisdiction: where it happened. Lizzie taped up a map of Blanton, a dot in the middle of the Inland Empire's largest wasteland.

She added photos of Blanton downloaded from the Web. They showed cracked runways, graffiti-covered concrete slabs pock-marked with bullet holes, and empty barracks. The local U.S. Air Force Base had been Blanton's number one employer. When it closed in the early 1990s, the population went from a high of 75,000 to 31,435. Bank-owned foreclosure photos featured tumbledown homes and streets without sidewalks; a dying desert town ready to blow away.

"It looks like a David Lynch movie," Berg said. "Have you visited?"

"Not yet," she said.

"Don't go," Berg advised. "It looks dangerous." Because Berg was her supervisor, Lizzie and Jones had to run the case by him. Not that he asked. He preferred not to get involved in cases if he could help it.

A second section of the wall was devoted to people. Stories needed characters. Law stories called them victims, criminals, and witnesses. Lizzie put photos of Joe Rincon, Lee, and Scanlon on the wall.

She left spaces for other characters she hadn't met but knew she would need.

One was Mrs. Rincon, Joe's grandmother. A good story makes you feel something. Lizzie wanted Mrs. Rincon to make the jury feel her grandson was a human being, a young man who didn't deserve to die.

Lizzie listed other characters by profession: a coroner to testify if Rincon had a head wound consistent with a flashlight blow, an expert to explain when it was legal for a cop to kill and when it was murder.

Below the place and people sections, Lizzie used a long piece of duct tape to divide the wall in half.

On one side of the tape she put her theory of the case. On the other side of the tape, she laid out what she thought the defense would be.

Lizzie's side was primarily based on what Scanlon saw:

Lee walked up to the pickup, yanked open the door, hit Rincon with the flashlight. Rincon stumbled but didn't fall. Lee drew his gun and pointed it at Rincon. Rincon had one hand to his head, another up and open and empty. A couple of seconds later, Lee shot him. There was nothing in the kid's hands.

The defense side was Lee's version, as told to the CHP and repeated by Det. Moeller and Deputy D.A. Seave:

Lee walked up to the pickup. Rincon hit him with the pickup's door then rushed at him with a knife. Lee pulled his gun and shot Rincon because he had no other choice.

"I wish Scanlon's version was simpler," Berg said. "Simple's easier to sell."

Lizzie knew a good storyteller can make anything simple. Anyway, she could only use what she had. Lawyer storytellers have to stick with the truth and the facts as given.

There was a blank space on the wall for Officer Lee's personnel file. The Blanton P.D. hadn't responded to Lizzie's subpoena.

"I wouldn't expect a lot of cooperation from them," Berg said. He suggested they check Lee's uniform pants to see if they had dirt on the back.

Lizzie said that was a good idea but she already knew the Blanton investigator never bothered to check Lee's uniform for stains and didn't inventory it with the rest of his equipment. Whatever evidence they might have found was gone now. Still, it was good to encourage Berg to get involved. It might help later on.

Berg was about to suggest places where they might look to find the flashlight when the receptionist interrupted.

"Your friend is here again, Lizzie."

Lizzie guessed who it was.

"It's my roommate Sarah," she said. "I'll be right back."

Berg and Jones stared at the wall.

"Is she gay? Is that what you have on her?"

Jones told Berg to shut up.

"It isn't sexual harassment if I ask *you*. It's only harassment if I ask her."

Jones said that wasn't true.

"No," Berg agreed, "but it should be."

Berg liked Lizzie. The only reason he hadn't asked her out is because he believed office romances were wrong. He also believed she would say no. Now, he wondered if her sexual orientation was another reason. Berg was a deep thinker.

Jones changed the subject.

"Do you know why nobody ever brings you a good case? Can I tell you?"

"Not if it's going to hurt my feelings."

"You're not seen as a good person, Davey."

"I'm perceived as a *bad person*?" Berg was shocked. He could acknowledge he was a bad prosecutor. He hadn't realized that was now a character flaw.

Jones tried to soften it. "Folks just don't see you as a guy they want to work with. The word is you're kind of lazy, a little gun-shy of trial, willing to throw people under the bus when things go bad."

"Wow," Berg said, shaking his head. "I sound horrible."

Jones told him he wasn't that bad.

"But, seriously," Berg asked, "*is* she gay?"

CHAPTER 12

Lizzie looked through the bulletproof glass separating her from the waiting area.

Sarah's back was turned, her face to the window, the curve of her neck making Lizzie's knees a little weak.

"Let her in, please."

The buzzing door made Sarah turn around.

"Friend," she said, about to cry. "My car got towed."

"Did you pay the tickets?"

"I meant to," Sarah said. "I really did."

They first met in the summer of 1989. The YMCA parking lot was jammed with church youth groups, setting off for a beach day. Convocation was still invited to things like this.

Lizzie made her Mom drop her off a block away so she could walk by herself. Lizzie was embarrassed Mom was so fat. So was Mom. They both felt guilty about it.

Sarah's parents slathered suntan lotion over her impossibly white skin and prayed for her safe return. They hadn't wanted to let her go. Elder Evans made them. Christ was a fisherman. God created the land *and* sea. All Convocation children must learn to swim.

The counselors organized the kids by age, pairing them off as buddies, responsible for one another. Sarah and Lizzie were the only girls their age.

"Friend?"

Sarah said it like a prayer. Lizzie nodded yes without thinking. They held hands and walked onto the school bus together.

They each needed a friend. Sarah spent most of the previous six months in the hospital. She would have died from meningitis but for Elder Evans, who interceded with God. She missed the whole school year, which was a shame, because she had been one of the smartest girls in her class. But her parents told her it didn't matter. Her life now belonged to God, who would direct it as He saw fit, through his servant, Elder Evans.

Lizzie went through something almost worse.

Two weeks earlier, Elder Evans administered her first public shaming.

It was done in front of the full Convocation, with her parents sitting in the front row, crying, but not doing a thing to protect her. At least she didn't need to go to the hospital afterward. Some kids did.

Her transgression was fighting. Lizzie bloodied the lip of an older boy in Convocation school. Elder Evans suspended her for a week.

"Why'd you do it, honey?" Mom wailed, as Dad held his face in his hands, moaning in shame. "Why'd you do something so ugly?"

Lizzie wouldn't tell them why. The boy called Mom a fat whale. She wouldn't hurt them by repeating it. During an all-day admonishment session, the boy stepped forward and admitted what he said. He came to their house. He went on his knees in their living room, apologizing for what he said.

Her parents forgave him.

Lizzie refused.

Nor would she admit why she hit him, even though everyone already knew. She didn't think it was fair to make her say bad things about Mom, even if she was just quoting. She refused even when Elder Evans threatened if she didn't confess and forgive the boy, she would force him to administer a loving rebuke.

The test of wills between 10-year-old Lizzie and 40-year-old Elder Evans went on for weeks. It ended at a Sunday service. Elder Evans's sermon was "Spare the rod."

Once upon a time, there was a mean little boy and a stubborn little girl . . .

Lizzie's stomach went tight. He was talking about her. When he repeated what the boy said about Mom, Lizzie's heart turned against him forever. Dad had to hold her back from rushing the stage. She wanted to scratch Elder Evans's eyes out.

"The boy repented and all that meanness just flowed right out of him. But the stubborn little girl wouldn't and didn't and still won't. And now she has to be corrected."

Elder Evans nodded to Dad. Dad wept as he dragged her to the stage, her screams drowned out by singing. Elder Evans was leading them in "The Easy Yoke."

Dad sat in a chair. They laid Lizzie over his lap. Elder Evans struck her hard, 10 times, with a paddle.

That night, Mom sat by her bed, holding her hand, begging her to forgive them for having failed to protect her. Lizzie thought Mom meant from Elder Evans. "The Devil's inside you, Lizzie," Mom said. "We didn't pray hard enough to keep him out."

Over time, because she loved them, Lizzie believed she forgave her parents.

She would never forgive Elder Evans.

She knew Mom and Dad would never leave Convocation. Neither would Sarah. She never did catch up academically after losing the year to illness. Not that her parents or anyone other than Lizzie ever encouraged her to try.

Lizzie would never abandon any of them. No matter how much she hated Elder Evans, she loved her family and Sarah more.

She turned down a scholarship to play basketball at Cal so she could stay in Orange County. She went to U.C. Irvine on a basketball scholarship, then graduated first in the first class of the new U.C. Irvine Law School.

But Jones wasn't wrong about her wanting to escape the Orange Curtain.

It was time.

If she could get a transfer to L.A., she would go. She was ready. The test of wills between her and Elder Evans couldn't go on forever.

CHAPTER 13

THE LOS ANGELES COUNTY CORONER'S OFFICE MAIN VAULT SMELLED like a bad meat market.

Lizzie stood in the middle of the room surrounded by 115 dead men.

The green and white floor tiles sloped down to a drain in the middle of the room. Fluorescent lights lit the bodies from above, leaving the corners of the room dark.

The men were stacked on metal trays, four bodies high. Each was wrapped in heavy industrial plastic, clear enough to make out the skin and hair color, the outline of faces and limbs. The plastic was tied loosely with rope, with openings for their heads and feet.

They were all unwashed.

"Sorry about the smell," Deputy Coroner Sal Gonzalez said. "The fridge isn't working too well today."

Part of Lizzie's job was casting: hiring the right people to tell parts of the story. Right now she was looking for a coroner. The Inland County Coroner's report didn't mention head wounds, but Lizzie heard they were a mediocre shop at best. If Scanlon was telling the truth about the flashlight, there had to be evidence of it.

Deputy Coroner Gonzalez looked good on paper. He testified in court before. He handled two autopsies of men shot to death by the LAPD. Both cases were deemed good shoots. Whoever Lee's lawyer turned out be, she wouldn't be able to label Gonzalez anticop.

In person, however, Gonzalez was creepy. He sported a Van Dyke beard and wore a white suit with a black shirt and red bow tie. Lizzie didn't think the hipster coroner would play well to an O.C. jury.

But she didn't have a lot of choices. San Bernardino, Riverside, and Ontario Counties had already turned down her request to meet on the case, having no interest in testifying against one of their own. It wasn't just the police who closed ranks in a cop case.

"You're probably asking yourself why we don't just freeze them," Gonzalez said. He was real chatty. "Obviously, the tissue would be damaged. That's why we can't clean them either. We could lose evidence."

Bad as it was in the vault, the smell in the corridor was worse. There, on hangars and in boxes, were the dead men's clothing and shoes, unwashed, preserved as they were when the men died in them. "Most of the guys were homeless, so it wasn't like they were clean to begin with," Gonzalez said. "Depending on how they died, there can also be a lot of soiling."

Elder Evans said the body was only a bag of bones. It was the soul that counted. Seeing these husks of human beings would have done his heart good.

"The guy I want to show you was beaten to death with an aluminum bat," Gonzalez said, checking name tags. "It's close enough to a flashlight to give you a sense of what I mean about the wound. Here he is."

Gonzalez peeled back the plastic to expose the man's head. His face was a mass of purple, matted hair and flesh, swollen and distended, a carnival nightmare.

"A smooth surface like a metal bat doesn't tear the skin."

Lizzie made herself look.

"*Nothing but a bag of bones.*"

Gonzalez pulled the plastic bag up over the dead man's head.

"Now, compare that guy to this guy over here."

Gonzalez walked Lizzie over to a different tower of bodies and peeled the plastic bag on another corpse. "This guy was hit with a hammer. That's not what killed him. Somebody strangled him after he got hit. But you'll see the difference."

The left side of the man's forehead had a knot the size of a fist. The flesh was blue, purple, and reddish-brown, flecked with thin, dried yellowish lines that seeped out of small seams around one side of the contusion.

"If you get hit with something that has edges, you get a wound like that," Gonzalez said, putting his nose an inch from the skin. "Smell that? That's pus."

He sniffs pus.

Lizzie tried not to think about it. "So if Rincon was hit with a flashlight, you'd see something like this? Because the Inland County Coroner didn't see it."

"Maybe she didn't look," Gonzalez said, straightening up. "They're not exactly the A Team over there."

Heavy plastic drapes, like the back of a butcher's shop, separated the main vault from the corridor leading to the various autopsy theaters. Gonzalez walked Lizzie down the hall past an open door.

There was a gurney with a body on it. The man was covered in gang tattoos. His chest cavity was split open. The counter and sink next to the body was spattered with blood. Nobody would keep their kitchen this filthy.

Lizzie would never eat ribs again.

"This guy was shot three times, we're digging out the bullets," Gonzalez said. "He's been manscaped. Seriously. His pubes are cut into a heart. We see lots of guys like that. You wouldn't expect it. Weird. You want to see?"

Jesus Christ . . .

Lizzie said no, thank you. The more Gonzalez talked, the creepier he got.

His office looked like her high school biology class. There was a chalkboard, metal stools, raised workspaces, a high ceiling, and the kind of windows you had to close with a long-handled wooden hook. His desk was covered with yellowing reports, files, medical instruments and manuals, cardboard boxes of files, and jars with organs floating in liquid.

His pencil container held fingers instead of pencils.

"I need to print those," he explained. "They came off John Does. We don't bother to autopsy them but we like to keep get their prints, just in case."

Lizzie waited as Gonzalez reviewed the Inland County Coroner's report.

"Okay," Gonzalez said, waving his fingers at her. "Gimme gimme gimme . . ."

She handed him the autopsy photos and X-rays.

"Yeah," he said. "I told you Inland County sucked. It's not in her report, but see this?"

Gonzalez showed Lizzie an autopsy photo of Rincon's head, taken from the side, the dead man in profile, eyes half-closed. Gonzalez used a metal probe to point out a line of purplish contusion at Rincon's scalp. "Most of it's hidden by the hair, but see that? Can't really tell how big the wound was, but I'd say it's consistent with Rincon being hit with something that has an edge. A big metal flashlight would work."

Lizzie asked if he would say it on the stand. He said he would.

"You're sure? You don't mind saying bad things about another county's office?"

Gonzalez had some swagger. "They did a shitty job. I have no problem saying that. We're scientists. We're not cops. We don't get all upset because we disagree. Trust me, if they thought we fucked up, they would be more than happy to testify."

● ● ●

JONES ASKED IF GONZALEZ GOT THE PART.

"He's kind of weird."

"He's a coroner," Jones said. "Of course he's weird."

Driving back to Orange County, her cell rang.

"Friend! Don't be mad, okay?"

Lizzie hadn't heard Sarah this excited since she got a summer job playing Snow White at Disneyland. Not that she ever got the chance.

Elder Evans killed it. He found the outfit immodest.

"I found my own place!"

Lizzie's jaw fell open in a silent, joyful scream.

"You're not mad about me for leaving?"

Lizzie said she would deal with it.

"Yay!" Sarah said, relieved. "It's going to be my first place. Can you believe it? The only thing is, could you help me move?"

Lizzie was happy to help and even happier to see the place was close to her place but not too close. The surprising thing was that there was a man living there.

"You said this was going to be your place," Lizzie said.

Sarah shrugged. "This is just Tom," Sarah said. "My roommate."

They were in the same class at Orange Coast Community College. "Introduction to Business." Tom had a tattoo of the Grim Reaper on his neck.

Did Sarah's parents know she was living with a man?

"We're not *living* together," Sarah said, blushing. "We're just sharing."

Lizzie suggested Sarah keep that to herself. This was a big step for Sarah, an act of independence. Lizzie didn't want to rain on it.

Instead, she went home that night and ran around her place naked, Bodhi chasing after her, both of them thrilled to have it all to themselves.

CHAPTER 14

LIZZIE AND JONES PUT OFF INTRODUCING THEMSELVES TO MRS. Rincon for as long as possible. Neither of them wanted to upset the woman unless they had a reason.

This time Lizzie took her own car. Mrs. Rincon's house was easy to find, just over the Inland County line, a two-hour drive away.

There was a bloody crucifix on the wall made of cheap wood. Jesus's face was contorted in pain, eyes to Heaven, real nails in red paint through hands and feet. Lizzie's Mom and Dad had a similar one over their bed.

Mrs. Rincon sat on the plastic-covered couch, her bone-thin brown arms wrapped tightly around her stomach. Tears streaked down her wrinkled face. She told them how she found out her grandson was dead.

"A policeman came to the door. He said, 'Why don't you have a phone?' I said, 'I don't know, why? Is something wrong with Joe?' The policeman said, 'You need to come with us to see if the man we have is Joe.' I thought he meant Joe was in jail . . .'"

The old lady doubled over in grief. The place smelled of fried oil, cigarettes, and disinfectant. Lizzie sat on the only chair in the room. Jones stood behind her. There was no other place to sit. An old television sat broken on the floor.

The old lady shook her head. She closed her eyes. Tears squeezed out.

"Later, they told me Joe tried to hurt a policeman and the policeman had to shoot Joe. But that's not right. Joe was a good boy."

He worked odd jobs, mostly construction when he could get it, laying carpet or moving furniture. The night he was killed, he spent the day moving car batteries to a junk yard.

Mrs. Rincon showed them Joe's birth certificate, photos of his first day of school, First Communion, sitting on Santa's lap, looking scared, his mom standing off to the side, trying to keep out of the picture while still holding his hand.

Lizzie knew what the bedroom would look like before Mrs. Rincon showed them.

There was the single bed, the Virgin of Guadalupe painting, the photo portrait of a young woman in a U.S. Army uniform ("That's Joe's cousin. She deployed."), a poster for Tecate beer ("Con Character") featuring swimsuit models draped around boxer Julio Caesar Chavez, Jr., the smell of Old Spice mixed with pot, sweat, and young man.

Not the bedroom of a Convocation boy. The bedroom of the local boys she'd sneak away to see, the brothers of her friends from public school, the boys she made out with when her parents thought she was at Convocation study.

With effort, the old woman kneeled down to pull a cigar box from under the bed. There was a prayer card from a funeral, a "Most Improved" ribbon from an eighth grade math teacher, a folded GED certificate. Underneath that was a small bag of weed, condoms, and a fake Arizona driver's license.

Lizzie's first unforced error.

The winner isn't the strongest or fastest. In the ring and in court, she's the one who makes the fewest mistakes. If Lizzie hadn't looked in the cigar box, she wouldn't have to show the defense lawyer what was inside.

It could have been worse. They were misdemeanors, penny-ante bullshit. Bad prosecutors would have pretended they hadn't seen it.

"Do a 302, please," she asked Jones. "For discovery." She couldn't see how a defense lawyer could use this to defend what Lee did that night, but she had an obligation to turn it over to the defense and let them try.

Grandma dabbed at her nose with a crumpled tissue.

They looked at high school yearbooks. Joe must have grown half a foot between ninth and tenth grades. The class photo showed him towering over his classmates.

"They wanted him to play football, but he didn't like it. He'd say, 'Grandma, I don't want to get hurt out there.'"

He smoked a little pot, everyone seemed to nowadays, but he wanted to learn how to fix cars. He also wanted to find a girlfriend.

"He was shy."

"Did he have a bad temper?" Jones asked.

The old lady shook her head. "He only fought that one time, when he had to, and he didn't like it. He was gentle. They didn't charge him. He was defending himself."

Lizzie already checked. She knew it was true. Rincon's assault arrest was for a fight outside a bar. He didn't start it or win it. The deputy who arrested Rincon admitted they never should have run him in.

"Mrs. Rincon, they say Joe pulled a knife on the police officer the night he was shot. Did the police show you the knife?"

Mrs. Rincon shook her head. She saw the photo of the knife in the paper, but she couldn't say if it was Joe's.

In the end, Lizzie thought Joe Rincon didn't sound like he was all one thing or another. He was a nondescript, not terribly successful, poor guy with few opportunities or skills. His grandmother loved him.

"Mrs. Rincon," Lizzie said, taking the old woman's hands. "Do you know why we're here?"

The old lady shrugged. It never occurred to her that anyone cared about what happened to her grandson.

Lizzie thought that was the saddest part of the whole thing.

CHAPTER 15

WHEN LIZZIE GOT HOME THAT NIGHT, SHE CHANGED INTO RUNNING gear, plugged into her headphones, and tried to get her mind off the case.

Sarah's voice came through her headphones. "Surprise! I stole your phone. Sorry! But I made you this playlist."

Classic Sarah. Lizzie spent the day frantically looking for her phone and was completely lost without it. Sarah meant well.

The first song was "I Miss My Friend." The next one was "I'll Be There for You," the theme to *Friends*.

Sarah was such a nerd.

When Lizzie was in college, Sarah came to every game, baked cookies for the team, and made signs: "Go Lady Anteaters!"

The team's point guard teased Lizzie. "Your wife's here."

"She's my best friend," Lizzie said. "We grew up together."

"Uh-huh," the point guard said. "If you say so."

The cloying words of a Convocation nursery song flashed in Lizzie's mind:

"When sinners mock, always grin, when they taunt, keep it in. Its only when you answer that you let the Devil in."

The worst earworm in the world. Elder Evans wrote them to be catchy.

The next song on Sarah's playlist was "You've Got a Friend in Me."

"Okay, I get it already!"

Lizzie went to the store, bought dog food, and ran home in silence, earphones in, but no more songs about friends.

She never even noticed Dwayne Lee sitting in the car down the block, watching her.

• • •

THEY PUT DWAYNE WAYNE LEE ON ADMINISTRATIVE LEAVE FOR A month after the shooting. He was back on the job the day after the Inland County D.A. cleared him, but he still wasn't sleeping well. He bet he had PTSD. Not that anybody gave a shit about him. Nobody ever cared about him.

Al Jenkins, senior man on the force, needed Lee. He was the only Blanton cop who could do paperwork. The others were too lazy or too stupid and that included Al.

Lee hated all of them.

Of the 30 officers on the force, he was the smartest. His scores on his intelligence and physical tests were in the top percentile of the whole state. He was this close to getting a job with the LAPD. He sailed through their Academy and scored the highest in his class on physical and intelligence tests.

All he had to do was pass a bullshit mental health examination.

He failed. Both times he took it.

There was no shame in it. Lots of guys on the Blanton force failed the intelligence or mental tests when they tried to get jobs elsewhere.

Still, Lee found himself envying the morons he worked with. Ignorance must be fucking bliss. Being smarter than the average bear just meant Lee knew exactly what a shit hole Blanton was. It made him angry. Many things made him angry lately.

At that moment, it was all this fucking paperwork. Just because he was good at it didn't mean he liked it. It was like doing a crossword, filling in the boxes, giving short answers to preprinted questions. The more forms or reports you did, the easier they became.

The only part he sort of liked was the Statement of Facts. It was all about what *he* said happened. He got really good at describing people and events in a strong cop way.

The bad guys were all SUSPECTS.

They acted "suspiciously," "nervously"; they drove "in a reckless manner." When he pulled up or approached them, they made "furtive movements," as if "concealing a weapon."

Once he got them out of the car or attempted to address them on the sidewalk, they didn't run from him. They "fled." He "gave chase." When he caught them, they almost never "complied with his verbal commands." Even if they did, that's not the story he always told. Sometimes, they "resisted arrest" or "used profanity and expectorated" at him. When that happened, the SUSPECTS often "slipped and fell, striking their heads on the ground," or "were restrained with intermediate, nonlethal force." A baton to the knee, a fist in the kidneys, broken fingers.

The fuckers were lucky he didn't shoot more of them.

OFFICER LEE was the good guy in these stories. VICTIMS or WITNESSES could be useful or sad, but they were never good guys.

Not that it mattered. Most cop paperwork never saw the light of day. Most cases never went up the line for prosecution. Only a fraction of those that did were ever charged.

Still, it had to be done, put in the database, kept in files. It was all cover your ass, in triplicate, in case anybody ever kicked up a complaint.

Once, when Lee was still bothering to send cases to the idiots in the Inland County D.A. for possible prosecution, the D.A. bitch had the nerve to compliment him.

"You write really well," she said.

Why wouldn't I write well? Because I'm a white trash piece of shit, you think I can't write well. Fuck you.

"Thanks," Lee mumbled instead.

. . .

AL JENKINS CAME IN TOTING A BAG OF GREASY BURGERS. "S'UP, Dwayne."

"Al."

Jenkins fell into a chair next to Dwayne's and plopped the bag in front of him. He never ate this slop in his office. He didn't want to stink it up.

"Heard your boy's doing real good," Jenkins said, unwrapping his burger.

Lee nodded.

"They say he's going to be okay," Jenkins said, taking a bite. "Hard to believe. Kids heal real fast, though."

Lee stapled two forms together and threw them in a file.

"Bad deal," Jenkins said, thoughtfully chewing. "Makes you sick thinking about it." Jenkins took another bite of his burger.

Lee turned to his computer to check the spelling of the word "notorious." As in "SUSPECT ONE, a 'notorious meth dealer,' moved in a threatening manner toward OFFICER LEE."

"How's mommy doing? She doing okay?"

Lee stopped writing and looked up. "What about her?"

Jenkins stopped chewing, aware he'd somehow pissed Lee off, which was never a good idea. "I asked how your wife was doing."

"She's a fucking animal, Al," Lee said.

Jenkins put down his burger and wiped his fingers on his pants. "It wasn't her fault, Lee," he said. "It could have happened to anybody. Don't forget, she's been there for you. You don't want to screw things up with her now. Marriage is tough."

He was tempted to point out Jenkins divorced his last wife 10 years ago.

Lee's private cell rang. He didn't recognize the number or the voice that went with it.

"Heya, Dwayne-o, my name is Joe Farley," he said, sounding like a used car salesman. "You don't know me, but I got a feeling you're going to."

"Why is that?"

"Well, sir, I'll tell you," Farley said. "A little birdie just told me the feds are looking at you on that Rincon deal. You're going to have to get yourself a lawyer, son."

Lee hung up on him.

CHAPTER 16

HANDSOME JACK HORTON SAT WITH HIS FEET ON THE DESK reading a suppression motion. The Chief of the Criminal Division stormed in.

"Get your feet off the desk."

But it's my desk.

Jack moved his feet.

Dante D'Ambrosio, The Chief, stood with his arms crossed over his barrel chest and his chin thrust up. Berg called it "doing a Mussolini." The Chief would have fired Berg if he knew. The Chief had a framed poster behind his desk of a scowling Winston Churchill ordering that they "Deserve Victory."

"Do I or do I *not* have the responsibility to approve all police brutality cases in the Central District of California?"

Jack said The Chief had the authority.

"Right!" The Chief barked. "Yet not more than five minutes ago I received a telephone call from the District Attorney of Inland asking about our investigation into a shooting in her county. I did not approve any such investigation."

Handsome Jack was the Deputy Chief of the Criminal Division. His job was to make sure The Chief knew what was going on in the largest, most spread out, most populous U.S. Attorney's Office in the country.

From the desert to the sea, to all of Southern California, only two hundred or so prosecutors were responsible for the federal crimes of close to twenty million people. Even a genius like Jack missed things.

"Chief, I'll be honest," Jack said, his head bowed. "I never heard a thing about any shooting in Inland County but I'm sure going to find out about it."

Contrition could lead to salvation. All it required was complete commitment. The Chief had no time for incompetence or ambition. The job was not a stepping stone. Prosecuting crimes against the United States of America was a privilege and the highest calling.

"Murder has no place in this office, Jack." The Chief uncrossed his arms. "The locals usually don't mess it up too badly. If you don't agree, let Main Justice do the case. They have a whole Civil Rights Division in D.C. This is what they're paid for."

Jack agreed that made perfect sense. The Chief was never wrong and never in doubt. He just celebrated his 37th year on the job. His retirement plan was to die in office.

Command delivered, The Chief relaxed, twirling his big, black glasses in his hand, turning his gaze to the ceiling, a professorial affectation Berg called "the Jaunty Raconteur."

"Let me tell you a little something about *the* District Attorney of Inland County," The Chief said. "The woman applied for a job in this office in 1998. Suffice to say, she did not merit an interview."

The Chief believed the office's mission was to do justice. His method was to maintain the highest intellectual and ethical standards. Their power was too precious to put in the hands of any but the best and brightest. If that made The Chief an elitist, so be it.

After The Chief left, Jack did some digging. Then he called Berg.

"What the fuck, Davey? You authorized a civil rights case? And don't lie to me, because I already know you did."

"Jack, if you're going to be that way about it, I might as well just tell you the truth."

Silence.

Berg got nervous. Being sentenced to Santa Ana was bad, but there were worse gulags. The office had satellite offices in Riverside and San Bernardino, too.

"Jones is the case agent. He's the best we got. Lizzie Scott wants to prosecute. I can't say no to her," Berg confessed. "I'm smitten."

Jack didn't say a word. What could he say?

Handsome Jack and Lizzie Scott had a little bit of history together.

CHAPTER 17

Lizzie walked into her office to find Jack staring at the wall with the Rincon evidence on it.

She actually gasped.

Breathe. Nothing bad has happened yet.

"Berg let me in," Jack said without looking at her. "You do know that you're supposed to get front-office approval to open a civil rights case, right?"

Lizzie stayed in the doorway, keeping the desk between them.

"Good to see you, too, Jack."

In the awkward silence that followed, an Elder Evans quote popped in her head. "Sin follows the sinner like a shadow follows the sun."

You follow me, too, because you implanted this shit in my brain when I was too young.

She spent *way* too much energy fighting Elder Evans in her mind.

Jack finally looked at her. She was ready for it this time and didn't gasp, but *goddamn* was he handsome. Berg never meant the nickname to be ironic.

She was thankful the whole thing only happened once.

It was after her first and last office social event. A mandatory beach party for new prosecutors. She had to go. She drove to Manhattan Beach, telling herself she would stay for an hour. But she made the mistake of wearing her favorite summer dress.

"Vanity, vanity, all is vanity. But the vanity of woman surpasses all."

Elder Evans based his sexism on Scripture.

But, then again, why *did* she have to make herself look so good that day? In all modesty, why *that* dress? She was no fashion model. You wouldn't think to call her small. But that dress fit just right. Life would have been simpler if she'd worn sweats.

Jack looked so much like a J.Crew model in khakis and a preppy button-down—he had a sweater tied around his neck, for god sake—she laughed at him.

"You must be Handsome Jack," she said. They shook hands. She was self-conscious her hand was as big as his. "I thought Berg was kidding."

Later, she was in the kitchen, getting a third margarita, and caught him staring at her.

She didn't drink often, but when she did, she drank a lot. "What are you looking at?"

He apologized. She smiled. Jack drew in a breath. She was gorgeous when she smiled. She punched his arm a little too hard. "I've got my eye on you, friend."

When the party was over, he offered to drive her home.

"In my role as a designated driver," he explained. "A DUI would be a bad way for you to start in the office."

She was drunk enough to say "yes" but not drunk enough to bring him to her place, not with Sarah staying there.

She asked him where he lived.

He flinched.

"Don't flatter yourself," she said. "I'm being considerate." She sacked out on more floors than she could remember: church events (she never said Convocation), high school basketball games, track meets.

"I only sleep with people I'm attracted to," she laughed. "You have nothing to worry about it." She meant it, too. Jack would have made a beautiful woman, maybe, but he was definitely not her type.

His apartment was on the border of Hancock Park and Koreatown. She never saw a straight man's place like it: hardwood floors, well-tended plants, stacks of art and poetry books, reproductions of nineteenth-century landscapes on the wall.

He offered her his bed. She took the couch.

"Would you like something to drink before you turn in?"

He'd meant water. She asked for Scotch.

They ended up at the kitchen table. They got through a third of the bottle. The conversation turned to boxing.

"You enjoy hitting people?"

"It's good for stress," she said. "And it's a great workout. Feel my arm."

He did, forgot himself, and left his hand on her bicep.

"Come on," she said, laughing and moving closer to him. "I'll arm wrestle you."

He grasped her hand without thinking.

She pinned him almost immediately then kept his hand pressed to the table.

He kissed her before he knew he was going to do it.

They never made it to the bed.

She spent the next day sparring against a bartender from Cudahy, knocking the woman halfway through the ropes.

He spent the next day listening to Chopin and staring into space.

And they say women are more romantic than men.

They never slept together again. One and done. He called, she ignored. Sex and work were a bad mix but more than anything, a relationship with Jack or anyone else in the office put her past and privacy at risk.

It wasn't hard. He was in L.A., she was in O.C., 30 miles away, doing the same job in different places. She dreamed about him, waking up feeling Convocation guilty.

Six months later, to the consternation of senior prosecutors, Chief D'Ambrosio picked Jack to be his Deputy Chief.

His rise was meteoric but not unexpected. The Chief admired intellect and credentials. Jack was always the smartest one in the room and the best papered: Phi Beta Kappa from Yale, a Marshall Scholar, Yale Law, editor of the law review, a U.S. Supreme Court Clerk to Anthony Kennedy.

The Chief forgave Jack for the last part. Even though they were both Californians, Stanford men, Anglophiles, and Catholics, The Chief couldn't stand Justice Kennedy's inconsistencies. "They call him the 'swing vote,'" The Chief said in Jaunty Raconteur mode. "What they mean is, he's all over the map, a will-o'-the-wisp, a weather vane. That makes him a poor institution man, in my book."

Lizzie consoled herself. Jack was only, *technically*, now her boss. As Deputy Chief of the Criminal Division, he was in charge of all the line assistants.

Now, Jack was in her office, because he had to be. It was his job. He scanned the wall.

"The kid was 17 years old," said Lizzie. "Still living at home with his grandma."

Jack wanted to talk about the bigger picture.

"Oh," Lizzie said. "*That.*"

He lectured her on the perils of handling a police shooting case. "Don't be fooled by cable news," he explained. "Every once in awhile when it helps ratings, they churn up outrage over a shooting. They cover the riots, too. But juries love the police, trust them; they have trouble imaging them as killers."

"I don't own a TV," she said. Convocation families never did. Not everything about Convocation was bad.

Jack said that wasn't the point. "State or federal, we need cops to do our job. They may not be the lead investigator, but they do *something* in every case, grabbing evidence or helping track down suspects—"

She held up her hand to stop him. "This is all really interesting, but are you saying I can't do the case or what? Because unless you're going to let me do it, I don't really want to sit here and be lectured to."

Jack flinched. Lizzie hadn't meant to hurt his feelings. "No, no, it's not you," she said. "It's me. I don't like being lectured to by anybody."

Berg stuck his head in the office, felt the chill, and scurried away.

"The thing is," Jack said, "our office does one or two police cases a year." He knew six more the office could bring but wouldn't. "If we're going to do one, it has to be a good one. This one isn't strong enough."

Lizzie said she wasn't done with it. It could get stronger. She owed it to Jones, Scanlon, Mrs. Rincon, but mostly, to Joe. "Are you saying I can't keep working on it?"

Jack wanted her to quit the case on her own. That way nobody could ever accuse him of killing it. That's what The Chief liked about Jack.

He thought ahead. "I'm looking out for you," Jack said. "Cop cases are career suicide. The cops don't forget. You'll be a pariah."

"They mocked Jesus Christ, too."

Elder Evans said it whenever Convocation was attacked. She thought it every time she was afraid of what people thought of her.

"Anyway," she said. "I'm going to keep working on it. Okay?"

Not knowing what else to do, Jack left without saying a word. She hadn't realized how much she wanted him until he left.

"Thanks, Davey," Jack said when he passed Berg's office. "I'm not going to forget this."

Berg hoped they wouldn't send him to San Berdoo. Not a lot of Jews in San Bernardino.

CHAPTER 18

JACK WASN'T WRONG. THE CASE WAS WEAK; A ONE-WITNESS CASE always is, especially when the witness is someone like Scanlon. He left drunken messages on her office machine.

"I don't want to testify!"

She asked him to stop. If they charged Lee, she would have to turn the messages over to his defense lawyer who would use them to cross-examine Scanlon at trial.

Scanlon didn't even remember making the call.

A week later, he'd do it again.

"The good news is, he hasn't retracted or changed what he said happened," she told Jones. "The bad news is, he sounds scary and crazy. Jury's not going to like it. He keeps saying he doesn't want to be involved; the cop is going to come out and kill him."

She wanted to go down to the crime scene. If she was going to tell a jury the story of what happened, she had to see it, to stand in the exact spot where Rincon died.

She also wanted to see Rincon's pickup which was still in the Blanton P.D. impound lot. She had to check the driver's side door to see if it was jammed. She also wanted Jones to interview Detective Moeller, the Blanton investigator who did such a lousy job. Jones wanted to surprise him. Otherwise, Moeller might get a lawyer and stonewall them.

Jones suggested they go on Sunday. No traffic, not that there was ever that much in Blanton, but he wanted to get down there early enough to catch Moeller at home. Detectives didn't work early Sunday mornings.

"What if we run into Lee?"

It happened. Prosecutors and defendants sometimes ran into one another. Berg once ran into a defendant when they were both naked in the showers of his local 24-Hour Fitness.

"Not much there, eh, Berg?"

The defendant and his lawyer laughed about it for the rest of the trial. Berg insisted it wasn't why he lost.

Jones thought Lee would run if he saw them. "He might want to talk to us, but I doubt it."

Lizzie agreed to meet Jones at the Blanton P.D. They could then drive to the other locations. She had something she had to take care of first. Jones knew enough not to ask.

. . .

EARLY SUNDAY MORNING, LIZZIE PICKED SARAH UP AT HER NEW place. Tom waved good-bye from the window. He was just wearing a towel.

"Does he walk around like that all the time?"

Sarah blushed. They were sleeping together. She stared out of the window, embarrassed, miserable.

"You're entitled to have sex, Sarah," Lizzie said. "Sex is a good thing."

"I know, I know. Everything's okay when we're doing it, but then afterward, I feel so guilty. Do you ever feel that way?" Sarah asked. "About sex?"

"Nope," Lizzie lied. She denied Convocation's teachings exerted any influence on her even if they did. "You'll get over it."

They picked up Lizzie's parents. Sarah got in the back with Dad to give Mom more room.

"Aren't the girls beautiful, Dad?" Mom said. "They look like movie stars; they're so pretty." When they got to Convocation Hall, Mom begged Lizzie to join them.

"Not this week, Mom. I've got work to do. I'll pick you up tonight."

Lizzie hadn't stepped foot in Convocation Hall for 10 years. She never would.

She gunned the engine out of the parking lot and headed for Blanton.

CHAPTER 19

SOMEBODY WAS POUNDING ON DETECTIVE VERN MOELLER'S DOOR.

"Who is it?"

"Good morning," Jones said. "I'm with the FBI. How are you?"

It was 6:00 A.M.

Moeller thought it was a joke, a bad one; it was way too early to be waking people up on a Sunday. He whipped the door open and was about to tell Al Jenkins to go fuck himself. Al was always doing stupid shit.

The guy at the door was not Al Jenkins.

"Detective Moeller, my name is John Paul Jones. This is for you."

Jones handed him a folded sheet of paper. Moeller, a mouth breather, was too surprised to refuse. It read: "Federal Grand Jury Witness Subpoena." The only name on it was his, right next to a date and time for him to show up and testify under oath.

"The fuck is this about?"

"It could be nothing," Jones said. "You may not even have to come up to L.A. to testify if we can work something out first."

Moeller stared at the subpoena like an ape handed a calculator.

"Work something out like how? I didn't do anything wrong."

"Ever?" Jones gave him the farmer's smile. "It's a crime to lie to a federal agent. Let's make that the last one you tell me."

Jones invited himself in for coffee.

"So, you were the detective on the Rincon shooting."

Moeller dropped his head and muttered a long, bitter string of profanity.

"That's some poker face you got there, detective," Jones said. This was going to be a man Jones could work with.

Meanwhile, Lizzie crossed into the City of Blanton without knowing it. Someone stole the sign. The photos on her office wall didn't do the place justice. They couldn't convey the sour smell of uncollected trash and skunk.

Stray dogs slept in the parking lot of what used to be a video store. The walls of the two elementary schools—Calabash and Caesar Chavez—were covered in graffiti. The high school was shuttered. Stoner teens rode dirt bikes over the ripped-up football field. Blanton's high school kids were bused 20 miles each way to another Inland city.

Only two buildings in town were built in this century: the Indian casino and the Blanton Police Department. Lizzie parked in front of the new steel and glass headquarters. Jones was waiting for her.

"How did it go with Detective Moeller?"

"He wants to meet with you," Jones said. "He wants his lawyer there and he wants immunity, too."

"Awesome," Lizzie said. "It's got to be good if he needs all that."

They walked into the lobby, unannounced and unexpected.

"I help you?" the bored junior desk officer asked.

Jones handed him his badge, making the kid open it up to look for himself.

"FBI?"

"That's right. Now let me introduce you to Lizzie Scott. She's a federal prosecutor. We're here to see the boss."

The desk cop ran to get Al Jenkins.

"Al's what they call in baseball 'a player's manager,'" Jones said. "Just one of the guys; runs a loosey–goosey operation, not real strong with the discipline."

There was a skeletal morning crew. Before they could talk with any of them, Al Jenkins came out of his office, a feral little man with shiny black ears and a nervous laugh.

"Hey, guys, what's this about?"

Lizzie suggested they use his office.

When the door closed, Jones asked if Dwayne Wayne Lee was on duty.

"You're here about *Dwayne?*" Jenkins was shocked. "Dwayne's my best cop. The guy is a hero. Did you hear about the guy who attacked him with a knife?"

It hadn't dawned on Jenkins they were there about the shooting.

"I don't even have to check the roster," Jenkins said. "Unless he's in the hospital with his boy or asleep, Dwayne Wayne Lee is always on duty. That's why we call him 'Iron Man.' He's probably out on the highway right now. You want him here?"

Jones said they didn't.

Lizzie asked how Lee's little boy was doing.

"Toddler, just started to walk," Jenkins said. "Dwayne wasn't home, on duty like always, like I told you. The kid got out of the house and into the street. Got hit by a Mexican gal with no insurance. Poor kid almost died. Fucking uninsured drivers."

"A Mexican gal?"

The case was hard enough without adding race to it.

But there it was. Lee was white and Rincon was brown.

There was no evidence Lee beat or shot Rincon because of his race. So it didn't have to be part of the story. Excessive force was a federal crime. Period. If Lizzie charged a hate crime, it would make the case harder to win, not easier. It would also inject a whole lot of problems into the jury room. She hoped she could ignore it.

"How's the little boy now?" she asked.

"He was in the hospital for months. They didn't know if he'd ever walk again."

. . .

LIKE BLANTON, RINCON'S PICKUP LOOKED WORSE THAN ITS PICTURE. The front side of the driver's door was bent forward so far that it was impossible to push the door near the pickup's cab, let alone to close it. The interior door panel showed signs of a collision as well, as if someone had run into the door while it was open and snapped its hinges.

The impound supervisor said it came in like that. The tow truck driver had to tie the door shut with cable. "It got dinged up at the scene," the supervisor told them. "The tow guy did it." It wasn't going to be possible to tell if the pickup door had been jammed or not. Accidentally or on purpose, somebody destroyed evidence. They wouldn't be able to corroborate all of Scanlon's testimony.

. . .

THE HIGHWAY WHERE RINCON DIED BAKED IN THE SUN.

Lizzie and Jones used the crime-scene photos as their maps. They positioned their cars as models: Lizzie's Pontiac was Rincon's pickup; Jones's FBI's Crown Vic was Lee's Charger. Jones laid out flares and evidence tape to warn traffic. Nobody drove by the whole time they were there.

They reenacted Lee's version of what happened, Lizzie playing Rincon, Jones as Lee. They had a hard time recreating the moment when Rincon was supposed to have hit Lee with the pickup's door. The Crown Vic's door was lower than the pickup's. The door didn't seem to generate enough speed or force to have knocked Lee off his balance.

In the end, the only way they could choreograph it was by having Jones/Lee stand toward the front of the pickup, further away from the police cruiser, so the door had more distance to travel, more time to build momentum.

They reenacted Scanlon's version, too, videotaping both versions from where Scanlon claimed to have been. Then they sat in Lizzie's Pontiac, its air-conditioning blasting, comparing the video to the reports in the case file.

Lizzie was surprised there was so much overlap in the two stories. The descriptions of where the cars were on the road were the same. Lee said Rincon was approximately 10 feet away when he fired at him; Scanlon put it at 15 feet.

"Not a big difference," Jones said.

"Plus, Scanlon said Rincon was knocked a few feet by the flashlight, which could explain the difference." Five feet wasn't going to convince a jury either way.

Lizzie kept playing the video.

"In both versions, Lee goes to the window. Either he's hit with the car door or he falls back when it opens. My question is, why was he that close to it at all? Rincon could've had a gun. Is a cop supposed to go up to the window like that?"

Jones hadn't been trained to do it. He doubted any police officer had been.

"Lee was either really brave or really stupid," Lizzie said.

She lost track of time then realized she had to get back to pick up her parents and Sarah. They would be outside by the time she got there, having Sunday meal on long tables in the parking lot.

"I'm going to take one more look around to see if I can find any of Scanlon's stuff at the abutment," Jones said.

Lizzie pulled onto the highway and gunned it, eager to put Blanton behind her. The place made her want to shower.

Ten minutes later, she was doing 90, music blaring.

That's when she saw the cop lights in her rearview mirror.

No way.

It couldn't be Blanton. It must be Inland County or CHP.

She slowed down, too late, put on her signal to show she was a cautious driver (like it would help) and eased to the shoulder.

The police car slowed down. Rather than park behind her, the squad car passed her. It pulled in front of her car then backed up to block her exit.

Lizzie sped a lot and got pulled over a lot. She never saw a cop do anything like this.

She didn't get a look at the driver, but she was able to read the door shield on the car:

"Blanton Police Department." Underneath it, in script, the department's motto: "Service and honor."

There wasn't another car or soul in sight.

Breathe. Nothing bad has happened yet.

She found that if she said it enough, she started to believe it. It helped her stay calm and carry on, right up to the moment when the bad did happen and she had to be brave.

Lizzie punched Jones's number on her speed dial.

"I've just been pulled over by the Blanton P.D.," she said. "Thoughts?"

It was the first time Jones heard her scared.

"Is it Lee?" Jones had just left the shooting scene. He jammed his foot down hard on the accelerator.

"Couldn't tell you." The sun blazed off the squad car's window, blinding her.

"Well, I doubt it's Lee," Jones said, managing his best calm farmer. "He's not the only Blanton cop on the road, and I bet you were speeding. We're still in their jurisdiction, and it is a speed trap."

Jones had the Crown Vic doing just shy of 100 miles an hour.

"Lizzie, don't give him an excuse to do anything stupid."

He got her location. He figured he was five minutes behind her.

"He might not even know me," she said.

"Right," he said trying to sound convinced, "but keep your cell phone on."

She put the cell in the coffee holder and waited.

Breathe.

The squad car door opened. Sun flashed off the side mirror.

Dwayne Lee stepped out of the squad car.

CHAPTER 20

Lizzie just had time to realize the Rincon crime-scene photos were sitting on the passenger seat next to her. Before she could try to hide them, Lee was already at the car, rapping his knuckles on the window.

"License and registration."

Sunglasses hid his eyes. He needed a shave and looked thinner than his DMV photo.

"Do you know how fast you were going, ma'am?"

She dug through her wallet and handed him her papers without saying a word. She palmed her U.S. Attorney's Office credential. While he glanced at her license, she slipped the plastic badge into her jeans.

"Get out of the car."

She glanced in the rearview mirror. The highway was empty.

Lee yanked opened the door. "Get out *now*."

She stepped out, close enough to him that she could smell alcohol on his breath.

"I asked if you knew how fast you were going."

"Seventy, I think." Her voice sounded tight.

"I clocked you while I was driving. You were doing 85 on the radar gun."

That's not true she thought. Radar gun readings aren't done from a moving car.

"Step away from the vehicle," Lee said. "Stand over there."

"Why?"

Lee grinned. It was ugly; part sneer, part smirk, part facial tic.

Breathe.

"Move!"

She stepped back two paces.

"More," he said, flicking the back of his hand at her. "Keep going."
She took two more steps. He held up his hand. "Stay."

He got into her car. She couldn't see what he was doing inside. A
moment later, he tossed her cell phone out of the driver's side window.
It bounced off the hardpan, landing a few yards from where she stood.

"You left your cell on," he said, smart-ass. "I turned it off for you."

Lizzie went over and picked it up.

"Hey! I told you not to move. Don't do that again."

She scanned the road looking for Jones.

"I ran your license plates," Lee yelled from the car. "They came back
law enforcement. Your boyfriend must be a cop."

Nothing bad has happened yet.

"You're not going to talk to me, huh? Maybe I should put you
through a sobriety test. What do you think? Should we do that?"

He got out of her car and walked toward her, headed for the trunk.
She was now standing in his way. "You gonna make me go around
you?" he challenged her.

"You told me not to move."

He gave her the grin again, then brushed past her.

Lee opened the trunk. He pulled out her gym bag, then took her
boxing gear out. He dropped it piece by piece onto the side of the road.

"I guess I should've asked if your girlfriend is a cop. I'm not going
to find a strap-on in here, am I? I sure hope not."

He stopped when he found her briefcase.

It had the autopsy photos and copies of the witness interviews,
including Scanlon's. If Lee opened it, he would find the identity and
current location of the only eyewitness against him.

"Now, what's in here? Drugs? Guns? It's big enough for both."

Her briefcase was locked.

"Give me the key."

Never. Not without a warrant. Not even then.

"You understand English? I said give me the key!"

The rage in his voice was meant to scare her. It had the opposite effect. It always did.

"Get a warrant," she said.

He stepped toward her and thrust his face inches from hers. "What'd you fucking say to me?"

Don't speak, not a single word.

"Did you say get a warrant?" White specs of spit flew out of his mouth and onto her face. "Don't tell me my fucking job! Do it again and I'll fucking spread you over the hood! I'll take your fat ass to jail!"

Lizzie Scott hated bullies. She would not tolerate being bullied herself. Ask Elder Evans.

Her voice was quiet but seething. "I said get a search warrant. I said it because I don't think you know your job."

Lee thrust his arm over her shoulder and pointed to her Pontiac. "Move over there, tits to the car, ass facing me."

She didn't move.

He pushed her toward the car.

"Don't," she said.

"Or what!" he screamed, his face red, the veins on his neck popping. "I'm going to fucking search you and you're going to shut the fuck up!"

He grabbed her by the shoulder and spun her around so she now faced the Pontiac. Then he shoved her hard into it. "Get into the position!"

He kicked his boot between her ankles, forcing them apart. He hit her once in the small of her back, sending pain shooting through her kidney.

Something bad happened.

"Now just fucking stand there."

He slammed his hands against her buttocks then shoved them hard into the back pockets of her jeans, beginning to force them down.

She spun toward him, swinging her right fist. It caught him flush on the side of his jaw. It sent his sunglasses flying and staggered him so badly he almost fell. She squared up on him now, hands high and fists clenched, ready to hit him again.

"You fucking bitch." Lee pulled his gun.

She finally heard Jones's siren.

CHAPTER 21

LIZZIE DIDN'T DROP HER FISTS UNTIL JONES WAS OUT OF HIS CAR.

"Okay, okay," Jones said, holding his badge out so Lee got a good look. "Let's everybody calm down."

Lee holstered his gun.

Jones asked Lizzie if she was okay, then picked up Lee's sunglasses and handed them to him. Jones saw the gym clothes on the ground and the locked briefcase. The side of Lee's jaw was red and swelling. Lizzie was amped up ready to brawl.

"Anybody want to say anything?" Jones asked. He hadn't seen the punch but he had a pretty good idea who landed it.

Lizzie stared at Lee: *Go ahead. Tell him what you did.*

Lee's mind was clicking. He tried to figure the angles, going back over everything that happened, trying to remember if he said or did anything that would make things better or worse.

He blamed Jenkins. Lee almost never drank on the job. Jenkins called him earlier to tell him the feds were down asking questions. It made Lee nervous. He needed to calm his nerves. He bought a pint of bourbon at a gas station and downed half of it in the restroom.

Suddenly, finding this Lizzie Scott bitch on the road and pulling her over seemed like a great idea. Now, he had some doubts. The punch sobered him.

"You want to charge me with something, officer?" Lizzie dared him. "Do it. I want a record of everything *you* did, from the moment of the stop, to the rabbit punch, to you grabbing my ass. Maybe we should give *you* a sobriety test? Should we do that?"

72

Jones made a shushing sound. "Neither of us have the authority to handle DUI, Lizzie. Plus, you of all people should know, you have the right to remain silent."

She was a suspect here, too.

Jones *knew* she was speeding. She always drove too fast. He was pretty sure she hit Lee, too, though he guessed she had her reasons.

The question was, would either of them admit it happened? If one denied it, could the other one prove anything? Unless Lee's jaw or Lizzie's hand were broken, Jones had a hard time seeing how.

Lee already decided he didn't want to charge her.

What he wanted was to beat her bloody with his baton.

On the other hand, taking her in would embarrass her and her office. He might even get lucky. Maybe they'd drop the case against him altogether, or at least assign someone else instead of this bitch.

It finally dawned on him that he played this whole thing wrong. She would use it against him to make him look dirty, like he was some kind of out-of-control thug. It would be embarrassing too; he would look like a pussy for letting a woman kick his ass.

It still wasn't his fault. Not really. He was smarter than this. Nobody could handle all the shit he had to deal with. The worse things got at home, with his addict wife and crippled son, the worse things got at work. He wasn't himself.

"Do you know who Ms. Scott is, Officer Lee?"

Lee gave up. It was time he got some help.

"I'm going to make a call." Lee walked to his squad car.

Lizzie's hand was beginning to throb from the bare-knuckle punch.

"He knows who I am, Jones. If he runs me in, he'll get to search the briefcase. They'll know about Scanlon and where he is."

"We'll move him, don't worry about that." Jones called the U.S. Marshals to arrange for them to get Scanlon out of his trailer.

Jones kept his eyes on the squad car. Lee was talking to someone on his cell phone, not the car's radio unit. "You know. He's got a shotgun and MP-5 machine gun in the cruiser, plus his sidearm. I'm feeling kind of outgunned at the moment."

Suddenly, Lee hit the siren. It made Lizzie jump.

Lee gave her the grin again then pointed a gun finger at her.

He turned it into his middle finger.

Then he hit the accelerator, peeling out so fast Jones and Lizzie had jump out of the way of the car.

Lee left them in a cloud of dust on the side of the road.

CHAPTER 22

"DIDN'T I TELL YOU, DWAYNE-O? DIDN'T I SAY YOU'D NEED A lawyer?"

Don Farley gave Lee directions to Tommy Taylor's office.

They were an odd couple. Farley retired from the Inland County Sheriff's Department with full pension. Bored, he cold-called Taylor, a flashy defense lawyer who once humiliated him on the stand. Farley was surprised Taylor took his call.

"You ever play Brenford Oaks, Donnie?"

Farley hadn't. Membership was a million bucks. That was spare change for Taylor. Farley just hadn't heard Brenford Oaks started taking in blacks.

Taylor drove up in his big Bentley and hugged Farley like they were long-lost friends. Farley realized how small Taylor was. He seemed so much bigger in court.

They sat on the patio after their round. Taylor greeted the foot traffic; the man knew everybody. Over a bottle of pinot, Farley asked for a job.

"I hired you the day you called," Taylor said, drawing on his cigar. "You're advising me on law enforcement issues."

It is a crime for lawyers to pay someone to funnel them clients. It is not a crime for lawyers to hire consultants who *happen* to refer them clients.

Farley didn't think he would like working for a black guy, but it turned out he loved it. Taylor was funny and generous. The work was an excuse to do what Farley did most of the time anyway: golf with ex-colleagues, hang out in court, gossip about his old office.

75

Farley caught wind of Lee's troubles during a Sheriff's Association poker tournament. The feds were looking into the shooting. They had a witness.

The boss was interested. Every once in a while, Taylor defended a cop. It was good for business, an act of goodwill: a way to show the cop community Tommy Taylor wasn't their enemy.

The vast majority of Taylor's work involved trying to embarrass law enforcement on the stand in order to win an acquittal or big civil rights payoff. Doing something nice for a cop now and then was smart public relations. Like when Big Tobacco gives to charity. People remember the nice stuff.

"You let Officer Lee know that Tommy Taylor is a clean cop's best friend," Taylor said.

• • •

FARLEY MET LEE OUTSIDE TAYLOR'S NEWPORT BEACH OFFICES. There were ocean views and a Pilates studio next door. Taylor's blonde receptionist had the body of a suntan lotion model.

"That's the new Mrs. Taylor," Farley said, as they waited for in his enormous corner office. "She used to be a Pilates instructor."

Lee saw the UCLA Law School diploma, the photographs of Taylor with Presidents (Obama, Clinton, both Bushes), the bookcase covered with baseball hats from local police departments.

"You got to get me one from Blanton," Taylor said when he finally joined them. He was wearing a bespoke suit, Italian loafers, French cuffs and links, and cologne. Lee wondered if the lawyers on TV dressed like Taylor or if Taylor dressed like them.

"Call me Tommy," he said, shaking Lee's hand. "I'll call you Officer Lee, because I believe you deserve that."

Farley headed for the door. "Where are you headed to, Donnie?" Taylor waved Farley back and pointed to a chair. The lawyer sat down behind his desk.

"Forgive my appearance," Taylor said, picking lint off his sleeve. "I don't usually dress up over the weekend, but I have a client's funeral to go to later. Medical malpractice case. Would've been more money in it if she lived, what with the pain and suffering, but, really, it's a blessing she's gone."

Taylor asked Lee how he was doing. "It's stressful to be under a cloud like this, knowing they're looking at you, not sure what they're going to do," Taylor said. "You got to care take of yourself."

Lee asked if Taylor thought he'd be indicted.

"Oh, absolutely."

Jesus, Farley thought, *don't sugarcoat it.*

Taylor explained it was going to be a long haul. "The feds have all the time and money in the world. The important thing is for you to pace himself, take care of your family and—"

Lee cut him off.

"Just so you know, I will not spend one fucking night in custody."

Taylor smiled at Lee.

"You express yourself very well, Officer Lee. But we're not on the street right now, and I'm not some dumb ass nigger you just yanked out of his car. So why don't you shut the fuck up and let me talk now. Would that be *alright*? Would that *work* for you?"

Lee gave Taylor a cold stare and finally a small nod.

Taylor moved on. It wasn't personal. He wasn't the one looking at prison. "Life is timing, Officer Lee. Just a few years ago, this case would never be brought. A few years from now, who knows? Your bad luck is to be on the wrong side of history."

"I'm not going to jail."

"Yeah, you said that."

Farley jumped in.

"What Mr. Taylor is saying, Dwayne-o, is that right now the public is down on cops. The Justice Department needs to show that they're doing something."

Lee's mouth twisted into his grin. "Yeah, but when a cop gets killed, nobody marches for the dead cop's civil rights, do they?"

"True, true, very true," Taylor said. He was starting to dislike his new client. "But the point is, Officer Lee, when they do indict you, we've got options that—"

Lee cut him off again.

"I didn't do it."

"Quit interrupting me, goddammit!"

"You don't want to know I'm innocent?"

Taylor stared at Farley. Farley whispered into Lee's ear. Whatever he said made Lee grit his teeth and close his eyes. Farley finished and nodded to Taylor.

"Sorry," Lee made himself say.

"It's all good," Taylor said, back in friendly mode. "Look, I get it. It's no fun being a defendant. I've been there myself, believe me. God-damn IRS went after me. *Twice.* But you got to control yourself. First thing you got to do is promise me you won't do any more stupid shit like pulling the prosecutor over. Second thing is, you got to promise me you'll do exactly what I tell you."

Lee gave a reluctant nod yes.

"You also got to learn to say things out loud, for the record."

Lee gave him the grin.

"And take that goddamn grin off your face!" Taylor said. "I guess nobody ever told you this, but you got a real asshole grin. You got to learn to stop imposing it on people. If a jury sees that grin, they'll convict you. I would."

Farley cleared his throat.

Taylor held his hand up before he could say a word. "Goddamn, Donnie, if I'm going to do his case, I got to know the man under-stands how it works. If he can't take direction, I'm happy to refer him to Holscher—hell, he can go to Scheper for all I care—because I don't need this. I'm already taking a haircut on this case."

"The union appreciates you taking the case for less than usual, Tommy. And Dwayne-o hears you. He understands."

Taylor's eyes never left Lee's face.

"I'm sorry," Lee finally said.

Taylor nodded. This was part of the process, teaching the client who the boss was, training him. With cop clients, it meant getting them to let go of the notion they had any power in the process. Lee was going to be harder to train than most.

Taylor moved on again. "Can you trust the guys you work with? Are we going to have any trouble from anybody in your department?"

Lee said the department was behind him.

"They're always behind you in the beginning. It's funny how that sort of tails off as the case goes on. What I mean is, is there anybody in the department you're not sure of? Anybody who the feds could squeeze and use against you?"

Lee was said his department was clean.

"Bullshit," Taylor said. "There's no such thing as a clean police department. Not on this earth. Somebody's always cutting some corners, doing some shit he shouldn't be doing. Whoever it is, the feds are going to find out. Then they're going to go after him and cut him a deal to testify against you. Happens every single time."

Lee said they might have a problem with Detective Vern Moeller.

CHAPTER 23

THE STORY OF LIZZIE HITTING OFFICER LEE SPREAD FAST IN THE office.

Berg started calling her "The Prosecutioner."

Chief D'Ambrosio wanted her fired.

Jack reminded The Chief that Lizzie hadn't been charged with a crime. Nor did it seem she would be. Lee hadn't filed a complaint. He hadn't even put her speeding ticket through.

If Lizzie hadn't reported what happened to her bosses, including the United States Attorney herself, nobody would have even known about it.

The United States Attorney was intrigued. She summoned Lizzie to her office.

It would be the first time Lizzie met her. Recently appointed by the President and confirmed by the Senate, Mrs. Deborah Leonard was wealthy, connected, and The Chief's only boss. She hadn't visited the branch offices yet. Berg doubted she would.

"The stores in Costa Mesa don't have anything she can't get in Beverly Hills."

Mrs. Leonard's predecessor, Jimmy Walsh, hired Lizzie. Walsh was a fine lawyer but a prodigious fund-raiser, recently named Ambassador to Ireland.

Mrs. Leonard's secretary ushered Lizzie into the office.

Tiffany lamps graced the side tables and antique desk. A new skylight let in sun.

80

Mrs. Leonard's late husband had been the founder and president of Leonard Construction, a billion-dollar home-building empire.

Mrs. Leonard made other structural improvements to her office, much to the consternation of the General Service Administration and G.A.O. They were not used to members of the government spending vast sums of their own money to improve the quality of their surroundings.

Chief D'Ambrosio stood when Lizzie entered, formal in his buttoned coat and tie. At an office roast, Berg once joked that The Chief was "Nixon without a sense of humor." Berg was transferred to Santa Ana the next day.

Jack stood in the back of the room avoiding Lizzie's look.

Mrs. Leonard received Lizzie as if she were a visiting head of state. A small woman, she barely came up to Lizzie's shoulder, she was impeccably dressed in a St. John knit suit, antique brooch, and Hermes scarf.

A full tea was laid out on a side table; an antique china set, linen napkins, and scones.

"You should eat something before we get started," Mrs. Leonard said. "If you don't, you'll think I wasn't a good hostess. May I pour? A butler at the Dorchester taught me this *years* ago."

Mrs. Leonard's office window looked down on Boyle Heights. She and her late husband grew up on Breed Street long before it became Caesar E. Chavez Avenue.

"It's nice to see a girl with an appetite," Mrs. Leonard said. She had the bearing of a grand dame and the intrusive warmth of a Jewish mother. Lizzie stopped eating and tried not to blush in embarrassment. She did anyway.

The Chief got down to business.

"In light of the fact that Ms. Scott assaulted Officer Lee, I recommend we turn the case over to Main Justice, Civil Rights Division, for further action."

Lizzie noticed how Jack jumped on board when he saw where The Chief was headed.

"I agree with The Chief," Jack said. "The upside is, if the Justice Department prosecutor wants, he can call Lizzie as a witness against

Lee, have her testify about what happened, show the jury what Lee is capable of."

He's selling me out.

Berg always told her Jack was a yes-man. Who else would The Chief choose to be his deputy? Lizzie hadn't seen proof until now. She didn't like it.

"May I be heard on this?" Lizzie asked.

Mrs. Leonard said of course. "That's why you're here."

"I haven't been charged with assault and there's no reason to think I will be. Also, I've talked to Main Justice. They've looked at the case. They won't take it."

Chief D'Ambrosio jumped in. "If it's too weak for them, it's certainly too weak for us."

Lizzie corrected The Chief, which was never a good idea.

"They didn't say it was too weak. They said they didn't have an available prosecutor to send out from D.C. They're swamped. This isn't a high-profile case or priority for them. There's been no public outrage over Rincon, there's no video of the shooting, there's—"

"There is no case!" Chief D'Ambrosio yelled. "You have *one* eyewitness and he's *unsavory!* All you've developed is circumstantial evidence from an outside coroner. Even if there *were* a case, your assault on the target precludes our further involvement!"

It amazed Lizzie how men assumed yelling at a woman would make her back down.

"Lee hasn't said I *did* assault him."

The Chief was aghast. "Do you deny it happened?"

"*I'm* the one who told *you* about it." Lizzie's tone made Jack wince. "I can't *prove* it happened. Jack is just plain wrong about me testifying about what happened."

Jack shot her a glance. Lizzie hadn't realized Jack was so sensitive about being told he was wrong. So she said it again.

"Jack is wrong because no judge would let me testify as a witness in the Rincon case. That shooting had nothing to do with what happened between me and Officer Lee. Even if it did, it's way too prejudicial. And Lee would just deny it anyway."

Mrs. Leonard nodded. "She's right. I certainly can't see Lee's lawyer bringing it up. It would make his client look terrible. If I were Lee's lawyer, I would file a motion to keep us from mentioning it at trial."

Mrs. Leonard never handled a criminal case in her life. For years she was her husband's general counsel, handling everything from corporate mergers to negotiating international loans, to suing anyone who dared get in their way. Her skills as a lawyer were superb. It rarely takes a good lawyer long to get up to speed in a new area of the law.

"Mrs. Leonard," Lizzie said. "If we don't do this case, nobody else will. The local District Attorney already passed." The Chief was appalled. Lizzie was going over his head.

Even more galling, Mrs. Leonard seemed to be listening to her. "It does seem that Officer Lee has no business being a policeman."

The Chief was seething but kept a civil tongue, noting, with all due respect, Officer Lee's continued employment was a local concern, not a federal matter.

Lizzie kept pushing.

"But what about the victim? He was just a *kid*. He had no record. His grandmother—"

"Victims don't choose our workload, Ms. Scott." The Chief did not believe victims had *more* rights than anyone else. The whole "victims' rights movement" was, in The Chief's opinion, a ploy by cheap politicians to get votes, not a valid public policy.

Lizzie stared at Jack, looking for some help. Jack said nothing.

"I'm inclined to do the case," Mrs. Leonard said. "At least it would draw attention to what happened. It could lead to Blanton firing the officer."

The Chief maintained decorum. "Mrs. Leonard, we only have sufficient resources to prosecute a fraction of the federal crimes in the district. We don't do fraud cases of less than a million dollars, we don't do drug cases unless the amounts are vast or the perpetrators violent. Even then, we do a small number of them."

"How many unarmed guys does Lee have to kill before we do something here, Chief?"

Lizzie regretted saying it the moment the words left her mouth. The Chief would never forgive such disrespect. Jack was afraid he would storm out of the room. The Chief stayed calm.

"Let me tell you a little story about this office and a fellow by the name of Rodney King."

They knew the story. The Chief made them listen to it anyway. There was the videotape. The state brought charges and lost. The riot that followed destroyed a good chunk of L.A. The U.S. Attorney's Office and Justice Department charged the officers on federal civil rights charges. They did a *little* better than the state. Two of the four cops were convicted: hardly a clean sweep.

Many said it was the office's finest hour. What they didn't know was the rest of the story: the bad blood it generated between the office and every other law enforcement agency in Southern California. "Cases against the police are the most dangerous to bring," The Chief concluded.

"Thank you for your thoughts, Dante," Mrs. Leonard said.

The Chief bristled. No one used his first name except at church and in his home, and he hadn't suggested Mrs. Leonard start.

"I don't expect us to just do easy cases," Mrs. Leonard said. "I expect us to do hard ones, too. Even if we don't win, sometimes it's in the public interest to bring the case anyway, to send a message."

Jack cleared his throat and wondered aloud if Lizzie's confrontation with Lee ought to weigh against pursuing this *particular* case.

"Not at all," Mrs. Leonard said. "If we drop the case or remove Lizzie, Officer Lee will have won. I don't like to let bullies win. Anyway, I like a girl who stands up for herself; it shows character."

· · ·

Afterward, Lizzie caught Jack in the hallway.

"Thanks for the support. It meant a lot to me. Really."

"You didn't need my help," Jack said, head bowed.

She never said she *needed* his help, but it would have been nice to have.

Jack went to see The Chief.

"Call OPR," he fumed. "Have them open an investigation on your friend Lizzie Scott."

OPR, the Office of Professional Responsibility, is the internal affairs division for federal prosecutors. Housed in the Department of Justice in D.C., it investigates wrongdoing and misconduct. If they find it, the guilty prosecutor can lose his job or go to prison.

"I want her gone," The Chief said. "The minute this case is over, Lizzie Scott's tenure in this office is over, too. Is that clear?"

Jack wasn't proud of it, but he was more upset The Chief thought he and Lizzie were friends than he was that The Chief was trying to get Lizzie fired.

What did The Chief know about them? Did he know about their one night?

It mattered. The Chief was a prude. He hadn't opposed gender or sexual orientation equality. He was just appalled gender and sex were being discussed in the office. He complied with the law and wishes of the Justice Department, EEOC, and whomever the president got around to appointing as *the* United States Attorney.

But he still had the authority to impose a policy against office romances, particularly between those of different rank and responsibility. If The Chief found out Jack had slept with Lizzie, he'd strip him of the deputy chief title.

For a man who thought himself a keen observer of the human condition, The Chief didn't seem to appreciate the temptation of forbidden fruit. Or the undeniable fact, proven time and time again, that men and women who spent their lives condemning and convicting others were prone to let off steam by sleeping with one another at a shockingly high rate.

* * *

JACK MADE BERG GIVE LIZZIE THE BAD NEWS.

"They're putting me on leave?" Her hand was killing her. She hadn't been able to train the way she liked. She wanted to get back to the gym and to the Rincon case, not waste time on this.

"Think of it as a forced vacation," Berg said. "Just until the OPR investigators can come out from D.C. and talk with you."

She was suspended again, just like back in school. Once again, it was for fighting. Life was the same damn thing over and over again. Only the men in charge changed. And they didn't even change that much.

Sarah and Tom took her to Laguna for the day. It felt weird being there in the middle of the week. She ran five miles with Bodhi along the surf. Seeing Sarah and Tom kissing didn't make her feel better. Thinking about Jack just made her mad.

CHAPTER 24

THE OPR ATTORNEYS ARRIVED FROM D.C. A FEW DAYS INTO Lizzie's forced leave. Against everyone's advice, she went in for the interview without a lawyer. Her hand was still swollen and achy, but she wouldn't even take aspirin. Convocation was against medicine, but that's not why. The pain felt cleansing.

Jack felt guilty about not supporting her. He expedited a 24-hour turnaround on the transcript. He highlighted the parts he thought might help her with The Chief.

Q: Were you cited for speeding or assault on the police officer?
A: No, but I *was* speeding. The punch was self-defense. I was completely justified in hitting him.

"Self-serving," The Chief said when he read it. "She's a slippery one."

Q: Do you have any personal bias against Officer Lee?
A: I'm trying to convict him of murdering an unarmed man because I think he did that. I'm not going to say I like the guy. I don't. But it doesn't matter. The case is not personal.

The Chief slammed the file shut. "They won't fire her! They won't even recommend we take her off the case!"

They couldn't, Jack noted, not yet, anyway. It was a classic Catch-22. Under OPR's own rules, they couldn't complete the investigation without talking to the alleged victim of Lizzie's misconduct, Officer Lee. But until Lee's murder trial was finished, OPR couldn't reach out to him to ask him what happened. Even if they did, Lee's lawyer wouldn't allow it. Moreover, Lee hadn't complained about anything. The Chief had.

"This whole case belongs in state court," The Chief groused, referring to state court as if it was a sewer. The U.S. Attorney's Office is a prestige location. Its power lay in its integrity, seriousness of purpose, and lawyerly excellence. Its reputation is made as much by the cases it does *not* do as the cases it does.

Usually, The Chief could kill the weak ones. Yet despite his efforts, the Rincon case lived. He had to do *something*.

"I'm replacing Lizzie Scott with you, Jack," The Chief said.

That would remove any issue the defense could gin up to make this look like a vindictive prosecution. Avoid the embarrassment of the media doing a story on the prosecutor punching out the defendant. He could move Lizzie some place safe, like appeals. It would take her off the trial line until OPR got around to issuing a report he could use to fire her.

Jack gently explained why replacing Lizzie with anyone would be the wrong move. "She knows the facts, has established relationships with the victim's family—"

"Don't talk to me about victims' rights!"

"I'm just asking, why stick me or anybody else with what you think is a loser? If anybody is going to get hurt over what's happened, it's Lizzie, not the office. If she wins, great, no harm no foul. And if she loses, well . . . it's her fault. Anyway, she may not even get enough to evidence to indict it."

The Chief gave Jack a nod. Maybe there was hope for his protégé yet.

* * *

This time, Jack left a message on Lizzie's machine. She could come back to work. OPR cleared her for the time being. They wouldn't complete their investigation into her possible wrongdoing until the Lee case was over.

"More good news: The Chief is letting you keep the Rincon case."

Lizzie listened to the message three times. The fact that he hadn't come down to deliver this good news himself said a lot.

She was done with Handsome Jack for good.

CHAPTER 25

JONES KNOCKED ON DETECTIVE MOELLER'S DOOR AT 11:00 P.M. THE late-night knock wasn't nice but it got people's attention. Moeller was due in the grand jury the next morning. Jones didn't think he was going to get much sleep tonight anyway.

"Ready to go?" Jones asked.

"*Now?*"

"It was your lawyer's idea," Jones explained. He made Moeller put on a coat and tie. "You're meeting important people. We can't have you looking bad."

Lizzie's first act when she came back to work was to reach out to Moeller's lawyer and negotiate a Queen-for-a-Day.

It is a simple contract between a federal prosecutor and a potential witness. The deal lets the government hear what the witness knows about a crime on the promise that they won't prosecute the witness for what they tell them.

She needed Berg's sign-off.

"Who's the Queen?"

"Officer Moeller."

Berg shuddered. "Make sure he's not armed. That's another problem prosecuting the police, they're usually armed." Berg was afraid of guns.

Lizzie said Moeller wouldn't be there for hours. His lawyer was coming down from Fresno. She spent the time catching up on work. Counting the cases on appeal, ready to indict, in the early stages of

investigation, or set to be declined, Rincon was only the most complicated of the 50 or so active matters in her files.

At 1:00 A.M., Jones came in with bags of tacos from the truck on
Chestnut and Main.

"Moeller was hungry," Jones said. "Thought you might be, too."

She was beginning to love Jones. That he kept her fed was just one
of the reasons.

Around 2:00 A.M., Moeller's lawyer, Dickran Drooyan, arrived.
Traffic was worse than he expected. A sad-eyed, bald man with unnat-
urally tanned skin, Drooyan had the tired look of a low-end Vegas
Strip pit boss. He carried a briefcase and a bag from 7-Eleven. He
asked for a few minutes to meet with his client.

"You don't know him?" Lizzie thought that might be a problem.

"I know him," Drooyan said. "But I don't *know* him. We talked on
the phone. I like to get a feel for the guy I'm cooperating." Drooyan
had no moral issue with letting his client cooperate with the government. Many defense lawyers considered it a violation of their duty of
loyalty to the community of the accused. They would fire the client
rather than let them become a government witness.

"Okay," Drooyan said. "We're ready. Let's get going. I got to be back
in Fresno by 8:00 A.M. for court."

Moeller shuffled into Lizzie's office. "I didn't do anything wrong,"
Moeller said without being asked.

"Shut up," Drooyan said. He gave Lizzie a put-upon look: *Do you
see what I have to put up with?*

"I explained it to him," Drooyan said. "But you should do it again.
It couldn't hurt. He's slow." Moeller didn't seem to notice or care what
his lawyer thought of him.

Drooyan took a wrapped sandwich from the 7-Eleven bag. "Do you
mind? I missed dinner."

Lizzie explained the deal: Moeller would tell them everything he
knew about Lee and the shooting, including any crimes or efforts to
cover up crimes, as well as anything he said about it before or afterward.

In exchange, they wouldn't prosecute Moeller for any criminal
activity he confessed to.

Drooyan nodded and chewed his sandwich.

"But if you lie to us, Mr. Moeller . . ."

Drooyan glared at his client: "Are you listening to this part? This is the important part."

Lizzie told Moeller that if he lied to them about anything, the contract was broken, the deal was off, they could prosecute him for the crimes he admitted as well as for perjury and obstruction of justice for whatever lies he told them.

"Poof," Drooyan said, wiping his mouth. "You go from Queen-for-a-Day back to Cinderella. And they get to fuck you in the ass. Okay? You got it?"

Moeller said he got it.

"He's got it," Drooyan said.

The lawyers and Moeller signed the deal.

Jones started the questioning. According to the tapes of the radio calls, Moeller didn't arrive at the scene for two hours.

Moeller considered that quick. "When the call came in, I was on the other side of the county. Sometimes, I don't get to the scene until the next day."

By the time Moeller got there, the crime scene was already cleaned up. The Inland Coroner was ready to take Rincon's body away, the CHP had taken their photos and measurements, and a tow truck was ready to roll the pickup to the evidence lot.

"Did somebody run into the pickup out there?" Lizzie asked. "Because the door was dented when I saw it."

The tow truck driver did it before Moeller arrived. "The tow truck guy's name is Arnie something. He's not real good at his job."

Drooyan chuckled. "Neither are you, my friend." The lawyer from Fresno had no respect for white-trash shit kickers from the Inland Empire. They were still a bunch of Okies.

Moeller said he followed the tow truck to the impound lot. He drove Lee in the squad car. The ride took an hour or so. They didn't talk the whole way there.

"You were the investigator in the shooting but you didn't ask him about what happened?" Lizzie asked.

Moeller pulled out a laminated card from his wallet and handed it to her. It looked like the Miranda card except it was titled "California Police Officer's Bill of Rights." Among other things, it said that under the law, police officers had 24 hours before they were required to submit to questioning about any officer-involved shooting.

"Anyhow, Lee already told the CHP what happened before I got there. That's the stuff I used for my report. Everything I said happened that night came from the Chippy."

Jones already reached out and interviewed the CHP lieutenant who took the report. Lee told the same story to the lieutenant that he told Deputy D.A. Seave. If Lee was lying, he knew enough to at least be consistent.

Moeller explained that he inventoried the equipment Lee had on him that night. He then made Lee sign that the list was complete and accurate. Moeller didn't think to take or photograph Lee's uniform but hadn't remembered seeing any stains on them.

Before she met him, Lizzie suspected he was covering up for Lee. Now, she believed Moeller was just incompetent. In his defense, neither the CHP lieutenant nor Deputy D.A. Seave asked about Lee's uniform or flashlight. No one knew Lee fell on the ground when the pickup's door opened or that the flashlight was an issue in the case until Hoot Scanlon said so.

Scanlon could be lying, don't forget.

Lizzie caught Drooyan staring at her, eyebrows raised, like they were playing charades, and he wanted her to keep guessing.

"I'm starting to think nobody asked you the right question," Lizzie said. "Because they didn't know to ask. I'm going to try. Did you see Officer Lee with a flashlight that night?"

Moeller dropped his head to his chest and cursed. Drooyan smirked. "It's about time. I thought we'd be here all night."

Drooyan opened his briefcase. He pulled out a large toiletries bag and handed it to Jones.

The butt end of Officer Lee's flashlight was sticking out of it.

CHAPTER 26

MOELLER DIDN'T LIE. LEE *HADN'T* SAID A WORD TO HIM ABOUT THE shooting. When they got to the impound lot, Lee opened the squad car's and handed Moeller his toiletries bag. He asked Moeller to hold it for him. Moeller didn't ask why. He didn't ask about the flashlight either.

"Nobody ever said anything to me about a flashlight," Moeller said. It hadn't been in Lee's statement to the CHP report. "I can't ask about what I don't know." For a police detective, Moeller was surprisingly but sincerely incurious.

Jones sent the flashlight to the FBI lab. They found Lee's prints, as well as Moeller's, but no blood, and no Rincon DNA. Lee had plenty of time to wipe the flashlight down before he gave it to Moeller, and Moeller mishandled it when he got it.

It didn't matter. The fight is in rounds. Lizzie was beginning to win the first round, the investigation. If Scanlon was telling the truth, Rincon was standing outside the pickup with nothing in his hands. He was no threat to Lee. Lee had no right to hit him in the head. If Lee hadn't shot Rincon, Lizzie could still have charged him with excessive force based on what he did to Rincon with the flashlight.

More important was that Lee hid the flashlight. It was devastating evidence against him. It was the action of a guilty man trying to cover his tracks. It wasn't a smoking gun. There never was one. But it was more than enough to take to the grand jury.

. . .

MOST OF THE TIME, TO GET AN INDICTMENT, ALL A PROSECUTOR HAS to show is probable cause that a crime had been committed, and this was the person who committed it.

But whomever the idiot was who said a grand jury would indict a ham sandwich never prosecuted a police officer.

The police are not merely presumed innocent. They are presumed to be heroes. To accuse a police officer strikes the average citizen as a sacrilege.

Put on too little of a case against a cop in the grand jury and they vote a "no bill," rejecting the indictment. Show them too much and you create a lot of prior witness statements that can come back to haunt you at trial.

Lizzie wanted to keep it simple. She wanted to charge Lee with one count of using deadly force against Rincon when he shot him.

She would use the flashlight blow and Lee's attempt to hide it as proof of his guilt. It was always the cover-up that brought people down.

Chief D'Ambrosio didn't trust simple.

Assuming Scanlon was telling the truth, Lee broke the law when he used excessive force by smashing Rincon in the head with the flashlight even before he shot him.

The Chief agreed there was no point in charging it as a separate crime; the judge would probably just merge them into one count, and it wouldn't add much to Lee's sentence if he were convicted.

But The Chief was adamant that they charge a second count. Along with having the right not to be beaten and murdered, Rincon had the right to due process of law. Lee violated that right when he hid the flashlight and signed the false inventory report.

Lizzie thought it was a ticky-tack theory that would hurt her chances of convicting Lee of murder. "I'll be giving the jury an easy out. They'll split the baby. They'll convict Lee of the false report charge and let him walk on murder. Odds are Lee won't even serve a year for filing the false report."

"Doesn't matter," Jack said, "so long as you get him on something."

Lizzie stood her ground. "It's not justice. Rincon died. Convicting Lee of paperwork—"

"It's not paperwork," Jack said, "it's a false statement made under oath."

"Then let the state charge it," Lizzie said.

Jack was hoping Lizzie would agree to charge both counts. It was what The Chief wanted. If it turned out to be a mistake, she would own a part of the blame. But she was impossible. Stubborn. She gave him no choice. He would go around her.

"I'll really try to convince the Indictment Committee to let you just charge the one count," Jack lied.

"Wait. Can't I present my own case to the Indictment Committee? It's my case."

Jack lied again and said he was looking out for her. It was better to leave the decision over how to charge the case with somebody else. "This way Lee can't claim vindictive prosecution, based on your confrontation."

OPR was still going to issue a final report on her confrontation with Lee when the case was over.

The Indictment Committee met over sandwiches and beers in the conference room of the Major Crimes Section. They were the office's collective brain. Because he hand-selected the committee, The Chief respected them. He also respected the process. After all, he created it. The Chief never overruled the decision of the Committee.

Later that night, Jack called Lizzie with their decision.

"I tried. Really," he said for the third time. "You can indict both the shooting and the false statement or neither. It's the federal way. We're the people who did Al Capone on taxes, don't forget."

Silence.

She wanted to hang up, but she was enjoying his discomfort.

"I did what I could," Jack said. "I swear."

Lizzie no longer believed a word Handsome Jack said.

CHAPTER 27

"Henry? Are you going to be okay?" Lizzie stood with Scanlon in the grand jury hallway.

He bit his nails and made a low, whining sound. His clothes were too small. Lizzie borrowed them from the witness coordinator's emergency court clothing. His hair stuck up like corn stalks.

"I think I'm going to puke," he said.

Jones took him to the men's room.

Lizzie had agonized for days over whether to put Scanlon in the grand jury.

"I wouldn't risk it," Jack advised. "You don't need Scanlon to testify in person to get an indictment." There was an easier way to do it. Hearsay was legal in the grand jury. Jones could summarize what the witnesses told him, lay out the facts, then Lizzie could tell the grand jury the law, answer their questions, and put it to a vote.

That's how it worked in most cases. Jones already summarized the testimony of the coroner about the flashlight blow and showed them the flashlight, explaining Moeller's role in it.

But Lizzie worried if she didn't put Scanlon in the grand jury, the grand jurors would think she was hiding him.

"They'd be right," Mrs. Leonard said. She didn't get involved in many cases but Lizzie Scott still intrigued her. Like most strong women, Mrs. Leonard liked other strong woman and encouraged them, particularly when they were younger and just starting out.

"If you can't convince the grand jury Mr. Scanlon is believable, there is no way you are going to get a trial jury to convict," Mrs. Leonard said. "As I understand it, the upside of calling Mr. Scanlon is he'd be under oath and on the record. So if Mr. Scanlon drank himself to death or walked in front of a train before trial, you could read his grand jury testimony to the trial jury."

Lizzie started to think the late Mr. Leonard's enormous financial success had a lot to do with his wife being his lawyer.

Scanlon came out of the men's room looking worse than when he went in.

Jones handed him a box of Tic Tacs.

"Courtesy of the government," Jones smiled. "Now if they ask if you got anything for your testimony, you can say yes."

Scanlon emptied half the box into his mouth.

. . .

THE GRAND JURORS STARED AT SCANLON, UNSURE WHAT TO MAKE of him, but after an hour of testimony, many of them had gone from distrust to affection. Hoot Scanlon was a hard man to dislike when he was sober.

A number of the jurors managed it. They accused him of hating cops, of being too drunk to see what he claimed, of being on drugs.

"I don't do drugs anymore," Scanlon said. "Can't afford them. 'If I'm using, I'm losing; if I'm boozing, I'm fine.' And I wasn't even boozing that night. I left the vodka back at the damn trailer."

With Scanlon still in the room, one of the grand jurors, a retired L.A. fireman, asked the same question he always did, no matter how many times she explained it to him.

"I'd like to hear Officer Lee's side of things next," the grand juror said. "Can't you bring Officer Lee in here?"

Lizzie smiled. "Remember how we talked about the Fifth Amendment, how we can't compel someone to testify against himself? . . ." Federal grand juries are invitation only. The defendant has no obligation to appear, and the prosecutor cannot make him come in. It would violate his right against self-incrimination.

Another grand juror, a retired elementary schoolteacher, smiled in sympathy when Lizzie had to run through it again. He was used to dealing with students who didn't listen.

"Well, what about Officer Lee's boss then?" the ex-fireman asked. "Can't we hear from him? Maybe he's got something he could share with us about Officer Lee's character."

Lizzie said she would subpoena Al Jenkins, Lee's supervisor.

• • •

JONES WAS RELIEVED WHEN THE DOOR OPENED AND SCANLON walked out.

"I done good, boss," Scanlon told Jones.

"You did very well, Henry," Lizzie said when she joined them. "I'm proud of you."

Scanlon beamed.

"They want to hear from Jenkins next," Lizzie said. Jones frowned. He was hoping the grand jury would indict on his and Scanlon's testimony.

Lizzie didn't want to call Jenkins either. It would delay the grand jury's vote on the indictment, but she didn't want to say no to the ex-fireman. Turn down a grand juror too much and you get a runaway jury on your hands, demanding all sorts of evidence and witnesses. It is better to keep them happy.

What she didn't tell Jones was that she didn't think she had enough votes to get the indictment. She didn't need all the grand jurors, just most of them, and she didn't believe she was close.

CHAPTER 28

JENKINS ONLY AGREED TO APPEAR IN THE GRAND JURY IF THEY gave him a nontarget letter, assuring him he wasn't going to be indicted. Otherwise, he was going to take the Fifth.

"Gee, Al," Jones asked. "What could we indict you for?"

Lizzie gave Jenkins the letter so he would feel better. It didn't give him any kind of immunity, really, but he didn't know that.

The ex-fireman was wrong if he thought Jenkins was going to help Lee's case.

"Instead of a new headquarters, why don't you hire better police?" the ex-schoolteacher asked.

Jenkins explained that Inland County, like every other county in California, paid for construction to create jobs. They didn't give cities money to pay higher salaries.

The elderly Iranian man wondered why Lee was still on the police force.

"He hasn't done anything wrong, as far as I know," Jenkins said. "He hasn't even been arrested. If I fired him, he'd sue for wrongful termination. And we'd settle with him, too. It's too damn expensive to fight these things in trial, thanks to the lawyers."

"So if we indict him, you'll have to fire him?" the Iranian man asked.

Before Jenkins answered, Lizzie cut him off. "I have to instruct the grand jury, you can't indict Lee to get him off the force. You can only indict him if you think he committed a federal crime."

The Iranian man smiled and wagged a finger at her. "No, we would never do that."

When Lizzie walked out of the room, Jones was waiting for her.

He looked as shocked as Jones ever looked. Tommy Taylor was with him.

Down the hall, in a suit and tie, was Taylor's client, Dwayne Wayne Lee.

"What's he doing here?" Lizzie asked.

Jones said she wouldn't believe it.

"He wants to testify in the grand jury."

* * *

"I DISLIKE TOMMY TAYLOR," CHIEF D'AMBROSIO SAID. "I RESENT his involvement in this case."

Jack said they couldn't really control who the defense lawyer was.

The Chief didn't agree. "Bad cases bring out bad lawyers. You brought a bad case. Don't try to evade your responsibility for this!"

Lizzie asked what she should do. The law said she couldn't force Lee into the grand jury to testify *against* himself. Could Lee force her to let him in to the grand jury to testify *for* himself?

The federal system does not give grand jury targets the right to testify. A few state courts did but almost no target ever does, for one good reason: It is a trap.

The prosecutor conducting the grand jury investigation will ask the target if he committed the crime. The target is under oath. He is not allowed to have a defense lawyer with him. The target can confess his guilt, handing the prosecutor a conviction for whatever the grand jury is investigating, or he can lie in the hope that the grand jury won't indict him. When he's convicted, he'll then face additional perjury and obstructions charges.

If the target is really and truly not guilty of anything, he could conceivably take his chances and try to convince the grand jury not to charge him. But no lawyer would recommend it or condone taking such a risk.

"It's legal malpractice for Taylor to be trying this," Jack said.

Lizzie agreed. She thought it was also a brilliant strategy.

If she kept Lee from telling his side of the story, Taylor would spin it against her in trial: "Ms. Scott never cared about the truth. She wouldn't even let Officer Lee give his version of what happened to the grand jury."

"We have to let him testify," Lizzie said.

"No. That's not what we're going to do here," The Chief said to Jack.

"Look at me, Chief. Please," Lizzie said. The Chief rarely deigned to look at who he was talking to, especially if they were assistants. "This is my case, it should be my call."

The Chief raised his eyebrows to Jack. *You see how she talks to me?*

The Chief finally relented, but he still wouldn't look at her. He spoke to Jack. "Make sure she puts all the Fifth Amendment warnings on the record, make certain Lee knows whatever he says is going to be used against him, and tell him what happens if he lies."

Jack nodded to Lizzie. They made for the door. The Chief stopped them.

"Please mention to Ms. Scott that this may be her only chance to cross-examine the defendant, so I hope she's ready for it."

She wasn't. She never expected Lee to show up in the grand jury. This was part of Taylor's plan. A sucker punch before she was ready for it.

• • •

TAYLOR SAT IN A CORNER TABLE OF THE COURT CAFETERIA, entertaining a group of DEA agents waiting for arraignment court.

"There she is," Taylor said when he saw Lizzie. "Do you all know Ms. Scott? She's a wonderful prosecutor. Truly gifted."

Taylor knew nothing about Lizzie Scott as a prosecutor, but it didn't cost him anything to compliment opponents he was sure he could whip.

"Mr. Taylor, where's your client?"

Taylor nodded to a table across the way.

Lee sat with a man wearing a bolo tie and Stetson.

"Who's the cowboy?"

"Mr. Don Farley, my investigator. Are we ready to have our say?"

Lizzie nodded. Taylor flashed an okay sign to Farley. He and Lee walked to the elevators.

"Excuse me, gentlemen," Taylor said to the DEA agents, sliding out of the booth.

"No rest for the wicked." With a nifty piece of sleight of hand, Taylor made business cards appear, fanned out like a poker hand. He then dealt them to the agents. "Worked my way through law school dealing Pai Gow at the Bicycle Club."

Lizzie and Taylor rode up in the elevator together. "You know who else was a card dealer?" Taylor asked, making conversation. "The Chief Justice of the California State Supreme Court. She used to deal blackjack in Reno. True story. Check it out."

Lizzie asked Taylor if he knew how the grand jury worked, that he wouldn't be allowed in, that Lee was exposing himself to perjury charges. Taylor let her finish.

"I don't suppose we could talk about you not bringing this case at all, is there?"

Lizzie couldn't believe it. "Are you looking for a plea offer?"

Taylor laughed.

"If Officer Lee wanted a plea offer, why would he hire me? No, Ms. Scott, I'm just trying to save you from doing something you and your office are going to regret."

Lizzie thanked him for his concern. She was used to opponents trying to get under her skin. Trash talk was part of the game.

CHAPTER 29

LEE WALKED INTO THE GRAND JURY AND TOOK HIS SEAT IN THE witness stand.

The grand jurors were transfixed. In their six months' serving on the panel, hearing all kinds of cases, this was the first and last time the target came in to speak for himself.

The jury forewoman gave him the oath. Lizzie warned him that everything he said would be used against him if the grand jury indicted him.

"I understand," Lee said. "I hope it doesn't come to that."

He removed a piece of paper from his coat pocket. "I'm a little nervous," he said. He didn't sound it. Lizzie thought he sounded angry. "I wanted to make sure I said everything that needed to be said. May I read this, please?"

Lizzie nodded. He could read whatever he liked. He would still have to answer questions.

"Thank you for this opportunity to speak with you today," Lee read. "My name is Dwayne Wayne Lee, and I am proud to be a City of Blanton police officer. I consider it my calling. Other than my family, being an officer is the most important thing in my life, and I have tried to do my job to the best of my ability."

Lee glanced at Lizzie and asked if he could have some water. He kept his face neutral, but she thought she saw the hate in his eyes. She hoped the jury saw it, too. Lizzie poured water from the pitcher in front of her and handed Lee the Styrofoam cup.

"Thanks."

The old Iranian man smiled at Lizzie. *Don't worry. I see what he is.* Lee went back to reading his statement.

"My counsel advised me not to appear before you today. I have chosen to come anyway, against his advice. I believe it is important that you, the grand jury, hear what happened on the night when Mr. Joe Rincon was shot. And to hear it directly from me."

Lee took another sip of water.

"To be clear, for the record, on the night of my confrontation with Mr. Rincon, I discharged my firearm for one reason and one reason only: Mr. Rincon confronted me with deadly force. During a traffic stop, Mr. Rincon attacked me, leaving me no alternative but to shoot him."

Lizzie jotted notes: *"No mention of flashlight, no details of fight, no head blow."*

"I wish Mr. Rincon hadn't forced me to use deadly force, but based on my training and experience as an officer, I had no choice."

Several of the grand jurors—men—nodded. That's all they need to know. Lee was one of them. A man doing the best job he could.

Lee folded the paper and put it back into his coat pocket. "Thank you."

All eyes turned toward Lizzie. After months of investigation, this was her first and probably only chance to ask Lee what happened.

Lizzie never went straight out at an opponent. She liked to take angles, get them off balance, throw punches from places they didn't expect to see them coming from.

She was the same way when it came to cross-examination. She never started at the beginning of their story. She started in the middle or the end, with a question the witness would never expect her to lead with.

"Officer Lee," she began. "In which hand did Mr. Rincon hold the knife when you claimed he rushed you?"

She caught him flat-footed. Whatever he thought her first question was going to be, it wasn't this. He couldn't help it. He flashed the grin. He caught himself and forced his face back to neutral, but Lizzie thought the grand jurors caught it. The Foreperson clearly did. It made her cringe.

"May I go speak with my attorney?" Lee asked. He couldn't have his lawyer in the room, but Lee could excuse himself to consult with counsel. The whispered conversations took place in the hallway and were confidential.

Lee walked out. Lizzie wondered if he would come back. She stayed in the room and couldn't help but hear the grand jurors conversations. They didn't give her confidence.

"He looks a little like my grandson," one of the older men said. "Is he a veteran? He looks like he could've been in the army." Several other grand jurors discussed Lee's courage. "Never saw a defendant come in like this."

They like him. They don't want to charge him.

The door opened. Lee came back in and took his seat.

"Thank you for the chance to speak with counsel," he said. "At this point, on the advice of counsel, I wish to assert my right under the Fifth Amendment of the U.S. Constitution not to be compelled to become a witness against myself."

With that, Lee stood up and walked out of the room.

"He memorized that last part," the retired schoolteacher said. "Did you notice?"

Lizzie had to admit Taylor was creative. He managed to get his client's story in without subjecting him to cross-examination. Lizzie couldn't force Lee back into the room to take questions. She also couldn't erase his testimony from the grand jurors' minds.

She *could* explain what Lee did was wrong, but it was risky. Taylor would ask for and get the transcript of her comments. The more she derided Lee's testimony, the more unfair the process looked.

"The less said, the less mended."

It annoyed her that Elder Evans was often right.

Lee had his fans. The ex-fireman and several others would not indict him no matter what. His appearance in the grand jury strengthened his hold on them. Lizzie didn't think Lee swayed any of the jurors who were on the fence or had already decided he should be charged. By her count, she had just enough votes to get a true bill. But it was close.

"Officer Lee has the right to take the Fifth Amendment, so don't hold that against him," she said. "Had we known he wasn't going to take questions, perhaps we wouldn't have let him testify, but we thought it was important to give him every opportunity to speak with you."

One of the older men raised his hand. "Who's his lawyer?"

Tommy Taylor was a controversial figure. You loved him or hated him. Lizzie knew Lee's fans were probably Taylor haters. They might turn against Lee if they knew Taylor was on his team.

Lizzie told the jurors it wasn't relevant who Lee's lawyer was.

The ex-fireman raised his hand. "I just want to say, I understand why the officer didn't want to answer questions. I wouldn't either. I'd be scared of saying the wrong thing."

The retired schoolteacher told him that wasn't a question.

Lizzie read the indictment to them. She explained the law and told them it was now time for them to decide whether Lee stood trial for what he did to Rincon. No speeches, no pathos: just the facts. She then excused herself. The prosecutor is not allowed to sit in on deliberations.

• • •

JONES AND LIZZIE LEANED AGAINST THE WALL OUTSIDE THE grand jury room waiting for their decision. It amazed her more defense lawyers didn't do what Taylor had done.

"It would only work with a cop," Jones said. "Maybe an astronaut. It has to be somebody who comes into the room already respected, just because of what they do for a living."

Three hours later, the grand jury broke for the day without taking a vote on the indictment. They would continue their deliberations in the morning.

It was a bad sign.

CHAPTER 30

LIZZIE WENT HOME THAT NIGHT, TOOK A SHORT RUN, THEN WAS too tired to make dinner. She fell asleep on the couch.

She woke up afraid.

Someone was trying to break down her door.

She grabbed a softball bat from under the couch.

"Who is it?" she yelled.

Whoever it was stopped. She heard the tired voice of Sarah's father.

"Lizbeth Scott, honey? We're not here to hurt you."

A solid Convocation member, a good friend of Elder Evans, Sarah's father sounded terrible. Lizzie spoke to him with the chain still on the door.

"Sarah's not here, sir. She moved out a few weeks ago."

"I know," he said. "We just thought maybe you could help us get Sarah away from the man she's with."

"We?" "Us?"

Lizzie knew who Convocations members relied on in times of crises. She had no doubt who was with Sarah's father. Having him so close scared her. But she hated being scared.

So she undid the chain and opened the door, just to show herself she could.

There he was, standing in the hallway's shadows: Elder Evans himself.

Lizzie regripped the softball bat and raised it to her shoulder.

"Your light's out, daughter," Elder Evans said calmly, his low, deep voice rolling toward her like faraway thunder. "Invite us in. Let's talk about this. We're just here to save your friend. That's all."

Lizzie didn't move. "She's an adult, sir. You can't force her to do anything anymore."

Elder Evans stepped forward. A shaft of light fell from her apartment onto his face. Sarah held her breath. His face was part prophet, part madman, handsome, cruel, and too often in her mind.

"Look at this man. See his pain." Elder Evans held his long arm toward Sarah's father. "You grew up with this man. This man is your family. You would not stand idly by and let your family suffer."

She tried to laugh at him.

You're such a drama queen, I bet you broke the light yourself to make it scarier. You're a ham, a wannabe televangelist without a studio.

But she didn't laugh. She never could.

The voice rumbled again. "If you won't help us, will you pray for her with us?"

"I can pray without you, sir," Lizzie said. "I don't need you for that."

Elder Evans told Sarah's father to wait for him in the car.

Sarah's dad, exhausted and desperate, left without a word.

Elder Evans lifted his palms up and closed his eyes, silently bestowing a blessing on her. The same way he did every day from the morning she was born until she moved away to college.

"Please don't," Lizzie said, finally lowering the softball bat, fighting the urge to bow her head and accept his grace.

How fucked up is that?

When he was finished, he looked up, his face peaceful, his smile kind.

"You've fallen away from us, daughter," he said. "I hate your sin, but I love the sinner. You are always welcome back home."

Lizzie stopped herself from ordering him off her property.

He turned and left.

Lizzie closed the door behind her and slid to the floor, dropping the softball bat.

She grabbed her cell phone.

Sarah answered on the first ring.

She was weeping.

"Elder Evans is coming over there," Lizzie said. "Your dad, too. They're going to try to take you away from Tom. I'm going to call the police—"

"Don't," Sarah said. "Please, Lizzie. I'm the one who called my dad and Elder Evans. I'm sorry. I can't live this way. Convocation is who I am, you know?"

"It doesn't have to be," Lizzie said. "They don't own you, honey. Elder Evans didn't save your life when you were a kid. Antibiotics did. Doctors did. If you want to stay there—"

"I can't!" Sarah said, weeping, ashamed. "I just can't."

They brought Sarah back to Lizzie's house.

Lizzie had a roommate again.

But that's not what made her angry. For all the things she hated Elder Evans for, she hated him most for breaking her best friend.

CHAPTER 31

Berg called it the "Death Watch."

Lizzie and Jones paced the grand jury hallway, waiting.

"If they don't indict, I'm taking Mary to Mexico. So, really, I can't lose," Jones said.

By lunchtime, Lizzie was ready to rush in and ask them what the hell was taking so long.

"What did you get me into, Jones?"

"It'll sound kind of corny," he said, "but I happen to believe in the FBI's mission. That whole fidelity, bravery, and integrity thing."

"So? Meaning?"

Jones shrugged. "Bad cops offend me."

Thirty minutes later the door opened.

It had been one of the longest deliberations in recent memory.

The grand jury voted a true bill. The Foreperson looked spent. "God help you, Lizzie."

. . .

Lizzie wanted Jones to arrest Lee right away. The Chief wouldn't sign off on the warrant. "We're going to let Lee self-surrender," Jack said.

"That's bullshit, Jack."

Lizzie's nerves were frayed. The long deliberation wore her down. She was sleep-deprived. Sarah would not stop crying because she missed Tom. But it truly didn't seem fair to treat Lee better than other suspects. "If anything, we should treat him worse. What's more evil than a cop who kills people for no reason?"

Jack said the fact Lee was a police officer had nothing to do with it. "He has no record. Taylor called us, looking for a courtesy we normally would extend anyone. He's not a flight-risk and I don't see that he's a danger to the community."

Lizzie didn't buy it. It wouldn't be the only cop privilege Lee would get either.

. . .

FARLEY GAVE LEE THE BAD NEWS OVER THE PHONE, CATCHING Lee on his private cell as he was driving home from his last shift. Lee was now the defendant in a federal criminal prosecution. For a moment, Lee debated whether to drive the cruiser back to the station.

Fuck it. They can come tow it.

He pulled his police cruiser into the dirt driveway and killed the engine. He lit a cigarette and blew the blue smoke against the closed windshield.

Three little kids—two Mexican boys and a white girl—none of them wearing shirts or shoes, played in the mud, a broken sprinkler having turned the yard into brown sludge.

Lee didn't recognize the boys. The girl was Jill, his six-year-old daughter. His son, Pete, wasn't going to be playing outside for a long, long time.

Lee got out of his cruiser and grabbed his baton. His stomach was killing him. Lunch had been Circle K junk washed down with black coffee, bourbon, and aspirin.

"Hi, Daddy," Jill said.

Lee nodded and kept walking.

He pushed open the broken double doors of the apartment building, his polished black boots echoing on the concrete floor.

"Lisa!" he yelled, his voice boomed off the dirty gray walls.

He rapped the baton hard on the first door he passed. "Get the fuck out here, Lisa!"

He pounded on the next door. She was supposed to be watching Pete, changing his bag of shit and piss, being a caregiver. Instead, she was probably doping with one of the other bitches who lived here.

An old Mexican man opened his door a crack then shut it again when he saw Lee.

"Yeah, you keep your fucking head in there," Lee growled. His stomach was churning so much acid he could taste it in the back of his throat.

He reached the end of the hallway. He turned around and began kicking in doors. The first one gave way to his boot and splintered. Empty.

"Lisa! I will fucking break down every fucking door in here if you—"

The Mexican opened the door again, just wide enough to extend a frail arm, which he pointed to the door directly across from Lee's own apartment.

Lee marched toward the door. He kicked it open. Lisa stood inside, paralyzed with fear. She then ran past him like a scared rabbit. He followed her.

He caught her in the hallway and dragged her by her hair into their apartment.

"Why is your fucking daughter playing in the mud?" Lee yelled. "Why aren't you watching your fucking daughter? Why aren't you looking after Pete?"

Lisa went limp. He grabbed her shoulders, feeling her bones compress in his hands, shaking her until her eyes rolled to the back of her head. Then he pushed her to the floor.

He was gasping for air now, heart pounding like it would explode, stomach tearing him ribbons of pain.

Lee stared at his wife, crumpled on the floor. He didn't care that she was a shitty, flat-assed bitch.

What he couldn't stand was what a lousy mother she'd become. He couldn't do his job and do her job, too. It wasn't fair. It wasn't right.

"You *know* the animals out on the street," he growled. "If some fucking child molester grabs your daughter, it's on you! You hear me?"

Lee turned and left to check on his son.

Little Pete lay on top of the covers, mouth open, asleep.

The scars on his head and neck snaked below his shirt.

The braces on his atrophied legs looked like the struts of an old car, or the scaffolding at a construction site.

The boy's bag needed a change.

Lee walked out and ordered Lisa to do it.

"Bye, Daddy," Jill said as he walked by.

Lee didn't say a word.

CHAPTER 32

THE INDICTMENT MADE JOE RINCON A MINOR CAUSE.

Lizzie and Jack walked the five members of "Justice for Joe Rincon" through security to meet with the United States Attorney.

The committee was a week old. It included Rev. Julian Bull, Inland Episcopal Church, the county's religious leader based on years in service and enthusiasm for any worthy cause that would have him.

With him was George Roe-Hart, member of the governing board of the Blanton Band of Mission Indians; Father Beke Ankewe, St. Peter's Catholic; and Mrs. Rincon. Their founder and chairman was Indio plaintiff's lawyer Abe Ybarra.

Half Chilean, half Jewish, Ybarra was a one-eyed cancer survivor and recovered drug addict. His motto was "Hang around long enough, good things happen."

"This case is kind of outside your niche, Mr. Ybarra," Jack said.

Ybarra laughed. Jack would never be good with juries. He used words like niche. "I want to be the Mexican Al Sharpton," Ybarra joked, winking at Lizzie with his one eye.

Ybarra's law office was several hundred miles from Blanton. His expertise was medical malpractice, but he held strong opinions about the police. They were no better than Cossacks. He never doubted Joe Rincon was a victim of *something*.

"I've been keeping an eye on this case from the beginning," Ybarra said, his oldest joke.

In fact he called Mrs. Rincon when he first read the Web article about the shooting. She never called him back. When the indictment was announced, Ybarra went to her house, presenting himself as a civil rights activist, eager to advise her, act as her spokesman, and provide transportation to and from court.

"It's what I do," Ybarra explained to Mrs. Rincon. "I help people."

He never mentioned he was a lawyer. He didn't have to. Mrs. Rincon recognized him from his television and radio commercials. They ran throughout the Inland Empire.

Ybarra was just there, in everyone's car or living room, hanging around, waiting for something good to happen.

When colleagues teased him about his cheesy ads, he took *them* to task, reminding them that they were in a service business. It was a disservice to the public *not* to advertise.

How else would the poor and disenfranchised know where to find him? He grew up in the 1960s. "The people united can never be defeated." That's what they used to chant at Cal-State San Francisco, back when Ybarra had a full head of Jewfro and his goal was to be Steve Bingham, unofficial general counsel of The Movement, West Coast.

Ybarra also wanted to own a Mustang, but he kept that to himself.

Times changed. Steve Bingham slipped a gun to a Black Panther in San Quentin. Guards were shot and killed. Steve hit the road and stayed on the run for years.

Ybarra got a job in Oakland handling tenants' rights, working for less than minimum wage. Like every job, it became a grind. He and his fellow lawyers agreed on the big things—social justice, grape boycotts, end apartheid, gender equality for women, gay rights—then fought over who stole food from the office fridge, who got the closest parking space.

When a condemned building near Jack London Square went on the market, Ybarra borrowed money from his father and bought it for almost nothing.

"I'm turning it into a women's collective," Ybarra said.

"Uh-huh," his father said. "It's the land you want. They're not making new land. Keep the land. Good things happen to those who wait."

It was at the collective that Ybarra met Betsy. A beauty, she looked like Ali MacGraw—long dark hair, high cheekbones, a Jewess from

Indiana committed to AIM. Her college boyfriend, Alex, was Native American. How he got to Brandeis, Ybarra never knew.

Betsy followed Alex down to Inland County and his Inland Band of Mission Indians. Ybarra followed Betsy. "I love you," Ybarra told Betsy in bed. Alex was cool with it. Everyone was cooler with everything back then. Betsy said love was a material construct meant to control and oppress women. Ybarra couldn't agree more. If she loved Alex, so did Ybarra. The three of them could love and work together on behalf of Blanton's Native Americans. People did things like that back then.

Ybarra didn't have to hang around too long for something good to happen. Six months later, Betsy gave up on the Indians and moved back to Indiana. The last Ybarra heard, she was a Trustee of the Art Museum and a Republican. Her husband, George Newhouse, looked like a gentleman hair farmer and was rumored to be worth a hundred million.

Ybarra and Alex ended up being the couple. Lovers, best friends, and business partners. Poor Alex died of AIDS in the 1980s, long before the Blanton Indians finally got the respect and gambling license they deserved. Ybarra was their lawyer. He earned a fortune. It was more than enough to cover his expenses, which included the best seats to jazz festivals, cases of Parker 91 wine or higher, and increasingly rare evenings with high-priced sex workers.

"Prostitute" was a pejorative term, loaded with historical and religious baggage.

Ybarra only contracted mature sex workers between the ages of 35 and 50, adults who chose their profession. That was not always true, of course, but there was only so much justice Ybarra could do in an unjust world.

Mrs. Rincon had not said she wanted to sue the City of Blanton or Officer Lee. Ybarra didn't push it. Ethically, it was better for it to be the client's idea.

"I'm so pleased to meet you all," Mrs. Leonard greeted them. "I like to think that a case like this brings a community together rather than tear it apart."

Rev. Bull agreed.

"Have you ever been to Blanton?" the Nigerian priest asked.

Chief D'Ambrosio doubted Mrs. Leonard had ever been south of Anaheim, let alone journeyed to the far deserts of Inland County.

"Father, I have not had the pleasure of going down there myself yet," Mrs. Leonard said. "But I plan to go, soon."

Jack tried to imagine Mrs. Leonard doing the six-hour roundtrip in order to hold a presser for the benefit of the *Inland County Recorder.* He doubted Mrs. Leonard would ever get to Blanton.

Ybarra must've had the same thought. Because when the meeting ended and they were leaving, he made Lizzie take a photo of the group with the U.S. Attorney.

"Better get it while we can," Ybarra said, winking his one eye at Jack. "Mrs. Leonard will be too busy when she visits Blanton."

Mrs. Leonard never managed to fit it into her schedule.

CHAPTER 33

THE COURT HALLWAY WAS JAMMED WITH UNIFORMED POLICE. They always showed up en masse to support their fellow officers. Not nearly as many who show up for a funeral, but enough to send a message: We are here. We are watching.

Lizzie tried not to let it bother her. She was used to playing away games in basketball or fighting in someone else's gym.

Never let the fans get inside your head.

She walked through the cop wall, giving them time to step out of her way, thanking them when they did. They ignored her, nodding respectfully at Jones.

Everybody has the right to a public trial, cops included. Some jurors don't like this show of unity. They see it as intimidation. Americans love the police. They don't love being leaned on.

Tommy Taylor stood down the hall, huddled with a radio reporter, giving an interview for the rush hour report. It is still the most effective way to reach potential jurors in Southern California.

Two "blue coats," retired sheriff deputies working as court security officers, stood guard to make sure no one interrupted.

Lizzie walked by, catching some of Taylor's spiel: ". . . Ms. Scott is one of those federal prosecutors looking to make a name for herself . . ."

Nice.

She ignored it and walked into the courtroom.

Jones ambled over to one of the blue coats. "Hello, boys," he said, loud enough to ruin Taylor's interview. "It's still illegal to bring recording devices into federal court, right? Judge Letts isn't going to like hearing you guys broke the rules."

The blue coats told Taylor to shut it down.

"Mr. Jones," Taylor slapped Jones on the back and handed him a card. "I can always use another man from the Bureau when you retire."

"If I ever retire, you'll be the first man I see."

• • •

LUCK PLAYS A ROLE IN EVERYTHING, INCLUDING WHETHER JUSTICE is done.

When the trial assignment wheel spun after the case was indicted, it landed on the name of The Honorable Oren K. Letts.

Lizzie was sure she would like Judge Letts in any other context except as her trial judge.

A former seminarian, Letts had a kind face and the gentle manner of an aging folk singer. A nice man, Judge Letts believed the best in everyone.

"There are no defendants in this courtroom," Judge Letts told prospective jurors. "They're just regular folks who are presumed innocent and are having their day in court."

Judge Letts occasionally took his obligation to protect the rights of the accused to what prosecutors viewed as absurd lengths. The government was entitled to a fair trial, too. But sometimes it felt as if Judge Letts was the second defense lawyer in the room.

Lizzie hated people who blamed the referee for losing. She won her only trial in front of Judge Letts, despite his never sustaining one of her objections. Sometimes you had to win *despite* the referee. She refused to "lay a mattress," the office's term for setting up an excuse for losing ahead of time. Judge Letts was not going to determine the outcome of this trial.

"Thank you so much for joining us today," Judge Letts said to a potential juror. The man wore shorts, a T-shirt, and flip-flops. He claimed he could not serve on the jury because of a scheduling conflict.

"Would you mind sharing with us what your conflict is?" Judge Letts asked.

The man mumbled something about a vacation.

Some judges in the courthouse would have demanded proof, airline tickets, hotel booking confirmations. A few judges would not have dismissed the man under any circumstances. Jury service was a civic duty, vacation was a privilege. Judge Letts wished the man a pleasant trip and excused him.

Lizzie didn't get upset.

Better one idiot goes free than 12 idiots get sworn in as jurors.

What bothered her was the slow speed of the process. Prosecutors like quick trials. The longer a trial goes, the more things can go wrong. In most federal courts, jury selection last a few days at most. Jury selection for Officer Lee's panel dragged on for two weeks.

Finally, when the panel was down to 30, Judge Letts turned things over to the lawyers so they could exercise their preemptory strikes. The goal was to shape the perfect jury panel. Each side had 10 strikes. The law allowed them to strike anyone without giving a reason.

Lizzie used her strikes to lose the woman who was married to a deputy, the man who wanted to become a crime-scene technician, and the older woman from Stanton who confessed to "having a problem" with Latinos. Lizzie also struck the man who stared at her breasts and a few others who just seemed wrong.

She had two strikes left.

"Your Honor, the government asks the Court to thank and excuse Mr. Sinek."

Judge Letts was surprised. The judge never tried a case as a lawyer but thought Mr. Sinek would be an ideal juror.

What Judge Letts did not know was that Jones went by the Juror's Parking Lot during jury selection. He checked out the cars and looked through the windows, just to find out what he could about the people who drove them. The blue-ribbon bumper sticker on the black Lexus caught his eye: "I Support the Fullerton Police." It was Mr. Sinek's car.

Jones ran into Farley doing the same thing.

There wasn't anything illegal about it. Cars parked in a lot were in plain, public view and both sides had the list of jurors. But jurors and judges wouldn't like it if they knew it happened. It would feel like an invasion of privacy. People were so sensitive.

"I won't say anything if you won't," Farley said.

Lizzie was about to accept the panel, leaving her last strikes on the table, but something about the Lady with the French Manicure worried her.

A beautiful woman in an expensive dress suit, she'd left the "occupation" box blank on her questionnaire. She was married to a surgeon and lived in a gated beachfront community in Laguna. She'd spent the day reading on her Louis Vuitton-covered iPad.

I bet she's never played on a team in her life.

Lizzie needed a jury that would convict. She wanted people who would gel over the course of trial: like a basketball team during a tournament. They didn't have to fall in love with one another. They just had to learn to work together and strive for a common goal: in this case, a unanimous verdict of guilty.

On her basketball teams, the unity killers were ball hogs, girls who wouldn't pass and didn't care about their teammates. They might have been better athletes, but their teams never shined because they never made the players around them better.

Lizzie wanted team players, not standouts or superstars. People who could get along and be part of the group. That meant losing the outliers. Lizzie always struck very pretty or very rich people, obvious freaks, probable narcissists, or anyone else who seemed like they would rub people the wrong way.

"Your Honor," Lizzie stood. "The government thanks and excuses Mrs. Meagher."

Good-bye Lady with the French Manicure.

Mrs. Meagher began to gather her things.

"Objection," Taylor said. "May we approach?"

The lawyers huddled beneath the judge's bench. Judge Letts leaned down, apologizing for being higher than they were, wondering if they'd prefer to go to his chambers. This was fine, the lawyers said. Judge Letts was such a nice man.

"What's the basis for you objection, Mr. Taylor?" The judge and lawyers whispered, their heads close together so the jurors couldn't hear.

"Ms. Scott struck Mrs. Meagher on the basis of race. That's not proper."

Lizzie thought she heard him wrong. "Whose race?"

Taylor pointed at Mrs. Meagher as she made her way out of the courtroom.

"Mrs. Meagher is white. My client is white. Mr. Sinek is white. The Supreme Court says you can't strike a juror based on the color of their skin. White counts as a color."

"I didn't do that," Lizzie said, louder than she meant. "Race had nothing to do with why I struck anyone. It's completely irrelevant."

Taylor gave her a sad, patronizing smile. "Race is *always* relevant, Ms. Scott. That's a historical fact."

Lizzie could feel the blood rushing to her face. She hated how flushed she got. Bad enough in the gym or in the ring, worse in bed during sex, but horrible in court, where you hid how you felt so the other side didn't know they were getting to you.

"It never even occurred to me that Mrs. Meagher or anyone else was white. The defendant isn't charged with a hate crime or having had any kind of racial animus toward the victim."

Taylor snorted. "Your Honor, if that's true, then why did she strike three white people?"

"I don't have to give you a reason why I exercised a *peremptory* strike," Lizzie said. "It's a *peremptory* strike."

"Technically, that's true, Ms. Scott," Judge Letts said. "But why *did* you strike her?"

"Your honor," Lizzie said, blushing worse. "By making me give you a reason, you're basically suggesting I'm a racist or that I did something wrong here. I didn't."

"No one thinks you're a racist," Judge Letts said gently. "I just hate giving Mr. Taylor an issue on appeal."

Here was the ugly truth about Judge Letts. The idea of being reversed because he made a mistake paralyzed him. Everyone would read about it. Everyone would know. Nice men had egos, too. Lizzie suspected the nicest ones had the biggest egos.

The law offers judges one sure way to ensure they are never reversed. Never rule against the defense. Only the defense can appeal a conviction. Prosecutors have no right to appeal an acquittal. Judge Letts figured it out almost immediately.

"Unless you give me a reason, I'm going to grant Mr. Taylor's motion and put Mrs. Meagher back in the box. Not because you're a racist, Ms. Scott, but because I want to give Officer Lee the fairest trial possible."

Lizzie's cheeks were now hot and burning. "Fine, Your Honor, I struck Mrs. Meagher based on what I observed of her body language and behavior toward the other jurors. I don't think she'll work well with others. I sense she could alienate people. All of which is more than the court or Mr. Taylor are entitled to know."

Judge Letts looked to Taylor. Taylor shook his head, unconvinced. "I've made my record, Your Honor, if you let her strike this juror, I'm going to take it up on appeal if my guy is convicted."

Judge Letts looked as if he might cry. He hated being forced to make a decision. A lot of judges did. Lizzie wondered why they never thought about it before they took the job.

Taylor tried to be magnanimous. "For the record, I'm not saying Ms. Scott *is* a racist. I don't know what's in her heart."

Lizzie stared daggers at him. He put his hand on her shoulder. It took all she had not to knock it off. The jury was watching.

"Judge not the sinner," Taylor said. "For we're all sinners. But call out the sin so that she might reconcile her ways in the spirit and knowledge of Christ Lord."

Jones and the rest of the courtroom could not hear a word of this. But they could see Lizzie's face, her jaw set, angry, ready to punch someone's lights out.

"Mr. Taylor's objection is sustained," Judge Letts said. "Mrs. Meagher will be welcomed back to the panel with the court's thanks."

Mrs. Meagher was already outside the courtroom and down the hall. The clerk had to fetch her.

Jones asked Lizzie what happened.

Lizzie shook her head. She was too stunned to reply.

"Judge not the sinner. But call out the sin so that she might reconcile her ways in the spirit and knowledge of Christ Lord."

Tommy Taylor was quoting Elder Evans.

CHAPTER 34

FARLEY ALWAYS DID A BACKGROUND CHECK ON THE OPPOSING lawyer. Taylor liked to know the person he was facing. It helped him get into their heads.

Lizzie had almost too much to offer.

If Lee had known anything about her, he *never* would have staged the confrontation on the side of the road. She had a thing about being pushed around. She didn't like it. Most people didn't. With her, it was an obsession.

As Mrs. Leonard predicted, Taylor filed a pretrial motion, under seal so the press never got it, *precluding* Lizzie from mentioning the confrontation.

"It's too prejudicial," Taylor said. "If they want to charge my client with assaulting her, let them, but not in this trial. This trial is about Joe Rincon. It isn't about Lizzie Scott."

He was lying, of course. Taylor intended to make the case all about Lizzie Scott.

. . .

HER OPENING STATEMENT WAS SHORT AND TO THE POINT. SHE told the jury what she intended to prove and how she planned to prove it. They would hear from witnesses and review evidence. This was the story the evidence and witnesses would tell:

"One night last October, an elderly woman named Mrs. Rincon was worried. Her grandson, Joe, hadn't come home from work. He lived with her because he didn't have enough money for his own place. He was a good boy, quiet, shy, never in trouble. She loved him. She still does love him. But Joe's not here anymore because the defendant, Dwayne Wayne Lee, murdered him."

She turned and stared at Lee.

She did *not* point at him.

Pointing was rude. Elder Evans pointed at people he condemned. Lizzie didn't think pointing convinced anyone.

"The defendant is a police officer. He swore to uphold the law. Instead, he broke the law. He shot Mrs. Rincon's grandson Joe and let him die in the road. Joe hadn't done anything to justify the defendant shooting him. After he murdered Joe, the defendant lied about his crime and hid evidence to cover up what he did."

When all the witnesses were heard and all the evidence was in, Lizzie promised to come back to ask them to convict Officer Lee.

Lizzie sat down and waited for Taylor's opening. He stood and buttoned his coat. He thanked the jury for their patience then pointed out Lee's wife, Lisa, and their daughter, Jill, in the front row behind the defense table. "Their son, Pete, can't be here, he's still recovering from being struck by a car."

Taylor then thanked Judge Letts and announced he was going to waive the defense opening statement for the moment and deliver it after Ms. Scott's case was done.

The law allows a defense lawyer to waive his opening statement until after the government rests its case. It doesn't give anybody the right to give *two* openings. Taylor said enough to humanize his client without touching upon the facts of the case. Most judges would have treated it as an opening statement and denied Taylor the right to give one later. Judge Letts was not one of those judges.

Lizzie let it pass. It was early in the fight. The jury hadn't made up their minds about the lawyers yet. She didn't want to alienate them. Trials weren't a popularity contest, exactly, but they were close.

● ● ●

LIZZIE'S FIRST WITNESS WAS MRS. RINCON. THE OLD WOMAN SAT in the witness chair clutching a purse, looking bewildered. "Joe lived with me for the last five years. His mom and my son went back to live in Mexico."

"What kind of person was Joe?" Lizzie asked.

Mrs. Rincon took a tissue from her purse. "He was a good boy. Shy, like his daddy, never any problem to anybody." She wiped her tears.

"Did he have a temper?"

"He never started fights. He was afraid of getting hurt. He'd say to me, 'Grandma, I don't want ever to go to the hospital.' He was so scared of needles. He was like a big baby."

The trial was about three men. Lee sat at the defense table, impassive, taking notes. Scanlon would come later. Joe Rincon wasn't there at all. Mrs. Rincon was his stand-in.

"Sometimes Joe helped out at my day care center, washing the floors, cleaning the bathroom. The kids liked him, but he was too shy to play with them once he got older."

"Tell us about the night Joe died," Lizzie said, ignoring the twinge of guilt she always felt when she make a victim relive a tragedy. It was part of the job.

"He called me around lunchtime," Mrs. Rincon said sadly. "He got a job moving car batteries from a repair shop to a junkyard. He said he would be home around eight that night." He always called if he was going to be late. He knew how she worried.

"Did he call that night to say he was going to be late?"

Mrs. Rincon shook her head. She waited up all night for him. A police officer knocked on her door in the morning.

Lizzie's last questions focused on whether or not Rincon was the kind of man who would attack the police with a knife.

"Was your grandson a violent person?"

No, Mrs. Rincon said, he was scared of violence. "When that crazy boy killed all those kids in Sandy Hook, Joey said to me, 'Grandma, why would someone do that?' I think because he was thinking of my day care, and all my kids."

Lizzie showed her the knife from the crime scene. Had she ever seen her grandson with it? Mrs. Rincon shook her head. "I never saw Joe with that knife."

Did he hate the police?

"No. He respected everyone."

Lizzie thanked her and sat down, curious to see what Taylor would do.

Taylor stood, palms together, fingertips at his lips, in prayerful thought.

"Mrs. Rincon, I had a bunch of questions to ask you. But to be honest, you remind me so much of my own grandma, I think I know what the answers would be."

Lizzie admired Taylor's game. The man was an excellent actor and a superb storyteller.

"Joe would fight if he had to, wouldn't he?"

Mrs. Rincon stiffened, but nodded yes. "But he never started fights."

"I get it, ma'am. But Joe was a big boy, wasn't he?"

"That's why they picked on him. Because he was big."

"God love you, ma'am, you're just like my grandma," Taylor said. "One last question, if that's alright with you?"

Mrs. Rincon said it was fine.

"Do you know if Joe was drinking that night? I mean, would it surprise you if I told you they found some alcohol and marijuana in his system?"

Mrs. Rincon said she didn't know anything about it.

Taylor played it right down the middle of the fairway, nothing fancy. What else could you do with a sweet old lady who'd lost her grandson?

Lizzie stood for redirect. Her question wasn't relevant, but she didn't think Taylor could object. The jury wouldn't like it if he did.

"When you heard what happened to your grandson, what was your reaction?"

Mrs. Rincon started to weep. "I just kept asking. Why? Why would anyone hurt Joe like this? Joe was so sweet. He was such a sweet boy."

Lizzie sat down. Under any other circumstances, she would have gone to the old lady and hugged her. But, then, under any other circumstances, she would have never asked the question.

Trial was different.

CHAPTER 35

"Big day today, Henry." Scanlon was not a morning person. Jones made sure he got an early start.

They stood in the free breakfast line of the Hampton Inn, a quick hop to the courthouse. Scanlon mumbled he just wanted coffee. Jones put a bowl of oatmeal on Scanlon's tray and steered him to a table. Then Jones took out a comb and tried for the third time to lay Scanlon's hair closer to his skull.

A little kid at the next table stared at them.

"What!" Scanlon barked at the kid.

Jones laid a warning paw on his shoulder. "We'll have none of that today, Henry."

They arrived at Lizzie's office two hours before court started. "Looking good, Henry," she said. "You feeling good?"

"No."

Lizzie asked Berg to sit in the witness room with Scanlon until he was called to the stand.

"I'm not going to have to clean it or feed it, am I?" Berg asked.

"Him, not it," Lizzie said. Berg brought his history of the French Revolution and a George V. Higgins paperback for Scanlon. "It reads, right?"

At 10:35 A.M., Scanlon walked to the witness chair. He shot a nervous glance at the jury but didn't dare look at Lee or the judge. Lizzie made a note of the time. She would keep her direct to one hour. She didn't want to burn Scanlon out before Taylor got to him.

She started off with the easy stuff. She asked where Scanlon came from, how far he went in school, what he did for money, whether he had any family, and who his friends were. Scanlon answered each question, then summed it all up in case anyone missed anything.

"Born here, stayed here, probably die here. Bad at school, never liked to work that much, ain't got many friends. Been in and out of trouble a lot but nothing ever that serious." He paused. "That's about it."

His voice still went from too loud to too soft, but he seemed to enjoy the attention.

"Now, let's talk about the night of the shooting," Lizzie said. She walked him through it, setting the scene, having him explain why he was sleeping by the highway that night, what, exactly, he saw happen. She spent most of the hour breaking down the seconds before and after the shooting itself. At one point, she had Scanlon walk into the well of the courtroom to show how Rincon held his hands up.

"The cop was pointing the gun at the kid, and the kid's hands were up in the air, then he started to sway. He took a kind of side step to catch himself and then boom. The cop shot him. Shot him dead. I still don't know why."

"The cop you refer to, do you see him in the room?" She didn't do it for dramatic effect. By law, she needed someone to identify Lee as the shooter. Scanlon didn't want to do it. He looked sideways at Lee, then jabbed a finger toward him.

Lizzie used the last 10 minutes of her hour to focus on the aftermath.

"Why didn't you come forward in this case sooner?"

"I was scared shitless."

Judge Letts didn't ask Scanlon to clean up his language. He didn't think it was his place.

"What are you receiving from the government in return for testimony?" Lizzie asked.

Scanlon snorted. "Not much. You bought me lunch a few times, put me up in a motel, and you're going to tell the D.A. I helped you. But you can't guarantee they're going to drop the probation violation. I'm kind of fucked."

A few of jurors smiled.

Scanlon had a rough charm.

Mrs. Meagher and a few others seemed immune to it.

Lizzie was down to her last question: "Why did you eventually come forward and call the FBI, Mr. Scanlon?"

"I don't know," he said. It baffled him. "I felt bad for the kid. He didn't do anything to get killed over. He was just in the wrong place at the wrong time. I'm usually that guy."

Lizzie checked the time.

It was 11:50 A.M.

She assumed Judge Letts would adjourn for lunch rather than make Taylor start, then have to stop, his cross-examination. That would give Jones time to get Scanlon some food and let him calm down. Taylor would then have to deal with a postlunch, sleepy jury panel.

To her surprise, Taylor told the judge he wanted to start his cross now and go for as long as possible. Judge Letts said of course, whatever he'd like to do.

"Are you the kind of man who lies to help himself?" Taylor began.

"No," Scanlon said.

"You lied about what you saw to get yourself out of jail."

"No."

"You lied right here," Taylor said. "You called the FBI *from* jail and got yourself out of probation by lying about my client."

Scanlon sat up, his hair sticking out all over the place, offended. "You don't know what you're talking about. I still got the probation over my head. And I didn't lie about what I saw that night."

Taylor had thrown an opening flurry, a barrage of punches, hoping to catch Scanlon and score a quick knockout. Scanlon stood up to it. Even a cornered desert rat will fight back.

"Let me ask you this," Taylor said, starting another line of questions. "Did you ever tell anyone that you *hadn't* seen any shooting? That you didn't know anything *about* any shooting? That you hadn't even been on that highway that night?"

Lizzie glanced at Jones, who gave a slight shrug: *No idea what he's talking about.*

Scanlon closed his eyes tight and thought hard. Then he shook his head. "No. I never denied what I saw that night. Never."

Judge Letts suggested to Taylor it was time for lunch. Taylor agreed.

"How'd I do, boss?" Scanlon asked. He and Lizzie sat in the witness room. She was too keyed up to eat the sandwiches Jones brought them. Taylor had the whole afternoon to rip Scanlon apart.

"You were perfect," Lizzie said. "But what about the question Taylor asked, about you denying being at the shooting or knowing anything about it?

Scanlon shrugged. He never denied seeing what Lee did to Rincon.

"Then we've got nothing to worry about."

After lunch, Taylor asked Scanlon if he hated the police.

"Sure," Scanlon admitted. They moved him around, searched his stuff, hassled or arrested him, and sometimes jailed him. Why would he like them?

"In fact, you especially hate the Blanton Police."

"Yeah, but only because I live out there. They're my local department," Scanlon said.

A few jurors chuckled. Scanlon shot them a look. "What?! The Blanton cops fuck with me the most because I live out there. What's so damn funny about that?"

The jurors looked away, embarrassed. Mrs. Meagher jotted down a note.

"So," Taylor said, looking to drive the point home. "You have a motive to lie about the police. You don't like them."

"That's just ignorant," Scanlon said. "If I say bad shit about a cop, the cop is going to come after me *worse* than before. Whether I tell the truth or lie about him. The best thing to do is keep your mouth shut and not say a damn thing about them."

"You didn't do that," Taylor said.

"I wish to hell I had," Scanlon answered.

Even a great lawyer like Taylor leads with his chin once in awhile. It couldn't be helped. The only guarantee when you step into the ring is you're going to get hit.

Two hours of cross later, still Taylor hadn't caught Scanlon in any obvious lies.

Still, the lawyer did a good job showing the jury Scanlon was an unemployed, alcoholic loner who hated the police and hoped Lizzie Scott could convince the Inland County D.A. to drop the probation violation.

"Now," Taylor said, "let's talk about what you say happened that night." Taylor ran Scanlon through it from every angle, catching him in a few small inconsistencies.

"In the grand jury you said my client was 20 feet away from Mr. Rincon when the shot was fired. Today, you say they were closer. Which is it?"

"I'm not sure," Scanlon said. "I'm not good with distances."

Then, later:

"In the grand jury, you said Mr. Rincon's hands were already up and *then* my client fired his weapon. Today, you say his hands went up *as* my client shot him. Which was it?"

Scanlon closed his eyes. "His hands went up and then your client shot him."

"So they weren't up already?'

Scanlon shook his head. "Like I said, the kid put his hands up, and then the cop shot him."

Then, finally:

"Wasn't it true, Joey Rincon rushed at my client with a knife in his hand?"

"I didn't see a knife. The kid didn't have anything in his hands except air." Scanlon shook his head. "The kid never rushed the cop with a knife. That's just bullshit."

Two of the younger jurors smiled at one another. They loved Scanlon.

"You mention the word bullshit," Taylor said. He showed Scanlon Lee's flashlight. "Here's what I think is 'bullshit.' You telling this jury my client hit Mr. Rincon in the head with this."

Scanlon said that was exactly what Taylor's client did.

"Ah, c'mon, man," Taylor said. "If I hit somebody with this, I'd kill him."

Lizzie objected. Judge Letts overruled her. Lizzie chided herself. She drew more attention to the point with her objection. Judge Letts was never going to sustain it anyway. Taylor scored a solid punch. His argument would be that the lack of a more serious head wound on Rincon's head cast doubt on Scanlon's version of events.

On redirect, Lizzie got Scanlon to emphasize that he was sober that night, that the wind and siren made it impossible to hear what the men said to one another, and to remind the jury he received nothing tangible from the federal government for his testimony.

"I was hoping for something, yeah, but I didn't get it," he said. "I'm kind of sorry I called the FBI. But Agent Jones said there aren't any take-backs."

Lizzie hugged Scanlon when they were back in her office. He kept his arms straight out, too shy to hug her back.

"You did it, Henry," she said. "You got us this far. I think you were really brave up there. I think some of those jurors believed you, I truly do."

There were obvious exceptions. Mrs. Meagher stared at Scanlon like he was sewage. The five older men and women also weren't in love with him.

Walking back to the parking lot, Scanlon looked exhausted. "I could use a drink."

Lizzie handed Jones a twenty. "On me."

"We can do that," Jones said.

Jones drove Scanlon back to his temporary digs in Ventura County.

Lizzie thought Scanlon fought Taylor to a draw at best. Nobody scored a knockout. But then Taylor didn't have to. A draw would mean Lizzie lost. Ties went to the defendant. Right now, she didn't think she had more than six jurors willing to convict Officer Lee.

Stop it. Breathe. Nothing bad has happened yet.

Lizzie counted her blessings. Scanlon could have blown up on the stand. He did better than she could have hoped. Plus, no one knew anything about who or what the jury believed until they came back with a verdict.

Unfortunately, by then, it wouldn't matter anyway. The case would be over.

. . .

Lizzie might have felt better about her chances if she knew how badly Lee felt about his.

"Taylor didn't do shit to Scanlon," Lee said, chewing his nails.

"I wouldn't say that, Dwayne-o," Farley said as he drove Lee and his family back to Blanton. Lee's wife and daughter sat in the backseat, staring out of the window, quiet, afraid to talk.

"Now, I admit, the boss didn't blow that Scanlon guy out of the water, but he made some points," Farley assured him. "And Taylor planted some bombs for later. You just watch. Taylor knows what he's doing."

That night, Lee lay in bed, staring at the ceiling, planning for the worst.

I will not go to prison for a piece of shit like Joe Rincon.

CHAPTER 36

VERN MOELLER NEVER LOOKED HAPPY, BUT HE LOOKED ESPECIALLY miserable on the stand.

"What was inside the toiletries bag Officer Lee gave you that night?" Lizzie asked.

She couldn't believe he showed up for court dressed this way. No coat or tie, a short-sleeved golf shirt and stained khakis. She was about to send him home to change when Jones reminded her that Moeller represented the Blanton P.D. The worst he looked, the worse Lee looked.

"The toiletries bag had some cologne, shaving cream, razors, and the flashlight," he said.

Lizzie held up a plastic evidence bag containing the flashlight and handed it to Moeller who confirmed it was Lee's. How did he know for sure?

"Well, it's the one he handed me," he said. "It was department issue, every officer gets one; the serial number is recorded."

Did Officer Lee carry his flashlight every shift?

"It's policy that he does. He was supposed to," Moeller said. "Every officer I know does."

All Lee's equipment was inventoried the night of the shooting. The flashlight wasn't on the inventory list. Didn't that make Moeller suspicious, especially after Lee *gave* him the flashlight?

"No," Moeller said. The jurors stared at Moeller with amusement, disdain, or disbelief. He was unabashedly stupid, but it never hurt him on the job. His career was proof that incompetence rises to his own level, bureaucrats fall up, and bureaucracies never change. The senior detective who bumped Moeller to detective had his reasons. He didn't want any competition from the junior man.

"Looking back, do you think you maybe should have been suspicious that he left the flashlight off the inventory list?" Lizzie asked.

Moeller shifted in his seat and furrowed his brow. Thinking hurt. "Nobody ever said anything to me about a flashlight until you brought it up. I guess, now, looking back, maybe I should've asked about the flashlight, but it didn't occur to me at the time."

If Moeller was miserable before, Taylor's cross-examine made him feel worse.

"Let me ask you this, sir: Would you say you're a liar or just completely incompetent?"

Lizzie might have objected if she cared about Moeller's feelings. She also wondered if Moeller was pretending to be this stupid or really was. It couldn't hurt her case either way. Lee was on trial, not Moeller. It *was* Lee's flashlight. Lee *did* hide it. *Res ipsa loquitor.* The thing spoke for itself.

"I didn't lie about anything," Moeller said. "I wasn't thinking flashlight. I was thinking gun and shooting. Tell you the truth, as I sit here now, I don't even know why the flashlight is such a big issue."

Lizzie never told him. Moeller never asked.

"So you're totally incompetent, then, is that it?" Taylor asked.

Judge Letts looked at Lizzie for an objection. He hated to watch anyone be embarrassed. Lizzie stared back at him. It wasn't her job to protect Moeller's feelings.

"I'm not *totally* incompetent," Moeller said.

"I guess not," Taylor said. "You were able to get yourself immunity from Ms. Scott. You weren't charged with filing a false statement like my client was."

Moeller said he hadn't meant to do anything wrong, repeating that when he inventoried Lee's things, he didn't know the flashlight was relevant.

"It's not like Dwayne told me what it was all about." Moeller was angry now. It finally dawned on him. Lee screwed him on this deal. Moeller was being a good guy. He did Lee a favor taking his bag for him, not knowing Lee was using Moeller to hide evidence.

"If you hadn't been so incompetent," Taylor hammered Moeller, "you would have checked the bag that night. You would have *seen* the flashlight, *asked* my client about it, and he could've *told* you he didn't carry the flashlight that night because it didn't work or it needed new batteries."

Lizzie objected. Taylor was stating facts that were not in evidence and never would be. The flashlight worked fine. Judge Letts overruled her objection. Taylor moved on anyway.

"My point is, Detective Moeller, because you did a lousy job inventorying the evidence in this case, my client is accused of something he didn't do."

Lizzie objected. Taylor didn't ask a question. He gave a closing argument. Judge Letts overruled her, but it didn't matter. Taylor pushed Moeller too far. The detective's anger finally boiled all over the lawyer.

"*Me?* What did I do? I didn't shoot anybody. I didn't know he was hiding stuff," Moeller said. "Okay, maybe I didn't do a great investigation, but nobody can say I intended to break the law. Your client is the one who did bad shit, not me."

Great lawyers are not perfect. They don't have to be. They just have to make fewer mistakes than the other side. Great as he was, Taylor had the bad habit of asking too many questions. It made them mad. It gave them time to counterpunch.

On redirect, Lizzie asked what Moeller did with the bag and flashlight Lee gave to him.

"I took it home and left it in my garage."

"Did Lee ever ask for it back?"

"No."

Mrs. Meagher stared at Lee.

For the first time, Mrs. Meagher didn't seem to like what she saw.

CHAPTER 37

Lizzie and Jones fought only once during the whole investigation and trial.

"Don't call an expert," Jones said. "Everybody knows you can't shoot an unarmed guy. It's common sense. It's in the darn Cowboy Code."

"Not everyone was born with an FBI agent for a dad," she said. "Not everybody grew up with force continuum chart on his wall."

Jones hadn't either, but he liked to *say* he did.

The force continuum is a guide that shows when and how much force an officer can use in specific situations. It is standard material, used to train law enforcement throughout the country. Lizzie wanted an expert to explain what the force continuum is and how, like every other cop in California, Lee studied and was tested on his knowledge of it.

Jones was against it. "If you call an expert then Taylor's going to call an expert and then we got a darn battle of experts," Jones said. "You're making this darn thing more complicated than it is."

"Please just get me an expert. I think we need one." Lizzie never liked to pull rank. Jones was in charge everywhere else, but she made the calls in court.

Once she made the decision, Jones never said another word about it. A team player, he went out and found her the best expert he could.

LAPD Captain Ezekiel Borns marched into court looking like a movie star. He knew all about the force continuum. He taught it at the LAPD Training Academy. The fact he looked so good in his dark blue uniform with the silver stars and stripes didn't hurt either. He was the antithesis of Scanlon and Moeller.

As Lizzie walked him through his resume, the jury leaned forward, loving him. Some of that love was bound to rub off on the government's case. That was the whole point of calling an expert.

Captain Borns used a PowerPoint presentation to show Lee's personnel and training records. He pointed out how many hours of special training Lee received on the levels of force cops can legally use to detain a suspect.

"Lee was taught with Peace Officers Standards and Training materials. He was told police officers can only use the *minimal* force necessary to accomplish the goal of maintaining order. He swore he would follow the law."

The officer's mere presence at the scene, armed, in uniform, is considered a form of force by itself. "Most of the time, it's enough to keep the peace."

Sometimes more is needed. Verbal commands, for example. Lizzie had Captain Borns demonstrate the techniques Lee was trained to use. It was really just an excuse to let the captain unlimber his magnificent voice.

"Freeze! Hands up! Go to the ground!"

Mrs. Meagher even smiled.

Certain situations demanded more force. Unarmed suspects who pose a physical threat to the officer can be restrained with "hands only force." The officer can grapple, grab, kick, push, punch, twist arms, and fight a suspect to the ground.

Moving along the force continuum, a more serious threat demands the next level of force. Nonlethal weapons such as pepper spray, the Taser, and certain baton blows—except to the head—are legal when they are necessary. "The officer has to defend himself and the community," Captain Borns said.

Finally, at the end of the force continuum, there is deadly force. If an armed suspect threatened an officer with a weapon, the officer is legally entitled, professionally trained, and morally justified to respond with all the deadly force needed to end the threat.

Lizzie asked if a man holding a knife justified the officer using deadly force against him.

"Not necessarily," Captain Borns said. "It would depend on what the man was doing. If the man is just standing there, the officer is trained to maintain a 21-foot distance. He may use verbal commands to order the man to the ground. If the suspect doesn't comply, the officer may escalate the force as needed."

"What if the man wasn't holding the knife and was just standing there?"

"In that scenario," Captain Borns said, "the officer would not be justified in using very much force. He certainly could not use deadly force."

Lizzie added to the hypothetical. What if a man was pulled over in a traffic spot and didn't or wouldn't get out of the car. What is the officer trained to do then?

"Keep his distance from the vehicle and radio for backup," Captain Borns said. "Use verbal commands to order the person out of the vehicle. Wait. Be patient. A body at rest stays at rest. The car isn't going anywhere. If it does, you can chase him. But officers know not to get too close to the car."

"Why not?"

"That's how cops get killed."

Lizzie asked Captain Borns if Officer Lee's actions that night complied with the standard police procedure Lee was trained to follow.

"Absolutely not," Captain Borns said. "It makes no sense for an officer to approach the vehicle the way Lee did. Rincon could've had a gun. It was also wrong of Lee to try to extricate the suspect. That's just begging for a fight."

Lizzie asked if Captain Borns had an opinion about Lee's actions toward Rincon.

"I would say Officer Lee wasn't terribly afraid of the suspect. Otherwise, he wouldn't have approached the car. Or if he did, he would have drawn his weapon. Officer Lee says he only drew his weapon after the car door hit him. He didn't sound scared to me."

Lizzie picked up the flashlight from the evidence table. "The eyewitness, Mr. Scanlon, testified that he saw the defendant hit Mr. Rincon in the head with this. Assuming Rincon was unarmed and had his hands up, was there any justification for Officer Lee to hit him with this?"

"None whatsoever. Head blows with flashlights are considered deadly force."

"Should Officer Lee have mentioned the head blow in his report?"

"Absolutely," Captain Borns said. "Accurate and honest police reports are the lifeblood of the criminal justice system. It's the only record we have of what happened in the field. The whole system relies on it being the truth. If it isn't true, the system breaks down."

"In your opinion, based on what you know, were the reports signed by the defendant in this case accurate and true?"

Captain Borns turned to face the jury. "In my opinion, the reports signed by Officer Lee were intentionally inaccurate and false."

Lizzie finished up with her strongest evidence of guilt.

"Detective Moeller testified that Officer Lee gave him the flashlight rather than include it on the evidence inventory list. Was that standard procedure, in your opinion?"

Captain Borns paused for emphasis and stared Mrs. Meagher down.

"What Officer Lee did with the flashlight was garbage. He hid and possibly destroyed evidence. By not turning over that flashlight, he prevented us from looking for Rincon's DNA or blood. He caused false reports to taint the system."

Mrs. Meagher wrote it all down.

Lizzie sat down feeling good about her decision to call an expert witness.

Then Taylor stood up. He gave Captain Borns a long, hard stare that lasted long enough to be awkward. Finally, Taylor spoke in a serious voice: "You, sir, are one *good-looking* man. Truly. I can't take my damn eyes off you."

The jurors laughed. But it only seemed like a light moment in a tense trial. Everything Taylor did was part of game plan. The testimony of an expert like Captain Borns lived or died on credibility. Getting the jury to laugh about any part of an expert was a good start. It broke the spell.

"There are no Dashcams in Blanton cruisers, right?" Taylor asked.

Captain Borns believed that was true. Almost half of all police departments did not have them. The number was lower for smaller departments like Blanton.

"Too bad for my client," Taylor said. "If Blanton wasn't so damn cheap, we'd have a video of what happened that night and my client wouldn't have been charged with anything."

It was also possible the Dashcam would show Lee was guilty, but Captain Borns was too professional a witness to say so. Taylor hadn't asked a question and wasn't about to get into an argument with him.

"Just so we're clear, so there's no confusion in the jury's mind," Taylor said. "You would agree if a guy with a knife rushes at a cop, the cop can use deadly force to stop him."

"I would generally agree with that."

Taylor nodded. "And in situations like that, an officer would have to make a split-second decision, right?"

"That's often the case."

"Sometime he can't get to his gun. Sometimes he's got to grab what he can, defend himself with whatever he's got handy, right?"

Is Taylor going to admit the flashlight blow?

Lizzie couldn't believe Taylor would go that far. He could just be feigning a line of attack, or merely keeping his options open. Fights and trials were fluid, living things. They changed as they moved along. The game plan only worked for so long.

Taylor picked up a piece of paper from his table. "Have you ever heard of a use-of-force expert named Professor Dennis Kenney, John Jay College of Criminal Justice?"

Captain Borns said he was familiar with Professor Kenney and his work.

"Let me read you something Professor Kenney said in a newspaper article."

Taylor put on his reading glasses. "'If it's legally OK to shoot the guy, then it's legally OK for him to hit him with the car, particularly if he thinks that's the best tool to get the job done.'" Taylor removed his reading glasses. "Do you agree or disagree with that statement, Captain Borns?"

"Well, the question is whether the officer was entitled to use lethal force." Captain Borns said. "*If* it was legal to use deadly force and there were no alternatives, it might be reasonable to use a car or a gun."

Taylor smiled. "What about a flashlight?"

Captain Borns conceded that if the officer had nothing else, a flashlight might be legal and reasonable in certain circumstances.

"What about these circumstances?" Taylor caught himself. "Oh, right, sorry, my bad. You weren't there that night. You don't know what happened. And I *know* you didn't talk to my client. You can't read his mind or know what was in his heart, can you?"

Captain Borns conceded he was no mind reader. "I can only give an opinion based on the information I am given."

Taylor pointed his finger at Lizzie. "You mean, what *she* gave you."

Captain Borns was ready for it. "Mr. Taylor, I've read *all* the reports available in this case, including your papers."

Once again, Taylor asked one too many. He was about to sit down, then decided to make a last run at it. "I'm curious, Cap, since you're the expert and all, how many people were killed by the police last year?"

Captain Borns looked to Lizzie. Taylor's question wasn't relevant, but Judge Letts would never sustain an objection. He hadn't yet.

"The general view," Captain Borns said, "is that, on average, approximately 400 to 500 people are killed by the police in arrest-related homicides and legal interventions. That's based on the FBI's most recent Supplemental Homicide Report."

Taylor pulled the face of a confused, disappointed child. "Don't you know how many people were killed by the police last year?"

"I'm afraid there is no database that compiles that number."

"But what about the United States Department of Justice Bureau of Justice Statistics?"

Taylor spoke slowly, drawing out each official word in the title. "They got the word 'justice' and 'statistics' in their damn name! They must know how many people are killed by the cops each year, Cap."

"I'm afraid they don't," Captain Borns said. "Some people believe the number is a lot higher, closer to maybe 1,000 or more."

Taylor stared at Captain Borns with disdain. "So, you don't know what happened that night, didn't even *try* to ask my client about it, and don't even know how often something like this happens?"

"No, I'm afraid I don't."

Taylor shook his head. "Your Honor, the defense moves to strike Captain Borns' entire testimony as utterly irrelevant to this proceeding and wholly without basis."

"Objection," Lizzie said.

"Mr. Taylor, your motion is overruled. Captain Borns has been qualified to give expert opinion. The jury may give it whatever value they think it deserves."

Lizzie won her first objection. It didn't feel like much of a victory. Jones never said he told her so, but she probably shouldn't have called an expert. Taylor seemed to get more out of Captain Borns than she did.

CHAPTER 38

THE HIPSTER CORONER FROM L.A. DIDN'T DO LIZZIE MUCH GOOD either.

"I can't say beyond a reasonable doubt that Mr. Rincon was hit in the head with a flashlight," Lizzie's expert witness said.

Gonzalez of the Van Dyke beard talked a big game back in the L.A. morgue. On the stand, he turned into mush. They always did.

Forensic scientists all suck. They never come through in court. Never.

Lizzie had a theory. Forensic science is to law what romance literature is to sex. A misleading fantasy with no relevance to real life.

It was ironic. Lizzie loved science. Few 12-year-olds had a better grasp of evolution. She peppered Elder Evans with questions because it bothered him so much. When she first started trying cases, she couldn't wait to get a forensic scientist to testify. They would do whiz bang tests and produce rock solid, undeniable Truth.

Except they never did. There was never quite enough evidence to support a definitive answer. Even with DNA, there were problems with how the items were collected or tested, where they were stored, how they were sequenced.

In the Rincon case, neither of the two coroners who testified could say beyond a reasonable doubt that Rincon had or had not been hit with a flashlight.

Clear as mud.

Nor could they say anything definitive about what happened that night based on ballistics, spatter evidence, the lack of stippling patterns, or pathology. Rincon was dead, killed by a bullet. Everything else was speculation.

The only coroner who ever got to examine Rincon's body was the Inland County Coroner, Dr. Helen Jackson, a slovenly woman who looked like her feet hurt.

She hadn't noticed Rincon's head wound. She was focused on the gunshot to his chest.

Lizzie showed her the photographs of Rincon's head wound, as well as Gonzalez's report, stating the wound was caused by a hard object with an edge, like a flashlight.

"Okay," Dr. Jackson shrugged, "I could argue it either way. Rincon's body was cremated, so I guess we will never know." She wouldn't lose any sleep over it.

Lizzie didn't watch TV, but she suspected crime shows did not star coroners like Dr. Jackson. They paid her to cut people open and write reports. They didn't pay her enough to care.

The toxicology wasn't any better. Dr. Jackson took longer than usual to order tests. They were expensive, and Detective Moeller hadn't requested them. Eventually, she did order the tests at the request of the Inland County D.A.'s office. They showed Rincon had traces of marijuana in his system. How much Dr. Jackson couldn't say. "Past 48 hours, there is some degradation in the samples."

Lizzie's expert, Gonzalez from Los Angeles, explained why the head wound was *likely* caused by a flashlight. The only thing he was certain of was that drugs were not a factor in the case. But his reasons had nothing to do with science.

"Officer Lee himself didn't report Rincon's driving was erratic. He stopped him because of the broken taillight, not because he thought he was under the influence." It was a good point. It was also common sense. Lizzie didn't need to call a coroner to say it.

Taylor only bothered to ask Gonzalez one question. "You can't tell this jury beyond a reasonable doubt whether Rincon was hit with a flashlight or not."

Taylor didn't even hire his own expert.

"That's the difference between *CSI* and *Law and Order*," Jones said. He and Mary loved both shows. "On *CSI* they never go to court and have to actually *prove* anything."

. . .

LIZZIE WENT BACK TO HER OFFICE DURING THE TRIAL'S LUNCH break.

Inland County Deputy D.A. Dan Seave was waiting for her.

He looked like he might cry. "We fucked up."

He handed her a single-page Interview Report conducted by the Riverside Sheriff's Office. It was dated two days after Rincon was shot.

"Riverside? Not Inland?"

"Apparently," Seave said, "the call came into Riverside. It was the only thing they did in the case. It was in my file, but I didn't see it until this morning. I missed it. I'm sorry."

Lizzie didn't recognize the name of the deputy who conducted the interview. It was of an unidentified white male who refused to give his name. It was conducted at the man's home, a trailer outside of Blanton. The additional description of the man and trailer left no doubt it was Scanlon.

The man refused to provide his name. He was interviewed after he contacted the Riverside County Sheriff's Office to report that he had information about the officer involved shooting involving a member of the Blanton P.D.

Lizzie thought she would be sick.

A deputy responded to the location the man gave the deputy's office. The deputy found the man who admitted he made the call. He denied having any knowledge of the shooting and insisted he had been in his trailer that night, several miles from where the reported incident took place. He apologized for inconveniencing the deputy.

Scanlon lied to her. Lizzie's case was about to fall apart. Lee was going to walk free.

The bad thing happened.

"We weren't trying to hide anything," Seave said. "I swear."

Lizzie kept calm and called Jones. "Get Scanlon. He's going back on the stand."

She called Jack and told them what happened. "I'm turning the interview over to the defense right away."

Jack told The Chief. Chief D'Ambrosio took the news with equanimity. "Didn't I say this was a bad case? OPR is definitely going to fire your friend now. Assaulting the target was bad. Hiding evidence is worse."

CHAPTER 39

"THAT'S SHAMEFUL, MS. SCOTT," TAYLOR SAID. "OBVIOUSLY, I'M going to ask for a mistrial."

Lizzie held her head in her hands. She was devastated. She told Taylor to do what he thought was best. It was wrong for him not to get Scanlon's prior statement. He was entitled to it by law. She only discovered the interview herself a few minutes ago.

Jones sat in the desk in front of her. This was a bad, bad deal.

"I can't tell you how sorry I am," Lizzie told Taylor.

"I don't accept your apology," Taylor said. "I never thought you were capable of something like this. This is an outrage."

Taylor hung up on her. Then he laughed. Lizzie just handed them victory.

By law the prosecution had to turn over all of Scanlon's interviews so Taylor could use them for cross-examination, to find inconsistencies or lies in Scanlon's testimony.

"I'd say the fact Scanlon said he wasn't there and didn't see anything was a big goddamn inconsistency," Taylor joked.

Lee couldn't believe his luck. Because the jury had been impaneled and the discovery violation was the prosecutor's fault, the case would be dismissed *with* prejudice against the government. Meaning they couldn't indict him again; double jeopardy had attached: Lee would skate.

What Taylor didn't tell Lee or Lizzie Scott was that he knew about Scanlon's interview with the Riverside Sheriff's Department weeks ago.

Farley was worth every penny Taylor paid him.

If Lizzie or the judge knew Taylor already had the interview, Taylor wouldn't have a prayer of getting a mistrial. So Taylor wasn't going to tell them.

"Baby," Taylor called his wife/receptionist. "Call the press. We got some good stuff about to happen over here."

. . .

LIZZIE HANDED THE CLERK A COPY OF THE RIVERSIDE DEPUTY'S interview with Scanlon and a hastily written memo explaining that it hadn't been turned over to the defense until now.

"Oh, the judge is *not* going to like this," the clerk said.

Ten minutes later, Judge Letts walked slowly and sadly to the bench. "I'm very disappointed in the government, Ms. Scott."

Jones stood next to Lizzie. He asked the Ventura FBI office to drive Scanlon back to court. Jones made it his practice to be there for his prosecutor for the good and bad times, but especially the bad times.

"It's an outrage, Your Honor," Taylor fumed. "Somebody's head ought to roll over this. Ms. Scott and Agent Jones should lose their jobs or at least be ashamed. This is just gross incompetence."

I'm going to be sick.

Lizzie kept herself together. She was blushing violently, but her voice did not waver. She explained why she had no knowledge of Scanlon's interview with Riverside until now. The report was in the Inland County Deputy D.A.'s file. He only discovered it today.

"Ah. She's just playing games now," Taylor said, ginning up outrage. "It's *all* the government, Your Honor. C'mon now."

"Clearly, I'm not hiding anything," Lizzie said. "I gave Mr. Taylor the report. Furthermore, the state and federal governments are separate. I asked the Inland County Deputy D.A. for his complete file several times. Until today, he swore I already had it."

It didn't necessarily matter. The law often imputes the mistakes of the state to the federal government. Lizzie wasn't allowed to personally go through the D.A.'s office records. But she was responsible for the D.A.'s failure to go through them carefully enough.

151

Lizzie tried to keep the case from being dismissed.

"We can fix this," she said. "We have time to remedy the problem. Mr. Scanlon is returning to court. He will be available for Mr. Taylor to recall him and cross-examine him during the government's case. Deputy D.A. Seave is also available to explain what happened. Officer Lee won't be prejudiced."

"What about the Riverside deputy who did the interview?" Taylor pounded the table. "Where is he? Did she hide him, too? I have no idea who he is or where he works."

He did know, of course, but he didn't like where this was going. Judge Letts seemed open to Lizzie's suggestions to fix the problem. Lizzie was right. The record wouldn't support a reversal. So as long as the defense got to impeach Scanlon with the prior statement, Judge Letts could not see any way that Taylor could argue his client was denied his right to confront the witnesses against him.

Taylor saw his best chance for a mistrial slipping away.

He dialed up the outrage. "Don't let them get away with this, Your Honor. The court has a duty to penalize the government for this. Dismiss the case. Otherwise, they'll just do this sort of thing again."

Judge Letts said sanctions would only be appropriate if the misconduct was intentional. "There's no evidence that Ms. Scott hid the document."

"Of course she did," Taylor said. "For the record, I believe Ms. Scott knew that Scanlon was interviewed before. I believe she knew about this and hid it."

Lizzie could feel the blood pulsing in her forehead. "Is Mr. Taylor calling me a liar?"

"That's exactly what I am calling you, Ms. Scott. On the record."

One of the retired cops laughed.

I want to kill him.

Lizzie put her hands behind her back and held them tight.

Judge Letts looked crestfallen. He hated when people didn't get along. Now people were calling one another liars. It was very disappointing. He called a recess to let tempers cool.

Lizzie stormed out of the courtroom and went straight into the elevator, leaving Jones to deal with the media. By the time Jones got to her office, Lizzie was already on the phone. She was enraged. "He called me a *liar*, Jack."

"Of course he did, he's a defense lawyer. He's trying to rattle you, and you're letting him."

Lizzie punched the wall. The impact knocked an award from the ATF to the ground. A stab of pain went up her arm. It was the hand she hit Lee with. It still hadn't healed.

"I want to move to have Taylor held in contempt, then I'm going to file a complaint with the State Bar, then I'm going to go after him for obstruction of justice."

Jack told her to put Jones on the line.

"No, Jack! I don't need *you* to tell *him* to calm me *down*."

"Then calm yourself down," Jack said. "Get yourself under control."

"Do I have clearance to ask for contempt or not?"

Jack checked his watch, stalling for time.

"Jesus, Jack, have some guts," she said. She was due back in court in 45 minutes.

"Sure, what the hell, go ahead, write up the motion. But before you file, just think, is it really something worth—"

She hung up on him, then sat down at her computer and pulled up a contempt order.

Jones slipped out, bought her a sandwich and a Coke, and placed them two inches from her.

She punished the keyboard, banging the keys so hard the light on her desk shook, muttering to herself as she typed like a crazy woman. Her hand was aching again. She hadn't been able to spar or hit the bag for months.

"It's time we got back, Lizzie," Jones said. "You should eat something."

She hit print. As the pages spat out, she opened and drained the can of Coke in two sips, then pulled a wad of turkey from between the slices of bread. She chewed without tasting it, staring straight ahead, still seething. "I don't like being called a liar."

Jones nodded. He noticed.

They rushed back to court. It was empty but for Taylor, Lee, and the clerk.

"Have a good lunch?" Taylor asked, winking at Lizzie.

Lizzie slammed a copy of her motion to hold Taylor in contempt into Taylor's chest. He grunted then smiled.

I like Lizzie Scott. That Lizzie Scott is alright.

The clerk handed Lizzie a motion. It was Taylor's motion to dismiss the case for prosecutorial misconduct and to hold Lizzie in contempt. Clearly, she hadn't been the only one working over the break.

"Counsel," the clerk said. "Judge Letts wants to see you."

Lizzie and Taylor followed the clerk through the door to chambers, leaving Jones and Lee alone for the first time since the trial began.

Lee walked past Jones, headed for the hallway. As he did, he whispered low and menacing. "When this is over, that bitch and I are going to have a long talk."

Jones grabbed Lee's hand, ostensibly to shake it, but he held onto it squeezed hard. Lee winced. "We won't have any of that, Officer Lee."

There was hate in Lee's eyes. "Maybe I'll come see you instead."

Jones's face broke into a goofy grin. "You want my home address?" Jones said, tightening his vise grip for emphasis. "I'd love to see you."

Jones let go of Lee's hand.

Lee put his head down and stormed out of the room.

CHAPTER 40

THE JUDGE'S LAW CLERK HANDED TAYLOR AND LIZZIE A COPY OF a document, still warm from the printer. It was headed "Preliminary Ruling."

Lizzie skipped to the last page:

"And so, based on Ms. Scott's misconduct in failing to disclose Scanlon's prior interview, the defense's motion to dismiss the indictment is GRANTED."

Lizzie couldn't breathe. The case was about to be thrown out. Lee could never be tried for what he did to Rincon. OPR would can her.

She never heard Elder Evans in her head when she was in trial. She was too engaged in the fight. Now she heard him loud and clear:

"The sinner will always sin. Always."

But she had not sinned. This wasn't fair, and it wasn't her fault.

There was glee in Taylor's voice. "Thank you, Your Honor," he said. "I appreciate the Court's bravery in doing this."

Lizzie tried to say something. Nothing came out. It was a nightmare. The breath dried in her throat. Judge Letts was waiting, about to make this final—

There was a knock on the door.

The clerk came in.

"Sorry to disturb you, Your Honor." The clerk looked like someone had pinned his ears back. "The Chief is here."

Judge Letts stood up when he came in. There were plenty of federal judges. There was only one Dante D'Ambrosio. Had he ever even been down to Orange County?

"Your Honor, I appreciate you agreeing to see me."

Judge Letts hadn't agreed to see him, but he was as intimidated by The Chief as everyone else.

"I understand Mr. Taylor has made an allegation against our office." Jack told him about it, looking for advice on what to do. Instead, The Chief grabbed his coat and stormed out of the office.

"The allegation is about Ms. Scott, not your office," Judge Letts said.

"Your Honor, Ms. Scott *is* our office. Every assistant is our office. I take any allegation of dishonesty personally. Obviously, we will want a complete hearing on the issue. Including the chance to cross-examine Mr. Taylor and his investigator, Mr. Farley, to determine how and when they first learned of the Riverside interview with Scanlon."

From what Jack told him about Taylor's questions to Scanlon ("Have you ever told anyone this didn't happen . . .") and the speed in which Taylor got the press there—not to mention the fact he seemed to have had the mistrial motion prepped—The Chief guessed this was a setup job. He couldn't be sure, exactly, but he knew Taylor was capable of anything.

Judge Letts said The Chief's office was entitled to interview both Taylor and Farley.

"Right," The Chief said. "Why don't we do it right now, Your Honor? The parties are here. I'll handle the questioning myself since Ms. Scott will be a witness. Mr. Taylor can get Mr. Farley here, I'm sure."

The gig was up. Taylor wasn't about to risk losing his law license or being held in contempt. You try things; sometimes they work, sometimes they don't. It wasn't personal.

"Your Honor, I agree with Ms. Scott that this whole thing can be fixed," Taylor said. "To help move things along, I withdraw the allegation against her and apologize if anyone was offended by anything I might have said in the heat of the moment."

Judge Letts said, in that case, the defense's motion to dismiss was denied.

"Anything to make Chief D'Ambrosio happy," Taylor said. "I'm just honored to see him again. We met several years ago."

Taylor extended his hand. The Chief stared at it for a moment. Taylor applied for a job with the office in 1990. The Chief thought he lacked character. He shook his hand anyway. The Chief was a gentleman, albeit one from the nineteenth century.

The lawyers filed out of chambers.

Lizzie tried to thank The Chief.

He waved her off. "A ridiculous waste of time."

Scanlon arrived looking scared. "What? What I do?"

"Mr. Taylor," she said. "Mr. Scanlon is back. Shall we put him on the stand next so you can cross-examine him about the Riverside interview?"

Taylor waved Lizzie away. "I'm not giving you the chance to explain this thing away in *your* case. I'll impeach Scanlon in my case, in my own good time, in my own way."

Smart move.

Lizzie admired Taylor's game. He would wait to impeach Scanlon during the defense's case to make it look like Lizzie had been hiding bad evidence all along. Technically, she should have been allowed to recall Scanlon before she rested the prosecution's case, but Judge Letts would never allow it.

Still, she had survived. The case was still alive.

Meanwhile, Lee's rage was building. Taylor promised him he would get a mistrial. Maybe not promised, but he made it seem like it was going to happen. He lied. They all lied. This thing was going to keep going until it ran over Lee once and for all.

. . .

LATER ON, LONG AFTER IT WAS ALL OVER, LIZZIE REALIZED Scanlon *had* told her about the Riverside interview.

It was the first time she interviewed him, at the Arby's off the 5 Freeway.

Scanlon said he went back to his trailer after seeing Rincon get shot. He drank the Stater Brothers's vodka to black out. The cop came to him. Scanlon, terrified, told the cop he hadn't seen anything, he wasn't on the highway that night. But the cop couldn't hear him. It was too windy.

Scanlon was so drunk, he thought the deputy was a cop and the whole thing was a dream.

It never dawned on Lizzie that it actually happened.

CHAPTER 41

"Mr. Scanlon denied that he saw Officer Lee shoot anyone."

Riverside Sheriff Deputy Ken White was young and nervous. This was his first time testifying. The jury sat forward in their seats, transfixed. Real-life trials didn't offer many surprises. This was the real deal.

Lizzie had to admire Taylor's game. Rather than impeach Scanlon directly by putting him back on the stand in the defense case, Taylor was using the Riverside deputy who interviewed Scanlon to destroy his testimony instead.

"Mr. Scanlon swore he had been in his trailer on the night of the shooting and hadn't been anywhere near the road," White said.

The only audience that matters in trial is the jury. They hadn't been privy to any of the drama behind the scenes. They weren't in chambers to hear how close the case came to being dismissed. They knew nothing about the Riverside interview until now. From their standpoint, Taylor was eviscerating Lizzie's only eyewitness. It was great stuff.

White explained that his regular assignment was the Men's Facility, Violent Offender Unit. He had been pulled into the shooting investigation by a supervisor who wanted nothing to do with it.

The fight is in rounds. Taylor was winning this one. White was burying Scanlon.

"I asked him what the deal was, why he had called the Sheriff's Office if he didn't know anything about the shooting. He said he didn't know why he did it. As I recall, his exact words were something like, sometimes, he did stupid shit."

Lizzie heard Scanlon say similar things. She didn't have any doubt Deputy White was telling the truth.

"Do you think you would be able recognize the man you interviewed by the trailer if you saw him again?" Taylor wondered.

Deputy White said he was sure he could.

Taylor nodded to Farley, who stood and walked out of the courtroom. Lizzie could see the jurors staring at the courtroom doors, anticipating the next twist in the story. Like all great storytellers, Taylor understood the power of anticipation. Make them laugh, make them cry, but most of all, make them wait.

Lizzie looked at Lee's wife, Lisa, in the front row. She looked tired, like she was about to fall asleep. It looked like their daughter Jill had a cold; her nose was red and irritated.

Lizzie felt a surge of empathy. She always did for the defendant's family. Maybe, when this was over, something good would come of it. Maybe Lee would serve his time and come back changed or they would move on.

That's not your job.

Lizzie made herself stop thinking about it. She was great at compartmentalizing.

The door opened. Farley led Scanlon in. His hair stood up. His suit was wrinkled. His shirt collar was open. Lizzie and Jones weren't able to clean him up. At this moment, Scanlon wasn't their witness. He was a character in Taylor's story now.

Farley walked Scanlon into the well of the courtroom, positioning him in front of the jury so he faced Officer White on the witness stand.

Taylor pointed at Scanlon, hack prosecutors point at the defendant.

"Look at this man, Deputy White," Taylor said. "Is this the man you interviewed by the trailer who admitted he didn't see the shooting?"

"Yes," Deputy White said. "That's the man."

Scanlon ran his hand through his hair and scratched his chest, looking guilty.

"Let the record reflect," Taylor said, "the witness has identified the man who denied seeing the shooting as Henry Scanlon."

Farley walked Scanlon out of court. The jurors stared at them leaving. Then they stared at Lizzie.

They think I lied to them. They don't trust me now.

Taylor held Deputy White's report in front of the jury. "You wrote this all down in a report and gave it to the prosecutor?"

Lizzie objected that the question was misleading. "Mr. Taylor referred to the 'prosecutor' when he means the Inland County District Attorney, not me or my office."

"They're all prosecutors," Taylor said. "Her, the D.A.—"

"Objection sustained," Judge Letts said. Taylor could get on the nerves of a saint. Judge Letts turned to the witness and asked the question himself: "Did you give the report to the Inland County D.A.?"

"No," Deputy White said. He gave it to his boss at the Riverside County D.A. "I don't know where it went after that. Then I went back to my regular job at the jail. I never heard anything about it after that."

When exactly did he hear about this case again?

Lizzie passed a note to Jones. Jones had no idea how or when White got involved.

"So, now, Deputy White, let me ask you this," Taylor said, leaning on the lectern. "If I told you the man you interviewed—Henry Scanlon—testified that he saw the shooting, based on what you know, would he be lying?"

"I just know what he told me at the trailer."

Taylor tried again. "What you're saying is that Scanlon was lying either when he spoke to you or when he came into court."

"I just know what he told me."

Deputy White didn't like being pushed around by a smart-ass black defense lawyer, even if he was defending a cop. Deputy White hadn't been a *complete* racist when he joined the department. The job seemed to have pushed him over the line.

"I guess we can let the jury figure it out," Taylor said, thinking: *Racist cop won't give it up to me, no matter what I ask him.*

"Your witness, Ms. Scott."

Lizzie never cross-examined a law enforcement officer before. Prosecuting a cop was like fighting a southpaw. Everything was the opposite of what you trained to do.

"You're on probationary job status, Deputy White. You've had less than 12 months on the job. In fact, you'd only been a deputy for a few months when you interviewed Mr. Scanlon. Was this your first interview?"

"I'd conducted a few interviews with a senior deputy. This was my first one alone."

Lizzie jumped on the word. "When you say you 'conducted' a few interviews, what you mean is, you *watched* a senior deputy conduct them as part of your training, correct?"

White nodded. Lizzie said he had to say it out loud for the transcript.

"Yes," he said, peeved.

Lizzie liked cross-examining a cop. It turned out that she knew exactly which buttons to push. It's why all the best defense lawyers are former prosecutors.

"Did you tape record the interview with Mr. Scanlon?"

"No."

"Did you spend a lot of time doing the interview? I ask because your whole report is less than half a page long."

White guessed he was with Scanlon for 10 to 15 minutes, but it could have been less.

"How drunk was he when you talked to him?"

The Look crossed Deputy White's face. It always fascinated her. It was the exact moment when a witness realized he was in a tight spot. He was either going to admit to something he was ashamed or guilty of, or he was going to lie about it and take his chances.

For all her issues with Elder Evans, Lizzie recognized he did a good job preparing his people for a moment like this. He trained them to tell the truth and face the consequences. Convocation people never had The Look. They always told the truth. They didn't want to burn in Hell.

Deputy White was not Convocation.

His face said he was weighing his options.

Lizzie knew the truth. Scanlon had been very drunk when he was interviewed. Deputy White hadn't put it in his report. He knew he should admit the mistake, but people hated to do that. Men, in Lizzie's experience, hated it more than women. Cops hated it more than anyone.

"Yes," White said finally. "Mr. Scanlon had been drinking. Quite a bit, as I recall."

Lizzie held up a plastic one-gallon jug of Stater Brothers vodka. Jones brought it in a brown paper bag in anticipation of this moment.

"Did you see one of these at the trailer? Because Mr. Scanlon claims to have polished two off around the time you interviewed him."

Deputy White recalled seeing a number of empty alcohol containers, but it would not surprise him to hear Scanlon drank that much.

"Is it possible Scanlon called in his tip then got scared and refused to cooperate?"

Deputy White said anything was possible.

"Haven't you ever seen a witness who got too scared to testify?"

Deputy White hadn't personally seen such a thing, but he believed it happened.

Lizzie noted that Scanlon owned no computer or cell phone. The story of the shooting hadn't been in the newspaper, only the *Inland County Recorder* website. The fact Scanlon called in the tip to begin with showed he knew *something* about it.

"How else could he have known about it unless he was there?"

Taylor objected. The question called for speculation. Judge Letts sustained it. Lizzie wasn't above asking an improper question to make a point.

Lizzie was about to sit down when she remembered the note she passed to Jones. "Deputy White, you said after you gave your boss the interview report you never heard anything about this case."

"Right."

"Except you're here now. How did that happen? How did you get here? When was the next time anybody asked you about your interview with Mr. Scanlon?"

It's a lie that good lawyers never ask a question unless they know the answer. Sometimes you have to ask, especially on cross-examination. Lawyers don't know everything, no matter what they want clients to think.

Deputy White was struggling. The Look wasn't there. He was genuinely trying to remember something, not deciding whether to lie about it.

"It must've been two or three weeks ago," Deputy White said, squinting a bit, as if he was trying to read a distant wall calendar. "I was at work when Mr. Farley came by and asked about it."

No way! Taylor knew about the previous interview weeks ago!

This is why you have to ask questions when you don't know the answer. This was why Lizzie loved trying cases. This was awesome.

Judge Letts stared at Taylor like he just found out Taylor was having an affair with the judge's wife. *How could you? I trusted you!*

Taylor took notes, pretending not to notice.

"Mr. Farley is Mr. Taylor's investigator?" Lizzie asked. "Mr. Farley is the gentleman who brought Mr. Scanlon back into court a few minutes ago?"

"That's right."

Taylor pretended he wasn't paying attention and didn't notice Judge Letts, staring daggers at him.

"Where did Mr. Farley work before he worked for Mr. Taylor?"

"Objection," Taylor said, finally, as if the whole thing was boring. "This is so irrelevant; Ms. Scott is trying to confuse the jury."

Judge Letts overruled Taylor. He stared at Taylor like a man who'd been betrayed.

"Mr. Farley told me he was a retired deputy."

"Did Mr. Farley say how he got in contact with you?"

"I guess my supervisor and Mr. Farley are friends. They play golf together."

Lee glanced back at Lisa. She was nodding off in the first row. The bitch couldn't even stay awake to see him get his ass convicted.

．．．

AT THE END OF THE TRIAL DAY, JUDGE LETTS CALLED THE LAWYERS back to chambers. He didn't ask the court reporter to join them.

"What I'm about to say is off the record," Judge Letts said. "I prefer this stay between us." The judge stood behind his desk, hands at his hips, robe open, exposing a wrinkled shirt and limp old-school tie.

"You misled me, Mr. Taylor." The judge's hands were shaking. "You knew about the Scanlon interview all the time. I almost granted you a mistrial based on your deception." Lizzie was afraid the judge might cry.

Taylor stared at him, his face neutral. The room was silent.

"Aren't you going to at least apologize?" the judge said, his voice thick with hurt.

Taylor pursed his lips and thought about it.

"No," Taylor said, adding gently: "It's a trial, Judge. Shit happens."

Taylor walked out of chambers.

Judge Letts turned to Lizzie, looking for some kind of answer. How could Taylor do such a thing? What could be done about it?

Lizzie said good night and followed Taylor out.

Judge Letts was a good man, but he had no business running a trial court.

CHAPTER 42

JACK CAME DOWN TO WATCH TAYLOR PUT ON THE DEFENSE CASE.
Mrs. Leonard wanted reports on how Lizzie was doing. The Chief
wanted to make sure Taylor didn't insult the office again.

Abe Ybarra brought Jack up to speed. Along with hanging around
in court every day, Ybarra blasted "Justice for Rincon Committee"
e-mails to his list of contacts, drumming up stories in a few left-lean-
ing websites, giving KPFK radio interviews. Ybarra thought the jury
might hang, cop cases often did.

"Lizzie's case went in very nicely," Ybarra told Jack. "The jury likes
her except for Juror #6, which is too bad because I bet your Juror #6 is
the foreperson."

Juror #6 was Mrs. Meagher.

You couldn't tell how a jury might vote, but you could always tell
who their leader was. You saw it in their body language, their defer-
ence, the way they looked to one juror in particular to gauge their
reactions to things.

Mrs. Meagher was the go-to juror. Ybarra was pretty sure she
couldn't stand Lizzie Scott.

Jack asked if Mrs. Rincon decided to sue.

Not yet, Ybarra said, but he was a patient man.

• • •

Taylor also thought Mrs. Meagher was the Foreperson, but he still wasn't happy.

His mistrial play failed. Deputy White was a disappointment. If things didn't improve, Lee would have to testify.

In a cop case, the officer usually did. They had no choice. Whatever privilege a cop gets comes with a price. The jury expects the officer to take the oath and tell the truth.

Taylor wanted to avoid it. Lee looked and sounded like someone fully capable of shooting and killing an unarmed man. Was there anybody else they could call instead?

"I got a use-of-force expert witness on hold, boss," Farley said.

Unlike most defense lawyers, Taylor didn't like calling expert witnesses. They bit into his bottom line. Passing the costs on to the client didn't cover Taylor's time preparing the expert, negotiating the retainer agreement, bargaining over whether they would fly out business class or coach.

"I'm already doing this case for half off," Taylor said. "I'm not digging into my own damn pocket to call an expert."

Farley persisted. It wasn't just the money. He thought Taylor's ego was involved, too. The boss liked to be the only expert in the courtroom, the star of the show; he didn't like to cede authority or to share the spotlight with anyone.

If Farley were in Lee's shoes, he'd want as many witnesses on his side as possible. The court told jurors it didn't matter which side brought in the most witnesses, but Farley knew that was nonsense. There was strength in numbers.

The other reason Farley pushed for the expert was because so many of his old colleagues kept calling him, looking for the job. At $400 an hour, it was a good gig, even if they had to kick back a few bucks to Farley. Taylor didn't need to know about that part.

The day before he would have to call Lee to the stand or rest the defense case, Taylor called Farley at 3:00 A.M. "Have the expert there tomorrow morning."

Taylor shouldn't have been allowed to put any expert on the stand. Judge Letts' trial order said lawyers had to exchange expert resumes and reports two weeks before trial. Lizzie tried to exclude Taylor's expert on those grounds; she didn't have time to prepare for him.

Judge Letts agreed Taylor violated his order, but after a fitful night's sleep, his fear of being reversed returned.

"I don't see what I can do, Ms. Scott," Judge Letts said. "Mr. Taylor has put us all in a terrible position. If I deny him the chance to call the expert, it'll be an issue on appeal."

The expert was FBI Special Agent Carl Ross, retired.

Jones knew the name. Ross was a headquarters agent, the first line of the signature block on final dispositions of shooting cases. He never left D.C., never conducted field interviews or testified at hearings. Jones never met him, but he was the name on the final disposition of his own shooting case.

"They retired him early," Jones said, having made calls to D.C. "He got crosswise with the higher-ups. Now he's bitter."

Apparently, after the Ferguson, New York, and Cleveland shootings, the Attorney General's Office decided they needed to take a more aggressive approach to excessive-force cases. There would be more indictments.

Ross counseled caution. Charging bad cases was unethical. It only led to greater public outrage and disappointment. The prosecutors in the Civil Rights Division said he was in the way. The A.G.'s office said it was time for new blood.

The FBI offered to transfer Ross to a field office in Biloxi or Billings. He retired instead. He had silver hair and the patrician air of a retired senator, with the kind of gravitas that would have been wasted in Biloxi or Billings.

"I don't know how many cases I handled," Ross said modestly. "I suppose I oversaw close to a hundred FBI agent–shooting investigations over my tenure."

Taylor asked how many of those shootings proved to be unjustified.

Lizzie objected; the question was irrelevant to this case. She was overruled.

"All the shootings were deemed justified," he said. "The FBI never had an unjustified shooting during my time there."

Yeah, that's because you cover up all the bad shoots.

If Lizzie sometimes found prosecuting a cop weird, Taylor found defending one surreal.

"Why were all the shootings justified, do you think?" Taylor kept a straight face.

"The FBI has the best trained, most intelligent law enforcement agents in the field," Ross said with pride.

"So, if the FBI is the gold standard," Taylor said, "I'm guessing the Blanton P.D. is something a little less than that."

Lizzie was familiar with Taylor's fight plan by now. Blame others. The culprit wasn't Lee. First, it was Moeller, who was an idiot. Now it was the Blanton P.D., a lousy department with bad equipment and training.

"I'm not an expert on small police department practice," Ross admitted. "But I'm sure the Blanton Police Department does the best they can with what they have."

Taylor had Ross describe the dangers of traffic stops, noting how many officers had been killed over the course of what started as a routine event.

"It happens too often, unfortunately," Ross said.

Taylor described Lee's version of what happened the night of the shooting and asked Ross his opinion of Lee's actions that night.

Ross said that based on those facts, Lee was not only justified in using deadly force against Rincon, but he had shown remarkable restraint in not using it sooner.

"Officers are trained to let a suspect with a knife only get within 21 feet of them. Here, Officer Lee didn't fire his weapon until the suspect was within 15 feet, or as little as 10 feet. Frankly, I think Officer Lee waited too long to fire his weapon. I believe he should have shot Mr. Rincon sooner."

Mrs. Meagher wrote it down. Juror #7 noticed she wrote it down and wrote it down in her notebook, too. There was no question who the foreperson was.

"What if Officer Lee was wrong?" Taylor asked. "What if it turned out the suspect had no knife? Would he still be guilty of using excessive force?"

Are they admitting Rincon never had a knife?

Lizzie thought it would be crazy to do so. But maybe it wasn't. The law let the officer be wrong about whether or not the suspect really was armed. Ross explained:

"The only question is whether the officer's fear of death was justified at the moment he responded with deadly force himself. We don't Monday morning quarterback life-and-death situations. So long as he reasonably feared for his life at the time, he's allowed to be wrong."

"Thank you," Taylor said. "Last thing, I should've asked, do you know Agent Jones here?"

Lizzie ground her teeth. She was sure Taylor was going to ask about Jones's shooting.

"Agent Jones and I were colleagues for a number of years," Ross said.

For a moment, Lizzie was tempted not to cross him. If the jury believed Scanlon, none of what Ross said mattered. He hadn't even discussed the flashlight or Lee's efforts to hide it.

But the jurors were looking at her, waiting and expecting she would ask the expert *something*. If she didn't, Taylor would argue that Ross was so convincing that she couldn't touch him.

"Mr. Ross," she asked, "are you getting paid to be here?"

Taylor was supposed to disclose if and how much his expert was getting. That he hadn't didn't mean anything; Taylor didn't seem to care what the rules were. Either way, Lizzie thought she was safe in pursuing it. Whatever Ross answered, Lizzie could use it against him.

"I'm not getting compensated for being here today, other than my expenses," he said.

Even better.

Ross wasn't a hired gun. He was a bitter former employee, looking to embarrass his old bosses.

"You're here, testifying for the defense for free, because you no longer work with the FBI, is that right?"

"I'm here because the defense thought I could be helpful."

"How can you be helpful?" she asked. "You weren't there, you haven't heard the trial witnesses, haven't been to the scene, you certainly haven't spoken to the government expert or the FBI agent involved."

"My only purpose is to offer a fresh set of eyes and to offer my expertise on the question of the use of force."

Lizzie pushed it. "I ask only because, as I understand it, you were retired a bit earlier than you would have liked when the new director took over."

"I have nothing but respect and affection for the Bureau," Ross said.

"But you weren't happy about being forced out."

"No," Ross said. "I wasn't."

That was enough. There was no point going into the details.

Taylor didn't bother to stand up. "I have no redirect, Your Honor. She didn't touch him."

Let it go.

Lizzie knew Taylor was trying to steal the round with a low blow. It might offend anyone who knew what he was doing. Unfortunately, jurors were chosen because they did not appreciate the intricacies of fighting.

If Taylor said her cross-examination hadn't damaged the witness, there was a good chance one or two jurors would think so, too.

CHAPTER 43

FARLEY HAD A HARD TIME FINDING ANYONE TO SAY SOMETHING nice about Officer Lee.

Taylor insisted. He wanted a witness who might still let them keep Lee off the stand. Trial took it out of everybody, but the longer the case went on, the more exhausted and irritable Lee became.

"I told you when we first met," Taylor reminded him, "you got to get enough sleep, eat something, take care of yourself."

"I'm fine," Lee mumbled, downing another cup of coffee. He was living off caffeine. Taylor wondered if he was dipping into his wife's meth supply.

"Nah," Farley said. "He's getting drug tested every week. It's part of the bail conditions. Plus, Dwayne-o's very antidrug."

Farley finally found a character witness, Marge Cooley, Blanton City Manager. She was far from Lee's direct boss, but she was the best Farley could do. None of Lee's fellow officers were willing to do it. Taylor wouldn't have used them anyway. The Blanton P.D. was full of cops Taylor wouldn't want *near* the stand.

"During the time my client has worked for the City of Blanton, have you formed an opinion as to his character for truthfulness?" Taylor asked.

Cooley said Officer Lee had a fine character and was a truthful person.

"Did these charges do anything to change your opinion of Officer Lee?"

"No," Cooley said. "I was shocked Officer Lee was charged. To my knowledge, Officer Lee has always done a damn fine job for our city."

"Thank you for your service to your community," Taylor said.

Lizzie stood up so fast it made Taylor nervous. She had a feeling she could score a lot of points off of City Manager Cooley.

"You're here, because, why?" Lizzie asked. Juror #7 laughed. "Are you here because, as City Manager, you sign Lee's checks? Is that why? Because you don't have direct contact with Officer Lee, do you?"

"No," Cooley said, glaring at her.

"Am I correct, ma'am, that as City Manager, a big part of your job is overseeing the budget, handling Blanton's finances?"

"That's right, I handle the budget and the finances," Cooley said. The more annoyed the witness's answers became, the more sweetly Lizzie asked her questions.

"I wonder if it would change your opinion of Officer Lee's character or reputation if you knew he *did* shoot Joe Rincon without cause?"

Cooley looked at Lizzie as if the lawyer was wasting her time.

"Do you mean, if I knew he was guilty of what you claim he did, would that alter my view of him? Is that what you're asking me, Ms. Scott?"

Taylor wished there were "time-outs" in trial. He would take one now. He would woodshed Cooley. Make her change her attitude. Make her show Lizzie Scott some respect.

"Yes, that's right, thank you, ma'am," Lizzie said like she meant it. "That's exactly what I meant to ask you. If Officer Lee *was* guilty of these charges, would that change your opinion of him?"

Cooley smirked because it was the dumbest question she ever heard. "If he was guilty of what you say, Ms. Scott, of course it would change my opinion of him."

Taylor would definitely take a time-out now. He would explain to the City Manager that just because she was used to saying jump and her underlings asking how high, she wasn't the boss here, and Lizzie Scott wasn't her toady.

"Would it change your opinion of Officer Lee if you knew he failed to report that he struck Mr. Rincon with a flashlight, then gave another officer the flashlight so it wouldn't be part of the equipment on his inventory list the night of the shooting?"

Cooley crossed her arms. Bad body language. Defensive. Taylor had tried to meet with Cooley before she testified. The busy city manager never found the time.

"Naturally, if that were true—and I don't believe it is true—it would change my opinion, Ms. Scott. If you proved he did any number of bad things, it would change my opinion. That's obvious. It's not even a question."

Two of the women jurors were staring at Cooley, seeing their own bosses or mother or sister, hating on her. Taylor viewed it as the magic of trials. Unless you told people how to act on the stand, their real personalities came out every time.

"You didn't try to find out if Officer Lee did any of these bad things, did you, Ms. Cooley?"

"That's not my job. I'm not a lawyer." Cooley turned to the jury. "Thank God."

She got nothing back but stares.

Taylor's teeth hurt the way they always did whenever a witness tried to be funny on the stand. It was never the right time or place for humor.

"Isn't it possible, Ms. Cooley, that you didn't try to find out if the defendant was guilty because you didn't want to know the truth?"

"Objection," Taylor said, in part because Lizzie was being argumentative, but mostly because Cooley was giving him the "why don't you do something about this bullshit" look. Another piece of bad witness behavior. There wasn't much Taylor could do.

"I don't mean to be argumentative, Your Honor," Lizzie said. "I'm laying a foundation to explore Ms. Cooley's bias toward the defendant and Ms. Cooley's motive to lie for him."

Cooley glared at Lizzie. Apparently, the City Manager did not like to be called a liar any more than Lizzie did.

"Objection sustained," Judge Letts said. "But Ms. Scott is correct, bias and motive to lie are always appropriate subjects for cross-examination. Please rephrase the question."

Lizzie was happy to do so. Jurors never remember what the question was after an objection delay.

"I'll ask it another way," she said. "What did you mean when you said Officer Lee did a damn fine job for your city?"

"Just what I said," Cooley snapped. "I don't know him well, but from what I do know about him, he's one of the good guys."

"By good, you mean he makes the City of Blanton lots of money."

"No. What I mean is, he keeps us safe. He protects us."

"You say 'no,'" Lizzie held up a document Jones gave her, "but I have a breakdown of the City of Blanton's budgets over the last five fiscal years and—"

Cooley cut her off. "That has nothing to do with why I said he did a good job."

"Ms. Cooley, let me finish my question, please?"

Interrupting the question? Perfect, Taylor thought: Cooley managed to break every rule a witness could break. She hadn't lied yet, but Taylor felt sure she would if she had to.

Lizzie handed Cooley her own budget repots. "According to your city's budget numbers, almost a third of Blanton's revenues come from court fines and assessments. Your police department is one of your biggest moneymakers. If they didn't write people up and arrest them, you'd be bankrupt."

Cooley shrugged. "We're not unusual. Many cities are that way."

"Yes, but your department's number of citations and fines, and arrests and seizures, has gone up by 40 percent in the last two years."

Cooley was indignant. "The State of California has cut money to the counties and to us. If we didn't do better, we'd have no money for roads or schools."

"Yes, but your city also collects more of the fines than any city in the Inland Empire."

"We've been proactive on collections," Cooley shrugged. "So what?"

If there was a worse term for a witness to use other than "so what," Taylor didn't know it.

"So, Ms. Cooley," Lizzie said, sweet as ever, "the police department is not only a major source of revenue for your city, it's the only one that's growing. Officer Lee was the leader of arrests, seizures, and fines on the whole force. He was its biggest earner."

"Yeah? So? I don't see your point," Cooley said, seeing Lizzie's point clear as day.

Taylor saw Lee staring at him. He could tell what he was thinking: *Nice job, asshole, this bitch is killing me.*

"Is it possible you're here to say nice things about Officer Lee because Officer Lee makes your city a lot of money?"

"No," Ms. Cooley said. "It's not possible."

Taylor didn't have anything on redirect. The sooner Ms. Cooley got off the stand the better.

"Nine times out of ten, we win through the defense's case," The Chief said.

Lizzie's best moments came from Taylor's witnesses. She was a great counterpuncher.

CHAPTER 44

COURT ADJOURNED FOR THE WEEKEND. JACK ASKED LIZZIE WHAT her plans were.

"Sleep."

Trying a case is like running a marathon while doing math word problems: physically and mentally exhausting. It's why they call it *trial*. Lizzie lost weight, sleep, and stomach lining. It felt good when it was over but only if you won.

"I was thinking, maybe, we could have dinner or something," Jack said.

Unbelievable.

Had he not noticed how angry she was at him over his lack of support with The Chief, to the Indictment Committee, for the last few months? He turned out to be a liar, a phony, and a kiss ass. What possible good could come from having dinner with him?

Sex would not be so bad right about now.

It was one of the few things a lawyer can enjoy in the midst of trial. You can't get drunk, though some do, especially on weekends, which is why so many trial courts were dark Monday and didn't start up again until Tuesday.

Lizzie didn't like to get drunk that much. Life-affirming sex was a healthier alternative. Unfortunately, Jack was the last person she should have been having sex with.

"I can't," she said. "Family stuff."

"Bring me along," Jack said. "I'd love to meet your family."

No, no, no. Never. Not ever.

Jones went home to Palm Springs but told her to call him if she needed anything. He was going to drive up to Ventura on Saturday to check on Scanlon. They might need him for their rebuttal case.

"I kind of miss old Hoot," Jones said. "He's kind of like the sidekick in an old Western."

Lizzie slept until noon, cleaned up poor Bodhi's mistakes, and took him for a long run. She and Sarah went to their favorite happy hour to catch up. They were living together again, but hadn't seen one another for weeks.

"Do you miss Tom very much?"

Sarah said she did and she didn't.

"He wasn't good for me." She went back and got her old waitress job at Red Robin. She was happy to be back at Convocation, too.

Lizzie got mad. "You know, you don't *have* to stay in it, Sarah. You're allowed to live your own life."

"It's my choice," Sarah said.

Lizzie was about to call bullshit on that but couldn't. Challenging Sarah about Convocation always felt like bullying.

"Just tell me this," Lizzie pulled the punch. "What do you get out of Convocation, exactly?"

Sarah said it gave her "spiritual structure."

"That's new," Lizzie said, pouring Sarah a refill from the margarita pitcher. "Elder Evans must have new writers. What does it even mean?"

Sarah explained. Since Christ died, the human race has been lost. "Because we didn't *get* it, we didn't understand what Christ was *saying*. So God sent a revelation to Elder Evans, breaking it down, so that he could share it with everybody."

Lizzie said uh-huh.

"But we still don't get it," Sarah said. "So God broke it down even simpler, into structures, spiritual structures. Each of us fit into all kinds of these bigger structures."

Two Marines from Camp Pendleton interrupted to hit on them. "What do you girls do?"

Lizzie said they were followers of the Elder Ethan Evans, Founder and Leader of the Convocation of Christ in The Holy Spirit.

The Marines retreated.

"You're not Convocation anymore," Sarah said. "You shouldn't joke about it."

"I'm just curious how long Elder Evans has known about these structures, sweetie? Why didn't he tell us about them before?"

Sarah leaned forward, eyes shiny from the margaritas and Elder Evans's teachings.

"He's growing, Lizzie. He's changing. It's not like when we were kids. He's not against the gays or Catholics or the Jews or anybody anymore. Because he's seen the spiritual structures, and he knows what they're built on. Love. They're built on love."

He's Satan. He adapts. He lives.

"You should come to services tomorrow," Sarah said. "Please?"

Lizzie wouldn't go to the service, but she did agree to stay for dinner.

· · ·

THERE WAS TOO MUCH FOOD AS ALWAYS. MOM ONLY HAD FRUIT. God bless her. She was bigger than ever, but she was trying.

"Mr. Scott," Sarah asked. "Who is Lisbeth named for?"

"Queen Elizabeth," Dad said. "We couldn't afford the 'e.'"

Dad's oldest joke. Lizzie never asked where the "s" came from.

Dad and Mom met at BIOLA, the Bible Institute of Los Angeles, just across the Orange County border. He was majoring in church administration and finance; she was getting a teacher's certificate. Their first date was a prayer service led by Elder Evans.

"Talk about a good deal," Dad said. "I fell in love with Mom and Christ the same night."

He also fell in love with Elder Evans.

The feeling was mutual.

Dad became the Elder's right hand, "the rock upon which we built a church," the most loyal of his lieutenants, the defender of Convocation's money.

Dad joked that his business card should read "Christ's CPA."

On his twentieth anniversary as Convocation's treasurer, Elder Evans gave him a box of cards, upping Dad to "Christ's Number One CPA."

Mom said Lizzie got her height from her, but she got her brains from Dad.

Convocation had lots of issues, but finances were not one of them. Dad was an investment whiz. He got Elder Evans to let him use a small portion of the early budget to buy stock, starting with Apple at $93 a share.

"It was Biblical inspiration," Dad joked. "It's the first food mentioned in Genesis." Dad hid Kiplinger's under his bed the way some dads hid porn. Dad turned down a job with an Irvine-based hedge fund that guaranteed a six-figure salary.

Lizzie accused him of being afraid of the challenge, of hero worship, of giving too much to Elder Evans. Dad said she was probably right. "I am what I am."

She remembered what Dad looked like in Convocation services; a beatified smile on his face, enraptured, in prayer. There were times Lizzie envied his faith.

Elder Evans slid in the seat next to Lizzie.

Her stomach tightened. She fought the urge to run. Sarah's face lit up. So did Mom's and Dad's. Seeing Lizzie with Elder Evans was all they wanted.

"How's your trial going, daughter?" He absentmindedly picked up a knife and tapped the blunt edge on his knuckles.

Lizzie was surprised he knew about the trial. He didn't read anything but the Bible.

"The only news I need is the Good News of Christ," he liked to say. "Stories are lies. Every story that has ever been written contains lies."

"What about Jesus's stories?" 12-year-old Lizzie challenged him one Sunday in front of the whole Convocation.

"Parables," Elder Evans shot back. "Christ spoke in parables, not stories."

"The trial should be over in about a week," Lizzie said.

Elder Evans asked Mom and Dad how they were, asked Sarah if she enjoyed her waitress job, but then he turned back to Lizzie, as he always did.

He couldn't seem to help it. Mom and Dad always told her she should be flattered. Lizzie didn't tell them she and Elder Evans were engaged in a lifelong fight for Lizzie's soul.

"It must be a strain on you, daughter, to accuse a police officer." Elder Evans now tapped the knife on the table.

Lizzie ignored him.

"I pray you know what you're doing," he said. "When you accuse, you diminish. Don't I know it? Haven't I been in that officer's position myself, accused of a terrible crime?"

Lizzie couldn't stop herself. "I thought you weren't guilty of anything, Elder Evans."

They stared each other down.

"C'mon, Lizzie, let's go." Sarah put her hand on Lizzie's arm. Her hand was shaking.

Elder Evans stabbed the knife into the table. "I was innocent of all charges, as you well know, and as the City of Los Angeles admitted in open court." He always said it the same way whenever the subject came up.

He let go of the knife. It stayed upright in the table.

"I just pray, for your sake, that this officer is guilty," his voice rumbled. "I pray none of the Convocation ever unjustly accuses another or bears false witness against any man. For if one does, it is as if we all did."

"Okay, thanks," Lizzie said. But trying to get the last word with Elder Evans was like trying to outrun the wind.

"We'll pray for you, daughter," Elder Evans said. "We'll pray Jesus sends you wisdom."

Lizzie couldn't stop herself. "Since you know Jesus so well, let me ask you something: Is Jesus with Joe Rincon or Officer Lee on this? I'm just curious."

I sound like I'm 12 years old again.

Elder Evans gave her the sweet, satisfied smile of a man who had just gotten to her. "It feels so good to have you here again, asking your questions."

Lizzie drove home so fast Mom and Dad prayed she wouldn't kill them.

She and Sarah sat in the driveway.

"I hate him."

"No, you don't," Sarah said. "You wish you did, but you can't."

That night Sarah woke up screaming and crawled into Lizzie's bed.

Lizzie stared at the ceiling. Convocation hadn't cured Sarah of the nightmares.

It would have been so much easier if Elder Evans had been a thief or a molester or told us to drink the Kool-Aid.

L.A. County Social Services accused him of bad things. The issue was physical abuse, corporal punishment, though Elder Evans could cite the Biblical basis for it. Courts didn't generally refrain from getting involved unless there was serious, provable physical injury. There had been on occasion, but not often, and not to enough children.

Convocation children were taken into foster care. The day they came for Sarah, she screamed and wept and begged them to let her go with Lizzie. But because they were not related by blood, they were sent to different homes. Lizzie ran away from hers to find Sarah, was sent to Juvenile Detention for a week, and never forgave herself for not finding her.

"In America we have the right to believe crackpots," their pro bono ACLU lawyer said. "At worst, Elder Evans is a crackpot."

When it was over, the children were returned to their families. Elder Evans was released from jail. Convocation celebrated with an all-night prayer vigil.

Elder Evans fulminated against "the whorish legal system," "the Nazi District Attorney," and "the jackbooted LAPD."

But he never beat another child.

Instead, Elder Evans took the settlement money from the city and relocated to the middle of the high desert, preaching the same fundamentalist faith.

Convocation lost so many members they had to close their school. Lizzie went to public school instead. She learned things that contradicted Elder Evans. She wasn't shy about confronting him since he couldn't beat her anymore. She accused him of being a sexist, racist, homophobic, anti-Semitic egomaniac who misrepresented Christ's teachings and ignored basic scientific facts.

Elder Evans debated her on every point but never resorted to violence again. Mom and Dad were appalled. Elder Evans assured them God sent Lizzie to them as a test, to make their faith stronger.

She hated to admit it, but Elder Evans probably had something to do with her wanting to become a prosecutor. He taught her how to fight, how to win an argument.

What bothered her more was that being a prosecutor seemed to appeal to some need she had for certainty, for black-and-white boundaries of right and wrong, guilty and not guilty.

Was it weird she seemed to need that kind of certainty, that kind of structure?

The word "structure" reminded her of Elder Evans and his new teachings.

I should see a shrink.

The idea was so un-Convocation, so counter to how she was raised, that the very idea made her laugh, but not too loud.

Sarah had fallen asleep in her arms. She didn't want to wake her up.

CHAPTER 45

FARLEY SAT WITH LEE IN THE COURT CAFETERIA, DEBATING WHAT to do.

"I have to testify," Lee said. "The jury has to hear it from me."

"Dwayne-o, that just isn't so. We got a pretty good sense they're going to hang."

Lee shook his head. "I don't want them to hang. I want to walk out of here now, not be back for a retrial."

Taylor joined them. After a long night of thinking, he decided they had no choice. Lee had to testify. "You think you can do that without fucking it up?" Taylor asked.

Lee told Taylor he would take care of himself just fine.

Knowing it might come to this, Taylor tried to set it up in his favor. From the beginning, Taylor told Lizzie that his client would *not* testify. As a courtesy, he said, to keep her from wasting all those hours preparing to cross-examine him.

Taylor told Judge Letts the same thing, assuring the court that he had discussed the matter with Lee, explaining all the pros and cons, and Lee had decided *not* to testify.

Judge Letts had to make sure. That was the law. Otherwise, if Lee were convicted, it would be an issue on appeal, a way for Lee to get a new trial. He would say he didn't understand what was going on, his lawyer hadn't really explained it to him, and so he had been denied his constitutional right to be heard.

When court convened, before the defense rested, Judge Letts sent the jury out of the room and held a mini-hearing, pro forma, to make sure what Taylor told him was true.

"Mr. Lee, your attorney informs me that you have decided not to testify in this case."

"No, Your Honor, that's not right. I want to testify."

Lizzie wasn't surprised. She never believed a word Taylor said. She'd spent days prepping to cross Lee.

Judge Letts, however, was apoplectic, his face contorted in rage. "How does this keep happening, Mr. Taylor? How is it that you say one thing and do another? This court depends on good-faith representations, not these cheap tactics."

Taylor laughed. "*Cheap*? I haven't been called that before. I try to keep my fees in line with the biggest firms in this county, but if Your Honor thinks I'm not charging enough, I'll raise them."

Lizzie sucked her lips to stop herself from smiling. Taylor was entertaining, especially when he wasn't directing his efforts at her.

Judge Letts slammed his palms on the bench then pointed at Taylor. "For the record, it was not lost on this court that you misled me on the discovery issue, Mr. Taylor. You had plenty of notice about the Riverside interview with Mr. Scanlon."

Taylor pretended to be shocked. "May I be heard on that, Your Honor?"

"No," Judge Letts thundered. Lizzie recognized righteous anger; there was no rage quite like it. "I've had enough more than enough from you, Mr. Taylor. This is not a game. I don't like being lied to by counsel."

Taylor stiffened. "Oh, so I can't call Ms. Scott a liar without The Chief coming down, but it's okay for *you* to call me one?"

Judge Letts wasn't backing down this time. "She did not lie! You did!"

Taylor leaned forward as if he'd been hit in the stomach then put both fists on the table to steady himself. "Now, that *does* offend me, Your Honor. It really does. My client has the right to change his mind over whether to testify right up to the last minute—"

"I know what his rights are, counsel!" Judge Letts seemed to levitate over his chair. "This isn't about his rights. This is about your conduct in misleading this court by making claims that were obviously false."

Taylor held his hand, palm up, to the court reporter seated below Judge Letts. His voice was now almost a whisper. "Ma'am, please do me a favor; designate this hearing for overnight transcription. I'll pay to expedite it. We'll need it for the contempt hearing."

Judge Letts pounded his gavel. Lizzie wondered if judges realized nothing made them look more petulant or powerless. Real authority never needs to bang the table.

"The court has not held you in contempt, Mr. Taylor!"

"You did, sir, you did," Taylor said sadly. "When you called me a liar, you held me in the worst kind of contempt."

Lizzie disagreed when prosecutors accused Taylor of playing the race card. What Taylor played was the honor card, always managing to twist any criticism into an attack on his integrity. The genius of it was that it suggested Taylor *had* integrity, otherwise why would he seemingly fight so hard to protect it?

"I've had enough of this," Judge Letts said, looking to his clerk. "Bring down the jury."

"No, sir," Taylor said. "I want to be heard."

"You've been heard, sir," Judge Letts snapped.

"No, sir," Taylor said. "The court has not yet ruled on the contempt issue. I ask the court to either withdraw its contempt or schedule an immediate hearing on the matter."

Judge Letts busied himself with paperwork as if he didn't hear Taylor, hoping that ignoring him would make him go away, at least until the jury got down there.

"I'm not playing with you," Taylor said, a street tough now, angry, threatening.

Judge Letts looked up, stunned. Taylor kept going. "Look, Judge, I can't sue you for slander or defamation for what you say in court. You have immunity in here. So a contempt hearing is the only way to get my good name back."

Lizzie tensed. This was serious. Taylor wasn't afraid of Judge Letts. Judge Letts was about to lose his mind. What was he going to do to him? Throw him in jail? Taylor would love it. It would stop the trial, become news, and pull focus from his client. If Lee were convicted, he would argue he was denied due process because of the judge's hostility toward his lawyer.

Judge Letts's whole body seemed to be vibrating with rage: "Now you listen to me, Mr. Taylor, you are nothing more than a—"

Lizzie stood up fast. "Your Honor," she said. She had no idea what the next words coming out of her mouth were going to be. "For the record, Mr. Taylor indicated to me that his client might testify."

That was a lie. Elder Evans hated liars. Elder Evans wasn't here.

"I am completely prepared to cross the defendant now, so the government has no problem with Mr. Taylor's client changing his mind at the last minute. It's fine. Really. We're good. Everything is good. It's all good."

Lizzie sat back down. Jones hid his smile. She was the best.

It took Judge Letts a moment to see Lizzie was showing him a dignified way out.

"Thank you, Ms. Scott. Clearly, there was some miscommunication here."

Taylor was seeing his moment pass. "No, no, there wasn't any—"

"No, Mr. Taylor, I think Ms. Scott is exactly right. Any confusion about what you did or didn't say about your client testifying has been cleared up so—"

There was a knock. The door to the jury room opened. The jury filed in.

Judge Letts went back to his paperwork.

Taylor whispered to the clerk:

"Never mind about the transcripts."

CHAPTER 46

DWAYNE WAYNE LEE TOOK THE STAND WITH HIS OWN LIFE IN his hands.

He was almost glad it came down to this.

Taylor was a shit head, and the judge was a joke. Lizzie Scott didn't scare him. He watched her during trial. He could handle her. He'd spent years knowing what to say in reports. Nobody knew how to cover his ass better. He could be nice. He could even be sweet when he had to be. Lisa and the kids had seen it.

"Officer Lee, thank you for being willing to speak with us," Taylor said. "You have every right not to testify, and the jury could not hold that against you, so what you're doing here is pretty damn special."

Lee looked to the jury. "I'm not afraid of the truth," he said. "I've told it every chance I got. To the grand jury, even though I didn't have to, to the CHP, to the Deputy D.A.—"

"Objection."

She filed a pretrial motion to keep the defense from mentioning that the Inland County D.A. passed bringing the case. The jury might think it was relevant. It wasn't. Even Taylor knew enough not to bring it up. Lee slipped in without asking him.

"Sustained," Judge Letts said, glaring at Taylor. Taylor shrugged.

Don't look at me, boss. I didn't tell him to say it.

"Now, Officer, tell us about yourself. Where are you from?" Taylor had to humanize his client, to give the jury an image of his man, something they could take with them and relate to when it came time to decide his fate.

Lee turned to the jury and told them about growing up in Orange County, his single working mom, playing high school sports.

"Did you always want to be a police officer?"

"From the time I was a little kid, I guess my dream was always to be a baseball player or a police officer. I must like uniforms, I guess."

Lizzie checked out the jury.

No reaction. They hadn't quite made up their minds about Officer Lee yet.

"Right before this shooting, you had a tragedy in your family, I understand."

Lizzie assumed Taylor would bring up Lee's son. She wondered if he knew the issue could cut both ways.

Thanks to Jones, Lizzie knew things about the accident Taylor did not. They were ugly things. She didn't know if she should bring them up. She hoped she wouldn't have to.

"My son got out and ran into the street in front of our house," Lee said. His voice thickened. "He got hit by a car. The woman said she didn't see him . . ."

Lee clamped his jaw down, struggling to control himself. It was the first time Lizzie had seen any emotion from him other than rage. "They thought he was dead."

Mrs. Meagher was jotting notes. Juror #8 had her hand to her mouth, her eyes filled with compassion. All the men leaned forward, staring at Lee, moved by him.

"The shooting happened three weeks after your son was struck by the car. Did it still look like your boy might die?"

"Yes, sir. We didn't know what was going to happen to him."

"Were you sleeping, Officer Lee?"

"Not very much."

"Eating?"

"Not really. I lost about 10 pounds."

"Did you tell your supervisor what was going on?"

"He knew. The whole department knew. They sent flowers. They came by to visit. They sent their prayers."

Juror #8 nodded. Of course they had. *She* would have.

"Did anyone on the force say, 'take a night off, Officer Lee, stay home?'"

Lee said they had the first week. After that, however, he had to come in. The department was small. They needed him. "Tell you the truth, I was happy to go on duty. It took my mind off things. Work can be a great distraction sometimes."

"Looking back now, though, do you think you were really up to being on duty?"

Lee took a deep sigh. "I don't know."

Taylor made him describe the day of the shooting. Getting out of bed after another sleepless night, going to the hospital, realizing he hadn't eaten again, grabbing coffee and a candy bar on his way to the station, the hours on patrol.

"It turned out to be the worst day of my life," Lee said. "Worse even than when my son got hit by the car."

"Why was it so bad, Officer Lee?"

"Because that was the day I accidentally shot and killed someone."

Accidentally shot and killed someone? Is he saying it was an accident now?

Lizzie wasn't sure she heard it correctly.

"Why? Why did you shoot Joe Rincon?" Taylor asked.

"Because he attacked me with that knife. I thought he was going to kill me. That's all. That's the only reason I shot him."

The clock struck noon. Taylor hit his mark. Judge Letts dismissed the jury. His direct would continue after lunch. Lizzie wouldn't get to lay a hand on Lee for hours.

● ● ●

Jack watched as Lizzie paced her office.

"What's Taylor doing? Is Lee saying the shooting was an accident *and* it was justified?" Lizzie couldn't figure it out. "What is that? He's got to choose one or the other, doesn't he? I would."

Jack said he would, too. It was the only intelligent, logical thing to do. Arguing two theories at the same time was illogical, lacked credibility, made it seem like you were throwing everything against the wall hoping something—*anything*—would stick.

But that is exactly what Taylor was trying to do. "The great thing about a cop case," Taylor confided to Farley, "is the jury *wants* to find *something* to hang onto, to let them walk the guy. They don't want to do a cop. We just got to give them an excuse not to."

. . .

TOWARD THE END OF THE AFTERNOON, LEE STOOD IN THE MIDDLE of the courtroom, hands at shoulder level in a small crouch. "It all happened a lot faster than this."

Lee would be Rincon. Taylor would play Lee.

"Now!" Taylor yelled.

Lee rushed at his lawyer.

The jury was transfixed. The law calls it "demonstrative evidence" or "a pedagogical device," but it was live theater, and Taylor knew jurors ate it up.

Just as Lee got to Taylor, Lee stopped and moved slowly, demonstrating what Rincon did next. "He started hitting me on my body and my head."

Lee delivered slow shots to Taylor, who fended them off.

"What happened next?"

Lee slow-motioned jabbed at Taylor with the pencil.

"He kept trying to stab me so I grabbed him."

Taylor grabbed Lee's arms, pinning them to his sides.

"Could you hold him?"

"No way," Lee shook out of Taylor's grasp and retreated a few steps. "He was bigger than I was and a lot stronger."

They stopped and switched sides. Lee handed Taylor the pencil.

Taylor was now Rincon. Lee was now playing himself.

"For the record, Officer Lee is standing where he was when the shot was fired, and I am standing where Mr. Rincon was. They are facing one another. I have the knife—pencil—in my hand. What was the distance between you and Rincon at this point?"

Lee said between 10 and 15 feet.

"When did you take your weapon out, Officer Lee?"

Lee said now; this was when he took his weapon from the holster.

He showed the jury how he did it, using his fingers to make the gun, then taking the classic shooting stance: legs spread, both hands on the weapon.

"What did Rincon do?"

"He came at me again with the knife," Lee said, facing the jury. "Except this time, he had the knife out to the side, like he was going to swing for my face."

"Did you fear for your life that moment?"

Lee swallowed and took a deep breath. "Honestly, I was afraid for my life from the minute he got out of the car and ran at me the first time. I just thought I'd never see my wife or kids again."

"Is that when you shot Mr. Rincon?"

"Yes, sir, that's when it happened."

Taylor asked Lee to return to the witness stand.

"Did you ever hit Rincon with a flashlight?"

"No. I didn't even have my flashlight on me that night."

"Why not?"

"It was in my squad car. I kept it in a bag with some other stuff. I didn't keep it on my tool belt because it got in my way when I got in and out of the cruiser. Also, it slowed me down if I had to run."

Why had he given it to Detective Moeller? Was he trying to hide it?

Lee shook his head. "No, of course not. I just thought, since the squad car might go into the evidence lot, I might not have access to the bag. I wasn't trying to hide anything."

Taylor thanked Lee for his service again and sat down.

The clock read 4:58 P.M.

Court adjourned for the day. The jury went home having heard Lee's story. Lizzie wouldn't get to challenge a word he said until the morning.

CHAPTER 47

LIZZIE RAN THE STREETS THAT NIGHT, MUSIC BLARING IN HER ears, going over her cross-examination. Bodhi had to lay out in full stride to keep up with her.

Taylor had Lee demonstrate how Rincon attacked Lee with a knife.

But he also brought up the tragedy of Lee's son and had Lee call the shooting an accident.

Why?

Part of it was a play for sympathy, she knew that, but there was more to it.

If the jury believed Lee's testimony, they had to find him not guilty. He was a hero. He stopped a knife-wielding attacker. Scanlon lied. There was never any flashlight blow.

If they believed Scanlon's testimony, they had to find Lee guilty. Rincon hadn't attacked him, didn't have a knife, the flashlight blow and shooting were unjustified. That's why Lee hid the flashlight. He was covering up his crime.

But what if they didn't *fully* believe either version? That's what happened in most cases.

"Tout comprendre, c'est tout pardonner," Berg said. "To understand all is to forgive all."

Taylor was hedging his bets. He wanted the jury to understand all about Lee and his state of mind, so that even if they didn't fully believe his version of events, they would still forgive his mistakes, all of them. After all, Lee was emotionally and physically exhausted because of his son's fate.

Lizzie had to admit Taylor played it just right.

That's why he called the City Manager, Cooley. To show the jury what a lousy department Blanton was, to put the blame on the department.

Jack said the jury would see through all this. Berg told Jack he was very naive. "Juries don't like to do that to cops. Especially not cops with sick kids."

Lizzie was never going to get Lee to admit to knowingly and intentionally killing an unarmed man, then trying to cover it up.

She had to do the harder thing. She had to make the jury understand the whole truth about Officer Lee, who he was and what he thought that night.

It was risky. It could blow up in her face.

It would also be about the cruelest thing she ever had to do.

CHAPTER 48

LIZZIE HELD THE KNIFE IN HER HAND.

An evidence sticker hung off the handle.

"Is this the knife you say Mr. Rincon had when you shot him?"

"It looks like it."

The courtroom was packed. It was also quiet. The battle between a prosecutor and a defendant is as close to life and death as the law allows. It's for all the stakes.

Jack sat in the back row, quietly thanking God it was Lizzie's case and not his.

Lizzie noted that Detective Moeller did not have the knife checked for fingerprints. Deputy D.A. Seave did. "They found Rincon's prints, which was no surprise: it was his knife. But they also found your prints as well. Why is that?"

Lee thought for a moment. "I must have touched it after I shot him, to secure it, make sure he couldn't cut me with it."

"While Mr. Rincon lay on the ground, dying, you moved the knife, Officer Lee?"

"It's part of our training, to neutralize the threat."

Lizzie glanced at the jury. Their eyes were on Lee. It gave Lizzie hope.

I was wrong. They haven't decided a thing about him yet. I'm still in this.

Lizzie took the pencil off the defense table. She held it up so the jury could see it next to Rincon's knife. The pencil was longer.

"The item you used to represent the knife was longer than the actual knife."

Lee almost grinned, but stopped himself. "Sorry. Was that a question?"

Just keep him up there. They'll see who he is.

"Were you trying to hide the actual size of the knife because you knew you couldn't have seen it in Rincon's hand that night?"

"I didn't suggest using the pencil to represent the knife."

Taylor stood up. "My bad, Your Honor."

He was looking for a smile or a laugh from the jury. He didn't get one. This was church time. This was serious time.

"Rincon was taller and heavier than you, wasn't he, sir?"

Lee agreed that he was. "That was partly why I was afraid of him."

"His hands were bigger than yours, too, right?"

Lee said yes.

Lizzie had him stand down from the witness box and hold the knife in his hand instead of the pencil. She then had him face the jury and hold up his hand. The knife was small and mostly handle. It disappeared in Lee's hand.

"Let the record reflect the knife can barely be seen in Officer Lee's hand."

Taylor objected. "I can see the knife just fine."

Judge Letts said the jury could judge it for themselves.

Lee hedged. "I knew he had some kind of weapon in his hand."

That's why he said the shooting was accidental. He's letting the jury acquit him even if he was wrong about Rincon having the knife.

Lizzie made him stand down from the witness box. "Imagine this lectern was Mr. Rincon's pickup. Show us exactly where you were and how you were standing when the door popped open."

"When he thrust the door into my chest?" Lee couldn't help himself.

Lizzie thought Lee's stance looked vaguely absurd. But it did suggest how he *could* have been pushed off balance by the pickup's door. Mrs. Meagher appeared to be sketching the scene in her notebook.

Lee got back on the stand. Lizzie glanced at Jones. He nodded. *Keep going. You're making some points.*

"Sir," she began, refusing him the dignity of his title or name. "You were supposed to hand over all equipment that night from your tool belt, correct?"

"Correct."

"You signed the inventory list under oath, swearing that you turned over everything?"

"Yes."

"You lied. When you said you turned over everything, when you signed the inventory list, you lied."

Lee turned to the jury. "I didn't mean to lie. I didn't even know I was lying. I just didn't remember the flashlight was in the bag. I didn't think it mattered. You got to remember, Ms. Scott, I didn't have the flashlight with me when I shot Mr. Rincon, so it just didn't seem that relevant."

There it is! Finally! There it is!

It was on Lee's face. The grin. Lee wiped it off, but the jury saw it.

"You watched Henry Scanlon testify, under oath, about what happened that night."

"Yes."

"You didn't know he was there, watching you that night, did you?"

"I don't know whether he was there or not. I know he *says* he was now."

"If he hadn't been there, you wouldn't be here," Lizzie said. "The D.A. didn't charge you. If Mr. Scanlon hadn't called the FBI, you would have gotten away with it."

Lee prepared for this moment. "I still have nightmares about that night. I wish it never happened. I didn't get away with anything, Ms. Scott."

I walked into that one.

Lizzie pushed on. "Mr. Scanlon testified that you fell on your backside when the door popped open."

"He was partially right about that," Lee said. "But it wasn't exactly like he said. Mr. Rincon thrust the door open. Basically, he used the door as a weapon. But I didn't fall to the ground."

"Is that when you hit Mr. Rincon with your flashlight?"

"I never hit him with a flashlight. I told you I didn't have one on me."

"Did you order Mr. Rincon to raise his hands over his head?"

Lee said he didn't have time. "Plus, with the wind that night, I doubt he would've heard me."

"Did he, in fact, raise his hands?"

Not that Lee recalled.

"How far away were you from Mr. Rincon when you shot him?"

"It seemed like he was right on top of me," Lee said. "I guess I had tunnel vision or something. He seemed a lot closer when he lunged at me."

Lee was staying on message. She wasn't drawing blood.

She had one more area to get into.

It was the dangerous one.

She had to do it. She had no choice.

"Let's talk about your state of mind when you shot Mr. Rincon."

"Okay," Lee said.

"Mr. Taylor asked you about your son," she said, choosing her words carefully. "You told your lawyer that you were tired and stressed, because of the condition of your son."

Lee sat up a bit. He didn't like her bringing up his son.

"That night," Lizzie said, "were you also angry about what happened to your son, sir?"

"Objection," Taylor said. "Irrelevant. Let's leave the man's boy out of it."

"The issue is the defendant's intent when he pulled the trigger," Lizzie said. "We have to be allowed to ask if the defendant was angry that night."

Judge Letts directed Lee to answer the question.

"I was angry at the situation with my son," Lee said, being careful, like a man walking on a ledge. "I wasn't angry at Mr. Rincon. The two had nothing to do with one another."

"Then why did Mr. Taylor spend so much time asking you about it?"

Taylor objected. Judge Letts sustained it. She moved on.

"So you were angry that night?"

"Anger has no place in my job," Lee said, then caught himself. "What I mean is, anger toward a suspect. That has no place in the job. Sometimes, you might be angry over other things, but you can't let it bleed into the work."

Keep talking, Officer Lee.

"So you were not angry at Mr. Rincon? Not even when Mr. Rincon refused to get out of the car, you weren't angry?"

"No."

"Or when he pushed—sorry, you said thrust—thrust the door into your chest? That didn't make you angry? Honestly?"

"I was surprised. I was scared. I was not angry."

"Even after Mr. Rincon pushed you back with the door—Mr. Scanlon says you fell on your butt—you weren't angry? That's hard to believe."

"We're trained to control our temper," Lee said.

The grin came out. It stayed out. Lizzie was finally getting to him.

Lizzie pressed him. "They train you not to walk up to a car door either, not to use your flashlight as a weapon, not to lie under oath in reports, not to hide evidence. You sure seem to pick and choose what part of the training you follow."

Lee kept grinning.

"Is it possible Mr. Rincon made you angry?"

"No."

"It is possible you were angry at someone else and took it out on Mr. Rincon?"

Lee looked at Taylor as if he expected an objection.

"Should I repeat the question?" Lizzie asked.

She glanced at the jury. The jurors got it. Even if they hadn't put together where Lizzie was going when she started this line of questions, they knew where she was now.

"I did my job that night, Ms. Scott, like I always did my job, to the best of my ability."

"Except when you hid evidence and destroyed potential evidence," Lizzie said. "Other than that."

Taylor objected. Judge Letts overruled him.

"How did your son get out of the house, sir?"

"Objection!" Taylor shot to his feet a little too fast.

Lizzie wasn't backing off. "This goes directly to the officer's state of mind, to his credibility and to whether he acted out of anger that night."

"It's completely irrelevant to—"

Overruled. Judge Letts ordered Lee to answer.

"We don't really know," Lee said. He looked like he was ready to blow.

"You told the ambulance crew that arrived to take care of your son that your wife left the front door open. That's how your son got out of the house."

For a split second, Lizzie feared Lee would jump over the witness rail and come at her.

"Objection," Taylor hadn't sat down. "Hearsay. I would like a sidebar—"

"Overruled," Judge Letts said. "Sit down, Mr. Taylor."

Lee's eyes hadn't left her face. "I don't remember what I may have said."

"Sir, you testified that your son's situation made you stressed, exhausted, and angry on the night of the shooting."

"Okay."

"If you weren't angry at Mr. Rincon, were you angry at your wife because you blamed her for your son's injuries? Did you take it out on Mr. Rincon? Is that possible, sir?"

For the first time, she saw it: The Look. Lee was debating whether to lie or admit the shameful thing.

You're damn right I blamed Lisa. You're damn right I was angry. I'm still angry. Right now I'm fucking enraged at you, Lizzie Scott.

"Like I said before," Lee said. "I wasn't angry at anybody."

Lee remembered the nurse at the hospital, the one who tried to calm him down, who told him if he didn't stop talking, she would have to file a report with Social Services, documenting his wife's neglect, her drug use, the fact that she was so fucked up that day she'd left the fucking door wide open, and Pete was crushed by that car.

"I'm not an angry person," Lee added. There wasn't a person in the courtroom who believed it. "But I guess I might have still been a little angry at my son's situation."

Lizzie tried one last time. "Was it possible you took out some of that anger on Mr. Rincon?"

Lee took a deep breath. "No. That's not possible."

Lizzie hadn't knocked him out but she'd hurt him.

It was still a close fight.

CHAPTER 49

Lizzie was driving home when Mom called.

She sounded scared.

"Honey, you should come over. There's a man here who says he knows you."

Lizzie didn't stop for red lights. She rushed through the front door and stopped just inside the house.

Jack was sitting on the white couch in the living room. Dad sat perched on the edge of his chair as if he was afraid to rub the fabric off.

"Lizzie, your friend Jack is here," Dad said, using his formal voice. "Come in, join us."

She hesitated.

Like a trained dog.

As a kid she was only allowed in the living room to vacuum. It was sacred space reserved for Bible study, funerals, or when Elder Evans came to deliver his annual blessing or to chastise Lizzie for taking Advanced Placement Biology in high school, or when she first insisted on playing competitive sports.

Lizzie sat next to Jack on the couch, keeping a six-inch space between their knees. She refused to look at him.

Unforgivable.

"Mother's bringing in snacks," Dad said, then fell silent.

"I happened to be in the neighborhood and came by," Jack said to the side of her face. "I guess I should have called."

"Definitely," she said, her voice flat. "It's incredibly rude to just drop in on people."

"It's fine," Dad said gently. Elder Evans taught them to always take in the stranger and welcome the traveler.

Lizzie wished Jack wasn't so good-looking. It was embarrassing. She wished he hadn't brought the bottle of wine sitting on the table. Alcohol was not Convocation.

She willed herself not to blush, not to show how angry she was, but the blood came into her cheeks anyway.

The soul always betrays the body.

The living room was very Elder Evans.

"You have a beautiful house," Jack said to Dad. "Really."

Lizzie gave an almost imperceptible shake of her head, enough to let Jack know he said the wrong thing. Convocation disavowed praise for worldly things. But even if her parents didn't like it, she resented his condescending tone.

Jack misread her color as embarrassment. He thought it was cute. It gave him confidence.

"I'm actually here to get information on your daughter," Jack said, trying to be funny.

Dad nodded, trying to be polite.

He thinks Dad has no sense of humor.

Lizzie had her issues with Convocation, but she hated how people like Jack assumed religious people were all humorless and stupid. Her parents weren't. She wasn't. Whatever issues she had with Convocation, she was loyal. How dare Jack judge them?

Take a breath. The bad thing already happened. Jack is here.

He now knew who she was, where she came from.

Mom came in wearing a candy-cane blouse Lizzie hadn't seen for years and a pair of enormous jeans, ironed, naturally, but with dirt stains at the knees, and cheap.

Oh, Mom.

Lizzie hated herself for hating how big Mom was.

"Isn't this nice, Lizzie?" Mom asked because she wasn't sure. Jack made her nervous. Handsome men always did. She carried a tray loaded down with homemade cookies and bottles of soda.

Without being asked Dad stood, took the towel off Mom's shoulder and spread it on the table. Lizzie leaned forward and moved the porcelains to the side. Mom collected religious figurines of the Holy Family. They filled the house. She kept her Marys in the living room.

Jack stood up to help.

"Don't," Lizzie said, sharp enough to make Jack sit down as if he'd been shot.

"I apologize for my appearance," Mom said, handling her good glasses and plates as if they were dynamite, her face set in concentration. "Your friend caught me gardening, Lizzie."

"That's no crime," Jack said. "You look great."

Dad didn't like to hear Mom's appearance discussed.

"I'll serve," Lizzie said. Mom sat down, relieved.

"Thank you, baby," she said. "I'm always afraid I'll break something."

"These porcelains are beautiful," Jack said. "Are they Lladró?"

Lizzie wanted to take Jack outside and give him a sound beating.

"We can't afford Lladró," Dad said.

The sound of tea pouring into cups and spoons scraping into the sugar bowl boomed in the silence. A roar went up outside. Some kid scored a goal in a pickup soccer game. The chime of the kitchen clock sounded loud as a church bell.

Mom poured herself a little bit of diet soda and took one small cookie. She tried so hard.

"How do you like working in Santa Ana?" Mom asked Jack.

Jack shifted uncomfortably. Clearly, Lizzie hadn't told her family about him.

It upset him. She wondered if it was because he cared about her, or because he assumed every woman would brag about being with Handsome Jack.

"Do you know Agent Jones, Jack?" Dad asked.

Jack looked surprised. "I do, indeed," he said. "How do you know him?"

"He did my background check," Lizzie said, looking at him for the first time. Jones interviewed her parents. He still sent them Christmas cards.

An hour later, they were saying their goodbyes.

Mom forced Jack to take a bag of cookies for the road.

"You might find this interesting," Dad said. He handed Jack a pamphlet: *The Seven Pillars of Convocation*. The cover showed a full-body portrait of Elder Evans in the desert, dressed like an apostle, in robe and sandals. He was pointing at the viewer.

The moment the front door closed, Lizzie was moving toward her car.

"I don't think they minded," Jack said. "They were so nice."

She turned on him. "That's because they're nice people, Jack. They're good people. If you showed up asking for money or food, they'd give it to you. They'd give it to anybody."

"I just wanted to meet them," Jack said.

She moved toward him so fast he flinched. "Why? Why was it so goddamn important that you needed to meet my parents, Jack? What possible good could it do you?"

Jack blinked, surprised she didn't know why. "I love you."

She snorted. Then she realized he meant it. Or thought he did. Men could be unbelievable. They said they loved you when what they should do is just apologize.

"I liked your parents a lot," he said. "They're great people. Really."

Jack's got a tell. Really. Every time he ends a sentence with it, what it means is he's lying or trying to convince himself of something he doesn't believe. Really.

She stared at him as angry as he had ever seen her.

"I'm sorry," he said. "I shouldn't have just shown up like this. Forgive me."

For the second time that afternoon, she hesitated.

Like a trained dog.

She saw the living room and thought about all the other rooms she hadn't been able to enter without feeling she wasn't supposed to be there.

"Please forgive me," he said.

Forgiveness was very Convocation.

"You must neither hate the sin nor the sinner, but rather love all Children of God. Bring them to your heart, as He brought humanity to His."

Handsome Jack was either lucky or cagey enough to catch on that Lizzie Scott was programmed to forgive.

Instead of hitting him, she took him back to her house.

When Sarah got home from her waitress job, Lizzie snuck out of the bedroom.

"Jack is *here*? Really? Can I meet him?"

"No," Lizzie said.

Afterward, Lizzie and Jack lay in bed, arms around one another, all problems resolved for the moment. His head was on her shoulder, his breath on her neck. They fit together so well. Sex was not the problem. Or maybe it was the whole problem.

He stirred. He was so beautiful it made it hard for her to breathe.

"You love me?" he asked, eyes still closed, groggy.

"Yes and no," she said.

"What's the 'yes' part?"

"What we just did, that's a yes. And I like that you're smart. And clean, you're very clean. You have good taste in clothes, art. But don't ever bring up Lladró again, okay. That's too much."

"What's the 'no' part?" Jack was drifting back to sleep.

"I don't have a lot of faith in you, Jack. I don't trust you."

She wanted to take it back. It was so harsh. If anyone ever said anything like that to her, she believed she would crumble.

Jack didn't even open his eyes.

"That's okay," he said, yawning. "I don't have a lot of faith in me either."

He turned over and went back to sleep.

Later, over breakfast, while Jack slept in, Sarah confessed that she snuck into the room and peeked in on them while they were asleep.

"Is that weird?"

"Yes," Lizzie said flatly. "That is very weird."

Sarah poured Lizzie a cup of coffee. "He is *so* handsome."

Lizzie didn't argue.

CHAPTER 50

TOMMY TAYLOR WAS STANDING IN THE PARKING LOT OF LIZZIE'S office, waiting for her the next day. Jones was with him.

"Sorry to bother you, Ms. Scott," Taylor said. "Could you do me the courtesy of having a little talk?"

Lizzie pretended she wasn't shocked. Jones gave her a slight shrug. *I have no idea why he's here.*

They went upstairs. Jones followed Taylor into Lizzie's office. Taylor tried to stop him. "Just the lawyers, please."

Jones walked in anyway. "It's for your safety, Mr. Taylor. You're not her favorite person."

Lizzie asked Taylor to state his business.

"First of all, you're trying a hell of a case, Ms. Scott. I've already told a bunch of people how good you are. Brave, too. Getting it this far, I know what a struggle that's been. I, for one, salute the hell out of you."

"That's nice," Lizzie said. "Was that it?"

"We're ready to take a plea deal," Taylor said.

She wasn't sure she heard him. Taylor looked annoyed.

"You want me to beg, is that it? We're ready to plead guilty. That's how good you are. We're folding. You won. Mazel tov."

Lizzie and Jones were shocked, but they kept superb poker faces.

"You're too late, Mr. Taylor. Our office has a policy—"

Taylor laughed. "Don't I know it? Your office has a damn policy for everything. But that's the federal government for you."

She laid the policy out in case he didn't know the details. "We don't offer plea deals in the middle of trial, except in rare situations, like when we're losing. We're not losing here."

"Get a load of 'The Prosecutioner' over here," Taylor said to Jones. Berg's nicknames had an annoying habit of getting around. Taylor turned serious.

"You're wrong, Ms. Scott, you're going to lose this case. You just don't know it. But you're young. I'm only here because my client is making me. Personally, I think we're kicking your ass, but I got to do what the client tells me to do."

Taylor was either baiting her, hoping she wouldn't make a deal, or he was bluffing, pretending to be more confident than he was in order to strike the best deal he could.

"I didn't like you quoting Elder Evans to me," she said.

Taylor glanced at Jones. Jones gave him back a blank stare.

"Sorry, Ms. Scott, I was just having some fun with you. I didn't mean to offend you." Nothing was personal with Taylor. That was his gift.

"What did you have in mind in terms of a deal?" Lizzie asked.

Taylor laughed. "No, no, I'm not going to start bargaining against myself. The way this works is you make the offer and I make a counter. Unless you don't want to, which is fine with me."

Lizzie said she was neither authorized nor inclined to offer any deal. "Agent Jones can walk you out, Mr. Taylor."

Taylor rolled his eyes and said Lee would plead guilty to Count Two, denying Rincon due process by filing a false report, if she would dismiss Count One, the murder charge.

"No," she said.

"Hold on now," Taylor said. "As part of the deal, Lee will quit the police force immediately. And he is willing to serve some significant period of home confinement."

Is he kidding? No jail? No prison?

"No deal," Lizzie said. "I won't even run that by Jack, forget The Chief."

"Good," Taylor said. "Great. Glad to hear it. I didn't want to plead this out anyhow."

Lizzie waited. Taylor got to his feet. But he didn't move to the door.

"Here's what I think," she said. "I think you want to plead this out because your client just went down in blue flames in front of the jury on cross, and you know he's going to get convicted."

Taylor chuckled. "Your cross wasn't all that but, as I understand your office policy, you have an obligation to convey our plea offer to your bosses. So I'll just leave you to it."

Jones walked Taylor out. Lizzie called Jack at her house.

So weird. He's in my bed. He loves me? He didn't say "really." Does that mean he means it or he doesn't mean it?

"I'll run it by The Chief," Jack said.

"Stay in bed, Jack. Don't call The Chief. I'm only calling you because I have to report it to a supervisor. This is a terrible deal. We would never take this deal in a million years."

Jack agreed, but said he had to run it by The Chief anyway.

"It's policy," he said.

She was about to hang up on him when she heard Sarah's voice in the background.

"Is Sarah in bed with you? Because that would not be okay with me."

Jack laughed. "We're having coffee in the kitchen, talking about Convocation. Pretty interesting."

The image of Jack and Sarah in her home having coffee, talking about Elder Evans, was beyond weird, a nightmare, really; almost as bad as Jack with her parents.

Trials were hard enough without a personal life.

Lizzie was headed to court when her cell rang. It was Jack again.

"The Chief says that if Lee pleads to the shooting, we might be willing to discuss a cap on his sentence. But the victim has to agree to it. Would Lee agree to five years in prison?"

Lizzie thought five years for murder was a little light. "I thought The Chief didn't think victims had rights."

"He doesn't," Jack said. "But if Mrs. Rincon is okay with it, The Chief said we'd be open to it. He said you could make the call."

"He's leaving it up to me?" Lizzie couldn't believe it.

Then it dawned on her.

"The Chief thinks I'm going to lose," she said.

Jack told her not to take it hard. "He thought you lost when you brought the case."

"That's not what bothers me," she said. "You're down here watching the trial and reporting back to him. You're telling him I'm losing, Jack."

Jack didn't even try to deny it. "You've done an amazing job, but—"

She cut him off. "I'm kind of angry about this, Jack. It seems kind of disloyal to me. And get the hell out of my house!"

Jack didn't know what to say. Lizzie hung up on him before he figured it out.

I will never, ever have anything to do with Jack again. Ever.

"Five years isn't enough," Jones said, changing the subject back to the case because he could see she was blushing over whatever happened with Jack. "I'm not looking for life, but if anyone deserves it, it's a bad cop."

. . .

LIZZIE MET WITH MRS. RINCON IN THE COURT CAFETERIA TO discuss whether she would even be open to a plea deal. Abe Ybarra hung around in case something good happened.

"I don't know," the old woman said. "It's okay so long as he admits he shot Joey."

Lizzie agreed. She would never take a deal that let Lee avoid taking responsibility for killing her grandson.

"Okay, then," Mrs. Rincon said. "If you can make him say he shot Joey for no reason, you can take any deal you think is right. You decide. It's up to you."

Jones got Taylor and walked him to a witness room where Lizzie was waiting. This time Taylor insisted Jones stay out. Lizzie agreed.

"What's the verdict?" Taylor asked. "Deal or not? Not that I care."

Lizzie said if it was up to her, there would be no offer. But if there had to be one, she was willing to dismiss Count Two of the indictment. She would let Lee plead to Count One, the shooting, and agree to a five-year prison sentence. "Which is ridiculously low."

Taylor made a counteroffer. "What if Lee eats the whole thing? He'll plead to both Counts One and Two. He'll admit he shot Rincon without cause. He'll apologize. Hell, he'll get on his goddamned hands and knees and beg forgiveness."

That sounds more like it.

Taylor was just warming up. "He'll quit the department, pay whatever restitution he can, take as many years on probation as you want, and serve a year, split sentence, half in jail, half in home confinement."

Lizzie said they were done talking. She wasn't accepting six months in jail for murder. Home confinement was a joke.

"Now, just wait a minute," Taylor said, pushing hard. "You get him on everything you charged him with. You got everything you wanted."

He was almost right.

She knew Jack would say take the deal. The Chief would, too, if Mrs. Rincon was okay with it. Mrs. Leonard would be happy they sent the message that cops can't use excessive force. Lizzie thought Mrs. Rincon would be fine, too. Ybarra would use the "Justice for Rincon Committee" to spin it as a win for civil rights. Then Ybarra would earn a bundle in the civil suit, most of it going to Mrs. Rincon. She could use it.

But six months for murder?

There was no way Lizzie could accept it.

"You need time to run it by your people?" Taylor asked.

Lizzie said no. Based on the previous conversations, the decision was hers. She rejected the deal.

"You're making a mistake," Taylor said. His tone surprised her. He sounded desperate. "You're holding out for something you're never going to get. I'm not just talking about the verdict either."

What the hell does that mean? What does Taylor know that I don't?

Taylor sat down at the table and rubbed his face. He looked drained. Trials take it out of everybody. "Shit. I know he's my client," Taylor said, his voice a whisper. "But I'm telling you, that man isn't screwed down right, Ms. Scott. I'm just telling you, lawyer to lawyer."

She didn't know what he was saying, but she didn't like the sound of it.

"What is this? A threat?"

"I'm warning you, my client is this close to the edge," Taylor said. "Hear what I'm saying. I'm not threatening you. If you say I am, I'll deny it. What I am saying is this is a good deal for everybody. Nobody gets hurt."

Lizzie gathered up papers and headed for court.

Taylor blocked the door.

"You're looking for a death sentence on this? You think my guy deserves to die for what happened out there? You think he deserves to leave his wife a widow and his children fatherless because he made a goddamn mistake?"

Lizzie got inches from Taylor's face. Her voice was quiet but firm. "I'm going to do my job and convict your client because he's guilty. Now get out of my way."

She left Taylor alone in the room.

Farley came in. "Did she take it?"

Taylor shook his head.

"Well, it's on her then, boss. You did what you could."

That's true. I did.

Plus, Taylor wasn't sure Lee would have agreed to the six months in jail. He never asked.

I wash my hands of it; whatever happens from here on out is Lizzie Scott's fault.

CHAPTER 51

"Did he threaten you?" Jones asked.

He and Jack stood with Lizzie in the hallway outside the witness room. Jack had his hand on her shoulder. Taylor's warning shook her up, but Jones clocked she was calm enough to step away from Jack's hand.

"No," she said. "Taylor's warning was about what Lee would do to himself, not to me or to anyone else."

"You should still notify the judge," Jones said.

She couldn't. The law didn't allow it. Taylor's warning came during a plea negotiation. By law, judges were not allowed to participate in them. They weren't even allowed to know what was said during the discussions.

"Even if I did say something, Taylor would just deny he said it."

It wasn't just because she thought Taylor was dishonest. Taylor probably shouldn't have said anything to her about his client's mental state. If it wasn't divulging attorney–client privilege, it was close enough that Taylor would have a problem with the California State Bar down the road. Not to mention his client. Lizzie didn't think Lee would like to hear what his lawyer said about him.

"Ah, you guys," Jones finally said, disgusted. "This is horse shit."

Lizzie was shocked. She never heard Jones use profanity before.

"I'm sorry, but it's true," Jones said. "Taylor's been playing games with you the whole time. Now, he's trying to get inside your head before closing arguments, make you think if you win, poor old Dwayne Lee is going to go all to pieces. Horse shit."

God bless him.

Jones was like a great corner man in the last round, reminding her to keep punching.

Jack said that if anything happened to Lizzie, he couldn't live with it. *Soft and clingy. I hate soft and clingy. I'm so glad I'm done with him.*

Jones excused himself, walked down the hall, and ducked into a witness room to call the U.S. Marshal's Office.

"I want to increase the security checks at Lizzie Scott's house," Jones said. He started them the day Lee said he was going to visit Lizzie when the case was over.

But Jones never told Lizzie what Lee said.

He had his reasons. He thought Lee was a coward. Only a coward shoots an unarmed man. He thought his threats were guff. He also didn't want to upset Lizzie during trial. And he certainly didn't want to do it now, right before closing arguments.

His wife, Mary, chided him for it. "You just don't want to distract Lizzie from winning the darn case," she said. "You're a devious man, John Paul Jones. If they only knew . . ."

It was true. People would be shocked to know how cold-blooded Jones could be when it came to pushing fidelity, bravery, and integrity.

He never broke the rules, of course. But sometimes he kept information to himself rather than share it with the prosecutor. Sometimes he even used information to get the prosecutor to do what he wanted.

For example, he hadn't lied to Lizzie when he said he brought her the case because she was ready to move up. He knew she was good, better than people realized, and tougher.

But he also knew she wasn't going to say "no" to him. Not that he would ever talk about her Convocation past with anyone. But she didn't know that.

He also knew about Lizzie and Jack. Like a lot of smart people, Lizzie thought her secrets were safe if she never revealed him. People had seen the two of them leave the Manhattan Beach party together. It was years ago, but there was no expiration date on gossip. Jones heard it from prosecutors who were not even at the party.

Jones figured if there were anything to it, Jack might back Lizzie up on the case. It hadn't worked out that way exactly, but Jack turned out to be a pretty good supporter.

But there was no way Jones was going to let Lizzie get hurt. Not by a horse-shit coward like Dwayne Wayne Lee.

CHAPTER 52

ON THE MORNING OF THE CLOSING ARGUMENTS, LEE WHEELED his son into the courtroom, putting him in the front row, in the space reserved for the handicapped. The boy looked fragile, a broken doll in metal braces, his face and head disfigured with ribbons of scars.

There wasn't an open seat in the place. The media table was packed. The rest of the crowd was split right down the middle of the room.

Behind the defense table and first row was a solid block of uniforms from police and sheriff departments throughout Southern California.

There were also retired cops wearing American flag lapel pins next to their old badges, members of the Blanton P.D., City Manager Cooley, and a few regular court watchers, retirees with nothing else to do.

The members of the "Justice for Rincon Committee" sat in the front row behind the prosecution table. They included Mrs. Rincon and her attorney, Abe Ybarra.

After that, it was row after row of Lizzie's colleagues: good-looking, young Assistant U.S. Attorneys in their suits and ties and dresses.

Jack sat in the back row of the prosecutors, thinking it was blue collars versus white collars, cops versus lawyers, Lizzie's people versus Lee's.

Lizzie loved the energy in a courtroom at this moment. It was the closest thing she ever felt to being on the court before a final game, or in the ring before a bout. After months of investigation, hundreds of decisions, large and small, emotional ups and downs, strategy sessions, arguments with supervisors, doubts, it came down to the final round.

The jury filed in. They dressed up for closing arguments. They always did. It was an occasion. Mrs. Meagher was in a Nancy Reagan red dress. None of the men wore shorts, which was rare in these parts.

Lizzie Scott rose and stood before them, a powerful woman, as striking a figure as the statue of Justice itself. Lizzie liked that Justice carried a sword. She was a fighter.

"When we began, I promised I would prove beyond a reasonable doubt that Officer Dwayne Lee murdered Joe Rincon. I kept my promise. I ask that you keep yours."

She broke the story down for them logically, focusing on her strongest evidence.

Lee wasn't scared of Rincon. If he had been, he wouldn't have gotten close to the pickup. Or he would have had his gun out. The experts didn't agree that the flashlight blow occurred. "But when you get back into the jury room, ask yourselves this: If it didn't happen, why did Lee hide his flashlight? Why did he leave the flashlight off the inventory list? He did it because he knows what he did with that flashlight."

She admitted the flaws in her case. That's what made her so credible. Henry Scanlon was not perfect. He didn't have to be. All he had to be was present that night and awake. "Mr. Scanlon had a clear, unobstructed, well-lit view of what happened. He remembered it clearly, it stayed with him; the way something horrible stays in your mind."

Yes, he had once denied what he saw to the Riverside County Sheriff's Deputy when he was drunk and scared, but that didn't mean he wasn't at the scene.

"Scanlon knew things he could *not* have known *unless* he had been there. He knew the positions of the pickup and the police cruiser, the distance between Lee and Rincon at the time of the shooting, about the flashlight. None of these details were ever made public. Scanlon only knew about them because he *saw* them."

Lizzie laid out the law, reminding them what Captain Borns said about deadly force, when and how it could be used, the hours Lee spent being trained to only shoot a suspect in a life-or-death situation. Again and again, she came back to the same theme: If this was a justified shooting, why did Lee hide evidence? Why hide the flashlight?

"The question is not whether or not Lee is guilty of Count Two. He is. No doubt about it. The question is what does that lie tell you about Count One. He wouldn't have hidden the flashlight unless he knew what he did in this case was a crime."

She finished with pathos. She earned the right to do so. She extended an open hand toward Mrs. Rincon.

"This is Joseph Rincon's grandmother. Her grandson was unarmed, complied with the officer's siren and pulled to the side of the road, and was shot for it. He was the victim of excessive, outrageous force, lethal, deadly force. If Mr. Scanlon had not seen it, we wouldn't know about it, we wouldn't be here, and this woman wouldn't have a chance for justice. She deserves it. Joseph Rincon deserves it."

The jury had listened to every word, absorbed, thoughtful, moved.

Jack and a few other prosecutors were not disappointed so much as underwhelmed. It had been a solid closing but not an overpowering one.

Taylor knew better. It was one of the best closings he ever heard. A jury begins its real work when they began to deliberate. Lizzie's job wasn't to convince all of them at once. It was to arm the jurors who agreed with her to win the case on their own by making arguments to convince the others.

And Taylor liked that she didn't overdo the emotion. Prosecutors hurt their credibility when they went for the heart. Passion was a defense tool, Taylor joked, because a lot of times, they didn't have anything else. "Most of these fuckers are guilty, you know."

Lee was not as impressed with Lizzie's performance. Or perhaps he was. It took everything he had not to rush across the courtroom and beat her to death.

· · ·

BOTH SIDES WERE GIVEN ONE HOUR TO MAKE THEIR CASE. ONLY state court judges let things go beyond that. Lizzie believed less was more. She didn't even use her whole hour.

Taylor talked for four hours.

Unlike Lizzie, he didn't need all 12 jurors. He only needed to arm one juror to hang all of them. According to Farley, the word was The Chief hated this case and wanted it gone. Taylor didn't see The Chief authorizing a retrial. A mistrial was as good as an acquittal. But if he should happen to convince all 12 to acquit, he wasn't opposed to that either.

Taylor's opening move was his usual one. He told the story of his boyhood friend.

"Cedric Clayton and I grew up together. One night, right before graduation, he was arrested for robbing a liquor store. There was an eyewitness who swore he saw what happened. Thank God, the jury saw the truth and acquitted Cedric because the actual robber was caught a month later. That's when I decided to become a lawyer. To help innocent people. That's why I'm standing before you today."

Lizzie wondered if any of it was true. Not that it mattered. Taylor wasn't under oath. Lawyer arguments weren't evidence. It certainly felt true. Jurors ate it up.

"Now, Ms. Scott says she told you a story, but that not's true. This was a puzzle. And there are a lot of pieces missing. Let's talk about one. Let's talk about motive."

Taylor took a sip of water to let the idea sink in.

"Ms. Scott never even *tried* to explain why my client would shoot and kill Mr. Rincon for no reason. I know, I know . . . the law says Ms. Scott doesn't have to prove motive. But don't you think she should have at least tried? Before she asks you to convict a man of murder, she should at least try to explain why he did it."

Now Taylor pointed at Lizzie.

"On the word of a low-life like Henry Scanlon, she wants to destroy the career and family of a cop who's never been in any kind of trouble. You saw Scanlon. Would you trust him with anything? She trusts him with Officer Lee's life, and the life of his and their two children."

Taylor took a moment to look at Lee's son in the wheelchair.

"Make no mistake. This case comes down to one question. Are you going to believe Officer Lee or Scanlon? It's got to be one or the other. Officer Lee shot a man who came at him with a knife. His mistake was to forget about his flashlight. That's not murder! It's a mistake!"

Taylor locked in on Mrs. Meagher.

"You can't convict him for a mistake. We don't claim Officer Lee is a perfect police officer. We don't claim the Blanton Police Department is perfect. Blanton is what it is: a poor town, in a poor county, struggling to survive, doing the best it can with what it has. Like all of us."

Taylor drew a handkerchief from his breast pocket and wiped his eyes. Lizzie was used to seeing Elder Evans move himself to tears.

"Did Officer Lee make mistakes that night? Who hasn't? I bet even Ms. Scott has made a mistake. In fact, I know she has. Indicting this case was a mistake." He turned to face her. "Human beings do that, Ms. Scott. They make mistakes. 'There was only one perfect man. And they crucified Him.'"

It was an Elder Evans favorite.

"All we ask is, do the right thing. Send Officer Lee back to his wife and kids. You can let the police department decide if he should continue to be a cop or not. Don't send him to prison with all those real killers."

Lizzie could have objected many times. Maybe she should have raised a number of objections, but she hated to object in closing arguments. Jurors hated it. And she had no faith that Judge Letts would have sustained any of them.

. . .

THE BEAUTY OF HAVING THE BURDEN OF PROOF IS YOU GET TO speak first and last. Lizzie got the last word. She stood up to give her rebuttal.

"Mr. Taylor is right. All of us make mistakes. If we're honest, we admit them. If we're dishonest, if we've done something wrong, we hide them. That's what Officer Lee did. It wasn't a mistake. It was murder. It wasn't a mistake. It was a cover-up."

Lizzie looked at Jones and nodded.

"I know the police are heroes. They risk their lives to protect people they don't even know. Nobody makes them do it. They're not drafted into it. It's a volunteer force. They choose to do it."

She picked up Lee's gun belt. "These are some of their tools."

She put the belt down and pointed at her head. "But what's in here . . ." She pointed to heart. "And what's in here are the tools that matter most."

Lizzie stared again at Dwayne Wayne Lee.

"Mr. Taylor is right. We don't have to prove motive. But we all have an idea why Lee did what he did. Lee told us himself. He was an angry man that night. He admitted the situation with his son made him angry. It would make anyone angry. But that's not the only reason he was angry."

The jury was listening intently now. They understood the importance of the point.

"Mr. Scanlon said that when the pickup door popped open, Officer Lee fell down. He got up angry at Rincon. Maybe he was embarrassed, too. That's when Mr. Scanlon saw Lee angrily grab his flashlight and hit Rincon on the head with it."

She picked up the flashlight from the evidence table and rapped it against the rail of the jury box, not hard, but enough to make a few jurors jump. "The expert told you a head blow with this was deadly force. Officer Lee was guilty of excessive force before he ever even shot Rincon."

She held the flashlight up in front of her so the jury could get a good look.

"The Inland County Coroner admitted she missed the evidence of the head blow and admitted this could have caused the wound on Rincon's head. Our expert coroner from Los Angeles testified that a blow with this flashlight was a reasonable explanation for the wound in the photos. Look at the photos yourself."

She took a breath to make sure they were all paying attention.

"Finally, when you get back in the jury room, ask yourself this: if there was nothing to hide about the flashlight . . . then why did he hide the flashlight?"

CHAPTER 53

DELIBERATIONS STARTED ON A WEDNESDAY. A WEEK LATER, THEY were still at it, or at least seemed to be. They hadn't sent out a single note.

Glenn Smitty, the big, bald, blue-coated U.S. Marshal in charge of ushering them to and from lunch every day, couldn't give Jones any insights. They were a quiet group. No yelling inside the room, no joking outside of it.

"They eat pretty good, though."

Judge Letts required the lawyers to be within ten minutes of the courtroom in case a question or verdict came back.

Jones spent the week back in Palm Springs, where he opened, investigated, and closed eight cases.

Taylor's blonde swimsuit model wife/receptionist spent the time convincing her husband to put down an offer on a much bigger house.

Lizzie caught up on paperwork and chewed through bottles of Tums. Waiting for verdicts never agreed with her, but this time was the worst.

Jack, realizing they had never been on an actual date, invited her to dinner. Against her better judgment and oath to stay away from him, she said yes. They agreed she wouldn't talk about the case if he agreed not to talk about their relationship.

The restaurant was quiet. So were they. Jack talked about the disappointing season the Angels were having. He didn't follow or understand sports. Berg said Lizzie did. She hadn't even noticed the baseball season had started.

Jack broke the promise first. "I miss you."

Lizzie jumped in. "I never should have called the expert."

She took him home that night. It had been a tough few weeks.

She was entitled to a mistake or two.

They slept late.

Her phone rang.

"Ms. Scott, we've been looking for you." It was the clerk. "We have a note from the jury."

She broke her own record for getting dressed and drove the five miles from her place to court. Judge Letts gave her a hard look. He could forgive anything but lateness.

Lizzie took the note from the clerk. Taylor read it over her shoulder:

"We need further instruction on the meaning of what 'reasonable doubt' means."

If they were thinking this hard about reasonable doubt, they were working on someone's theory of acquittal.

Taylor chuckled. "Hot damn." Clearly, he thought this was a pro-defense question, too.

The note was signed by the foreperson, Juror #6, Mrs. Meagher. Ybarra and Taylor guessed right, as they always did.

Judge Letts looked to the lawyers for help on how to answer the note. The jury had been instructed on reasonable doubt. They had a copy of the instruction in the jury room. By law, the court couldn't add anything more without risking problems on appeal.

On the other hand, saying nothing might lead them to give up and hang. "We could just bring them in and tell them to keep trying," Judge Letts suggested. Lizzie and Taylor were both against it.

In the end, they did what courts often do when the jury asks for help: they pretended not to have heard the question.

Lizzie walked back to her office, went into the restroom, and threw up.

●　●　●

THE NEXT JURY NOTE ARRIVED TWO DAYS LATER.

"We have reached a verdict."

222

Judge Letts delayed calling the case to give time for the press to arrive. By the time they did, the courtroom was full. Police officers and deputies far outnumbered everyone else. There is always a lot of law enforcement around a courthouse.

Lizzie and Jack ran over.

She was amazed to see how bad Lee looked. Deliberations always took the most out of the man facing a verdict.

Jones happened to be transferring a prisoner to Long Beach. He parked the guy in the Santa Ana jail and raced over. He made it in time, slipping into his seat next to Lizzie as Judge Letts took the bench.

"Has the jury reached a verdict?"

Mrs. Meagher stood up. "We have, Your Honor."

What happened next always struck Lizzie as its own form of cruel and unusual punishment. Mrs. Meagher, Juror #6 to the world, passed the note to the clerk. The clerk walked it over to Judge Letts, who put on a grim poker face to read it, then silently passed it back to the clerk. The clerk walked it back to the foreperson, Mrs. Meagher. The whole nonsensical dance served no purpose other than to heighten the mood and create unbearable tension.

Judge Letts asked Lee to rise. Taylor stood with him.

The judge instructed the clerk to record the verdict.

Breathe.

"Members of the jury," the clerk read, "as to Count One of the Indictment, charging Dwayne Lee with unlawful use of excessive force against one Joseph Rincon, how do you find?"

Mrs. Meagher unfolded the verdict form and read it out loud and clear. "We, the jury, find the defendant, Dwayne Wayne Lee . . ."

Breathe.

"Not guilty."

The gallery exploded in a muffled whoosh of expelled breath. Someone said "yes" and someone else clapped their hands. The room broke into a low, buzzing chatter. Lizzie could pick out the sound of Mrs. Rincon crying.

Judge Letts rapped the gavel once. The room went still.

Lizzie felt like she'd been punched in the throat. The bad thing happened. She didn't feel very brave.

The clerk continued:

"As to Count Two of the Indictment, charging Dwayne Lee with conspiracy to file a false statement, how do you find?"

Mrs. Meagher turned and looked directly at Lee.

"Guilty."

Maybe Mrs. Meagher hated Lee a little bit, too.

Lee flinched at the verdict, as if he'd touched a live wire.

The AP reporter was out of the door before the room quieted down again. He had drafted three versions of his story—one for guilty, one for not guilty, and one for a split—and now topped the appropriate one by phone text with a short lede:

"A Blanton City police officer was acquitted this morning of killing a motorist during a violent confrontation following a traffic stop."

He stuck the news of the guilty verdict on Count Two at the end of his story and hit send. By the time he got to the lobby, his editors were already proofing it. By the time he got to his car, the story had gone out to the world.

Lizzie felt woozy.

They split the baby. Just like I knew they would.

Lee stared at her. He didn't look like the winner. But, from a legal standpoint, he was one.

He'd been acquitted of the top charge. He was facing a sentence on the lower one, but the difference was night and day. On Count One, he could have gone away for life. On Count Two, even with adjustments, Lizzie doubted Judge Letts would give him more than two years, if that, and probably split it in half between custody and home confinement.

Jones touched her elbow. There was still work to be done.

"Does the government have anything to add?" Judge Letts asked.

"No, thank you, Your Honor," she said.

Judge Letts thanked the jury for their service and sent them home. The gallery thinned out. Only Jack, Mrs. Rincon, and Abe Ybarra stayed. Farley, Lisa Lee, and a few cops sat behind Lee.

Judge Letts went through the formalities, explaining to Lee that he had the right to appeal his conviction on Count Two. He then assigned the proper office to prepare a Pre-Sentence Report and scheduled Lee's sentencing six weeks from then.

The last issue was Lee's bail status.

Since Lee had been free during trial, Lizzie doubted Judge Letts would step him back now. But she wanted to at least try, if for no other reason, to let Mrs. Rincon see she did.

"Your Honor," Lizzie said. "We move that the defendant's trial bond be revoked and he be remanded into custody now."

Jack cleared his throat, trying to get her attention, wanting to remind her about office policy that you never ask for a remand when it's unlikely to be granted. She didn't look back at him.

Judge Letts shook his head. "I'm not going to remand him."

"I'll be heard anyway, Your Honor," she said. Lizzie didn't care about Judge Letts's feelings anymore or whether he made a mistake. It was too late for that.

"The defendant's current bail was set when he was presumed innocent. He's not innocent now. He's been found guilty and he's facing prison."

"Not much of it," Taylor said.

The *Inland County Recorder* chuckled. Taylor was a quote machine.

"My client has shown up every day on time without fail when he was facing a murder charge so he's not a flight-risk. And there's absolutely no evidence that he's a danger to the community. The jury just acquitted him of Count One."

Lizzie knew she should leave it there. She would have, too, but she'd looked at Mrs. Rincon, the old woman had stopped crying. She was listening, getting something good out of Lizzie's effort to put Lee behind bars.

"The defendant has every reason to flee now," Lizzie said. "As to whether Officer Lee is a risk to the community, the court might ask Mr. Rincon's grandmother here about that."

"That's it, Ms. Scott," Judge Letts said, angry now. "You're wrong on the law and the facts. I'm not supposed to remand someone as a form of punishment. Under the law, I'm only allowed to remand someone if I see evidence that he's a flight-risk or a danger."

"You heard the evidence, Your Honor, he shot an unarmed man. That makes him a risk."

"You lost, Lizzie," Taylor said in a stage whisper. Then addressing the court, "I hate to see Ms. Scott be a sore loser."

Lizzie fixed Taylor with a stare. She threw a haymaker. Just to see if it would land.

"Your Honor," she said. "I have reason to believe the defendant could be a threat to himself, if no one else, and should at least be required to—"

"Hold up!" Taylor said. "I don't know, but I think this may have something to do with a conversation we had during trial, in the witness room, am I right?"

Lizzie was surprised. She thought he'd deny the conversation.

"Mr. Taylor said his client posed a danger to himself."

"That was when he was facing a murder charge," Taylor said. "He's fine now."

Lizzie wondered if Taylor lied when he said Lee was on the edge, or if he was lying now, when he said Lee wasn't?

"On this record, I see no basis for altering the defendant's status," Judge Letts said. Lizzie had no other arguments left to make.

Judge Letts asked Lee if he understood his obligations to return to court.

"I do, Your Honor. Thank you."

Court was dismissed.

Lee walked out of the courtroom and up to the Probation Office to fill out forms. He was a free man, at least for another six weeks. His wife, Lisa, followed a few steps behind.

Lizzie couldn't imagine what was life going to be like for Lisa for the next six weeks, let alone after that.

Unlike other stories, there are no happy endings in criminal trials. Relief, sometimes, a grim sense of a wrong being righted, perhaps. Justice and injustice have their many consequences. Happiness is never one of them.

* * *

Lizzie, Jones, and Jack rode down the elevator with Mrs. Rincon. Lizzie put her arm around the old woman. "I'm sorry."

When the elevator opened, Abe Ybarra was there, waiting to take Mrs. Rincon home. If she were going to get any justice out of this, it would have to be in civil court, in a lawsuit. A week ago she said she was ready to talk about it.

"She thinks it's blood money," Abe said. "Blood or not, it's still money."

Mrs. Rincon hugged Lizzie. "I'm sorry we didn't do better for Joe," she said. Mrs. Rincon kissed her cheek.

Lizzie didn't go back to her office. She walked to her car, ignoring Jack's offer to drive her home.

"It was the right verdict," Berg said. "If I were on the jury, I'd have come out the same way they did."

"Yeah?" Jones said flatly. "Who asked you?"

Jones went looking for Farley. He found him in the Probation Office, finishing up Lee's paperwork, arranging for his presentence interview.

"Where's your client, Farley?"

"You just missed him." Lee and Taylor left a few minutes earlier.

Jones said he hoped they're not going to have any problems with Lee.

"What sort of problems?"

Jones said he didn't like the way Lee was staring at his prosecutor. "We're not going to have any of that nonsense, are we? Because I wouldn't like it."

Farley assured him that if he got a sniff that Lee was even thinking of doing something stupid, old Jonesy would be the first to know.

"I wouldn't worry about it, though," Farley said. "If Dwayne-o was going to do something, he'd have done it already. Trust me."

Jones didn't. He convinced the U.S. Marshals and the Santa Ana P.D. to step up their drive-bys around Lizzie's house.

CHAPTER 54

LIZZIE SCOTT WAS NOT THE KIND OF GIRL WHO CRIED WHEN SHE got hurt. Instead, she pulled her car out of the lot, roaring past the security guard, then tore down 17th Street, daring a cop to pull her over.

He got away with murder.

She blew through a red.

I let him get away with murder.

Windows down, wind roaring, she blew past cars in the fast lane, passing on the right when she could, taking the left-side breakdown lane when she couldn't. She was lucky not to crash but didn't care if she did.

She snapped out of it when she hit the San Diego County line. Her stomach hurt. She hadn't eaten all day. Pulling off the freeway, she went looking for food and spotted a taco truck parked in front of a CVS.

The line snaked half way down the block. That was a good sign, but it was the smell that sold her.

A few regulars brought beach chairs but most of the customers sat on the curb. Lizzie ate her food off the trunk of her car.

A CAL-TRANS road crew stood in line in dust-covered work boots and jeans, dented hard hats, sun-faded orange vests, and T-shirts.

The two in front were young, athletic; Lizzie would've bet they played high school basketball. Now they were using their butts to block out their boss, an older Chinese man who was trying to hand the counter girl cash.

"Let me pay for everybody," the boss was saying. "I want to pay."

Another member of the crew put his arm around the boss's shoulder. "We got you, jefe, don't worry about it. You're going to need it when you retire."

The boss mumbled thanks and put his money back in his wallet.

Lizzie started to cry.

What the fuck is this?

She wiped her eyes and stared at her fingers.

Then she left her food sitting on the trunk and walked over to the CVS.

CHAPTER 55

PREGNANT.

"I'm going to have it," Lizzie said, precluding any discussion of her alternatives. Not that Sarah would have raised any.

"Oh, my God," Sarah said, her big eyes wider than seemed humanly possible. "Friend is going to be a mommy. Before me."

They hugged and cried.

"It is Handsome Jack's, right?" Sarah asked.

"Yes, it's Handsome Jack's," Lizzie said, pretending to be offended. For the first time, she laughed, all the tension and disappointment of the trial forgotten for a moment.

Lizzie couldn't stop crying. "Oh, fuck this," Lizzie said, rubbing the tears away. "If it's going to be like this, maybe I won't have it after all. My hormones are killing me."

Sarah wiped Lizzie's eyes with the sleeve of her sweatshirt. "Have you told Handsome Jack?"

"That's not actually his name, Sarah, you know that, right?"

Lizzie hadn't told Jack yet. "After the Lee sentencing," she said. "I want to get through that first."

Sarah said she understood, but she looked confused. "It just seems mean. Jack has a right to know. He's the daddy."

Just hearing the word made Lizzie wince. Jack was the dad. She was the mom. None of it seemed real. Finding out she was pregnant scrambled her brains like no punch ever had.

"I just need time to process all of it," Lizzie said.

"Friend?" Sarah asked. "Do you want to pray?"

"No," Lizzie said. That would not be necessary.

Without being asked, Sarah made an appointment for Lizzie with the OB-GYN. Then she picked a date for Lizzie's baby shower.

"How did I let this happen?" Lizzie asked.

"It's meant to be," Sarah said. "It's your spiritual structure."

Lizzie couldn't stand it. She was no smarter than the girls she pitied in high school, too dumb to use a condom, too stupid to think beyond the moment. She looked down on them then. But she chastised herself worse now. She knew better. She had no excuse.

"So you're not as smart as you thought," Sarah said. "You're still *really* smart."

Lizzie made Sarah swear she wouldn't tell anyone, especially not Mom and Dad.

"After the sentencing," she said.

Six weeks weren't going to make that big a difference.

CHAPTER 56

THE CHIEF'S TICKETS WERE NOT IN THE FOUNDER'S CIRCLE. THEY were high up in the balcony. He could afford better, but these had sentimental value. He and his brother bought them. When his brother died, he kept the empty seat in memory of him.

Also, he didn't like to bring people. They would want to chat. The Chief didn't approve of chatting at the opera.

He was walking to his car after what he considered to a disappointing *Don Carlo* when a familiar voice offended him.

"Dante?"

The Chief bowed to Mrs. Leonard. Her seats were in the Founder's Circle. "Did you enjoy the performance, Madam U.S. Attorney?"

"Oh, I loved it. Such voices!"

Mrs. Leonard introduced him to her granddaughter. (Sierra? Sienna? The Chief never bothered to remember names he deemed unconventional.)

"Our Lizzie Scott did a wonderful job on the use of force case," Mrs. Leonard said. "You must be very proud of her."

"She lost the top count," The Chief said. "I don't consider that a win."

"I think she's wonderful, Dante. I think she should be in Los Angeles. You should move her up here. I think she'd be happier."

The Chief had no interest in the happiness of the young people who worked for him. Doing the job well should have made them happy enough.

He had no desire to see Lizzie Scott in Los Angeles. The further away she was from him—and Jack—the better. The Chief didn't know the nature of their relationship. He didn't want to know. But he did not think she was a good influence on him. Until he found better, Jack remained his protégé.

He wished Mrs. Leonard a good night.

Mrs. Leonard could not understand how an intelligent, sophisticated man like The Chief who loved opera and the law so much could be so cold-hearted.

"It's the Scalia syndrome," she told her granddaughter, Sierra. "It makes no sense."

CHAPTER 57

"THE JURY DIDN'T BELIEVE ME," SCANLON SAID.

He and Lizzie sat at a coffee shop by the Ventura County Pier on a gray day. The ocean was as flat and monotonous as the desert.

Lizzie told Scanlon it wasn't his fault. He'd been a hero. Thanks to him, Lee wouldn't be a police officer anymore. Mrs. Rincon was grateful to him.

Lizzie put her hand on his. "You came through for us, Henry. You showed a lot of guts coming forward."

Scanlon ran his hand through his hair and scratched his chest and blushed. "Yeah. I just wished I did better for the kid."

Lizzie wished she could have done better for Scanlon. She tried to get him a new start. But it was harder to get into Harvard than Federal Witness Protection. The best she could do was a few bucks from Witness Assistance.

Lizzie took out a pen and card. "This is my cell and home number. If you ever need me for anything, anytime, call."

Henry took the card and mumbled thank you.

"Where are you going to go now?"

Scanlon looked around and shrugged. "Here's good. Better weather. Never lived by the beach before. The cops are nicer."

• • •

ON HER WAY OUT OF VENTURA, BERG CALLED. THE CHIEF WAS looking for her. "You've been summoned. So be nice," Berg said.

"I'm always nice," she said. "Until provoked."

Jack wasn't in his office. The Chief sent him up to San Francisco at the last minute to handle an appellate argument in the Ninth Circuit.

She was shown in. The Chief was standing behind his desk. For the first time ever, he looked her straight in the eye.

"Well done, Ms. Scott," he said shaking her hand. "Well done indeed."

He's going to fire me.

She had no reason to think so other than the fact he was being so nice. He asked her to take a seat. He twirled his glasses in his hand and stared at the ceiling and launched into a long discourse on the nature of justice, comparing Spinoza's view to St. Augustine's.

Then he got down to business.

"Ms. Scott, I have good news," The Chief said. "Based on your work in the Rincon matter, I've recommended—and you've been accepted—to become a Trial Attorney in the U.S. Department of Justice Civil Rights Division, Washington D.C. Congratulations."

She was finally getting her transfer.

He's not firing me, he's kicking me back East.

She told The Chief she'd think about it.

. . .

WHEN JACK HEARD ABOUT THE TRANSFER, HIS HEART SANK. He did love her, he was almost certain of it. Really. She couldn't leave him, could she?

How could The Chief do this without asking Jack about it? *Did* The Chief know about them? Was he trying to keep them apart?

The ambitious part of Jack's brain alerted him to the fact that Lizzie moving to D.C. might be the best thing in the world for their careers and their relationship.

The battle between Jack's head and heart was always fierce.

CHAPTER 58

DURING THE NEXT SIX WEEKS, LIZZIE HIT THE GYM EVERY DAY but passed on the chance to spar, much to the owner's relief. Sarah cooked constantly, making too much food, forcing folic acid tablets down her throat.

"Baby needs nutrients," Sarah said.

Lizzie begged her not to refer to "baby."

She worked on the Lee case, filing the government's position paper, calling for the highest possible sentence, but there wasn't much she could do. What Lee got was out of her hands. But anyone who thought Judge Letts made the decision didn't understand federal justice. Federal judges don't give sentences. Congress does.

Through a complicated, points system–based matrix, with tables and charts, Congress tries to ensure that no matter where you commit a crime, and no matter whom the judge is you end up in front of, you get the same sentence for the same conduct.

The U.S. Probation Office prepares a Pre-Sentence Report, a criminal biography of who the defendant is, what he did, and what should happen to him now. It includes an in-depth analysis of the crime itself, adding and subtracting points based on the conduct.

Did the defendant abuse a position of trust when he committed the crime? Add two points to the sentencing range.

Did he accept responsibility for what he did? Take two points off the sentencing range.

It is all laid out in the U.S. Sentencing Guidelines, two fat manuals that purport to contain all the possible variables and crimes, with corresponding mathematical formulas to determine what the final sentence should be.

Like every other congressional effort to make things simple, the sentencing guidelines are a jumbled mess, as likely to produce good results as bad. Too many exceptions are built into it, too many variables, the biggest being who was assigned to write the Pre-Sentence Report. Because how they interpret things determine what the sentencing range will be.

Magda Krinsky was considered the softest touch in the Probation Office. An unpublished novelist, she felt great empathy for the condemned. Judge Letts adored her.

"So many of them never had a chance," she said. They were victims of abuse, poverty; it was no wonder they turned to crime. "There but for the grace of God—"

"Lee was a cop!" Lizzie yelled. "Don't you see the difference between Lee and a gang-banger or a drug dealer?"

Krinsky said she did, of course she did, but she believed Lee was remorseful. Like all defendants, he had the right to refuse to a sit-down interview with her, but he came to her office and was forthcoming and sincere.

"I saw real sadness in his eyes," Krinsky said. "I saw a man wrestling with what he did, accepting responsibility for it."

Krinsky wasn't supposed to, but she told Lizzie that Lee's sentencing range was going to come out between 12 and 18 months. It was heavy for what amounted to a false statement case where the defendant had no previous criminal record, but ridiculously light for murder.

"They didn't find him guilty of murder, Lizzie."

Magda Krinsky agreed with Mr. Taylor. She was going to suggest Judge Letts depart downward from the sentencing range. She was recommending that Lee receive a six month sentence, split: half in jail, half in home confinement.

"That's ridiculous," Lizzie said, her face flushed, thinking.

Jesus Christ, please don't let me start crying in front of her.
"It is not ridiculous," Krinsky said. "It's justice."

• • •

"I TOLD YOU BEFORE, I'M NOT GOING TO JAIL." LEE REFUSED TO DO even three months, not that he was going to have a choice.

Taylor was used to clients being ungrateful. Always get the money up front, he told Farley. They don't want to pay you when it's over. No matter how much good you to do for them.

"Dwayne-o, listen to me," Farley said, leaning forward in his chair. "Three months in jail is nothing."

"Then you serve it, asshole." Lee ripped up the Pre-Sentence Report and threw it on Taylor's desk. Taylor shook his head. It figured a bully like Lee would turn to jelly over a nothing sentence.

Farley patted Lee's knee. "You could do three months in your sleep. Literally. We got this doctor, he can get you prescriptions—anxiety pills, sleeping pills, antidepressants, whatever you want—all legal. And the dispensary's got to let you have them. It's your right as a prisoner."

And if they don't give him the pills, Taylor thought, he would sue the state for violating Lee's civil rights, and he would win, too.

But Taylor kept it to himself. He almost never met a defendant he didn't like. Repeat customers are a big part of every good lawyer's business. But he was sick of Officer Lee.

Still, he gave him the sentencing pep talk. He owed him that much.

"Look, Officer Lee, I understand how you feel, but you got to think about your wife, your kids. They need you to be strong. They need you to keep your head up, do your time, and come back to them a better man than when you went in. I know you can do it."

Farley nodded in agreement, but he could tell the boss was phoning it in.

Lee gave him the grin. "That just means the world to me, Mr. Taylor," he said, sarcastic, seething. "Now, try to hear what I'm saying. I'm not some white trash piece of shit who belongs in jail. Okay? And I'm not going to jail. So you need to figure a way out of this."

Lee got up and left.

Farley apologized. "He's real worried about his wife taking care of the kids by herself."

Taylor nodded. He always tried to find something good in every client, even the ones he hated. It made him try harder.

"At least he didn't call me the N-word."

CHAPTER 59

LIZZIE'S SIX WEEKS WENT BY IN A BLUR. LEE'S DRAGGED LIKE A KIND of torture.

He spent his days at home waiting and hoping Taylor would work some kind of magic. He spent his nights worrying about how Lisa was going to manage the kids without him.

He walked her around the house, explaining where to turn off the gas if there was an earthquake and the water if there was a leak, going over the bills she had to pay, how to check the balance on their account.

"Lisa, are you fucking paying attention?"

She nodded. Math was not her strong suit. Plus, it seemed like she was using again.

Other than meeting with the Probation Office once a week, peeing in a cup when they made him, and dealing with the fucking electronic ankle bracelet, he had nothing to do.

"Dwayne-o," Farley called, checking in on him. "I'm going to send over a catalog of stuff Lisa can buy for you through the prison commissary. Toilet paper, books, things like that, just let me know what you need, I'll set you up."

Lee mumbled thanks. Farley said he had friends in the sheriff's department who would look out for Lee once he went inside.

. . .

THE DAY BEFORE THE SENTENCING, WHEN IT WAS CLEAR TAYLOR wasn't going to being pulling any rabbits out of hats, Lee just wanted to get it all over with, once and for all.

Sentencing was set for 11:00 A.M.

Lizzie was awake and throwing up at 4:00 A.M.

So far, she hadn't really enjoyed being pregnant.

Jones called the Marshals to make sure everything was okay. They called the private company that monitored Lee's ankle bracelet. Everything looked fine: no alarms. Lee was at home, where he should be, no problem.

The Santa Ana cops said Lizzie's house was quiet, too.

At 6:30 A.M., Jones called her cell just to make sure. "Everything good?"

"Everything's good. Meet you in my office."

An hour later, her phone rang again.

"Jones, I'm fine—"

But it wasn't Jones.

It was the Clerk's Office.

Dwayne Lee didn't show up for his presentence drug test at 7:00 A.M.

"Did his lawyer show up?"

"Mr. Taylor was here with Mr. Farley. They didn't seem happy."

Lizzie called Jones. "Lee's AWOL."

While they were on the phone, they both got texts: Lee's ankle bracelet had stopped functioning. He wasn't being tracked anymore.

Jones told Lizzie to stay put. He would grab the Marshals and go to Lee's house. In the meantime, he was getting a couple of Santa Ana P.D. squad cars in front of her house.

"He's not coming here," Lizzie said. "He would've done it already. Just make sure Moeller is safe. He's the one I'd be worried about. I'll call Henry."

Jones said he would take care of both of them. Then he called Jack.

He got him on the cell, driving down from L.A. for the sentencing. Not because anyone needed him there. He just wanted to see Lizzie, even from the back row of the courtroom.

For the last six weeks, she refused to see him, ignored his texts, and wouldn't take his phone calls.

He couldn't figure out what he'd done wrong.

He sent her a long e-mail, explaining that he had nothing to do with the job offer in D.C., although he certainly would understand if she wanted to take it. In fact, it might be the best thing for her career and their relationship.

Jones told Jack about Lee and suggested Jack go stay with Lizzie. He didn't think Lizzie needed protection. But he thought Jack would want to be there for her.

CHAPTER 60

Jones pulled up to the Lee house as the Marshals got to the door. Smitty didn't figure Lee was dangerous, but just to be safe, he brought Rory Holmes with him, a new Marshal but a former U.S.C. linebacker.

Holmes banged on the door. Jones heard something and made him stop.

"Who is it?" said the voice of a little girl. It was Jill Lee.

Jones leaned down so the girl could hear him clearly without him having to yell. "Honey, is your daddy home?"

"No."

"How 'bout your mommy?"

The Marshals looked at one another. By law they could break down the door; they didn't need a warrant for a guy on release. And at a combined weight of 500 or so pounds, it wouldn't take but shoulders and a push. But Jones didn't want to scare the girl.

"Honey, could you open the door for us? We want to see your mommy."

Silence.

The little girl said she couldn't open the door to strangers.

Smitty gave it a try. "We're not strangers; we're friends of your daddy. We're policemen, too. Just like him."

Rory shook his finger at Smitty and made a tsk-tsk sound.

Smitty hissed at him to quit fucking around.

The little girl opened the door.

She wore a filthy T-shirt for pajamas, her face and hair needing a wash.

Lisa Lee was still in bed, under the influence of something. She had no idea where her husband was. He'd been sleeping on the couch for the last three months.

Jones asked if she would mind taking a look around and let them know what Dwayne might have taken with him.

She stumbled out of bed and around the room, checking drawers and closets. "Dwayne hid about $1400 in his closet. It's gone now."

"Anything else, ma'am?"

"Like what?" she said, hand to her forehead, wincing from the headache.

Jones played a hunch. "What about the gun?"

Rory shot Smitty a look:

What gun?

In order to get bail and remain free during trial, Lee turned over his service revolver and personal shotgun. Farley turned the weapons over to Court Services. They still had them.

Lee's wife stared at Jones, trying to sort out what her husband told her she could say or not say if anybody asked her about guns.

"I'm not asking about the guns Dwayne turned over to the court," Jones said. "I'm talking about the guns we don't know about."

Her mind clicked into gear. She spewed what her husband told her to say. "It's my gun. Dwayne bought it for me when we got married, for protection, when he was on duty. When they said he had to turn over all the guns, we figured that didn't mean my gun."

Jones nodded as if that made perfect sense. "So Dwayne just has the one gun."

"Yeah," she said. "But no ammo. He never let me buy bullets for it." Jones thought that was wise. Lee was probably afraid she would kill him with it.

* * *

JONES DROVE TO TAYLOR'S OFFICE WHILE ORGANIZING THE manhunt via cell. The Ventura FBI went to see Scanlon but couldn't find him. Jones sent a squad of FBI agents down to Blanton. They hit the police department unannounced, taking positions at the exits, demanding to know if anyone had seen or heard from Lee in the last six hours.

"Dwayne ain't been here," Al Jenkins said. "He knows better."

Jones also sent two agents to find Vern Moeller, the detective who testified against Lee. There was a chance Lee wanted to get even with him. They hadn't found him yet.

Meanwhile, Lizzie was on the phone with the Resident Agent in Charge of the Ventura FBI office, suggesting where they might find Scanlon.

"There's a liquor store on the corner across from the pier. I'd start there."

Lizzie bit her nails.

"What's wrong?" Sarah said. She was up early.

Lizzie didn't want to scare her. "It's all good," she said. "Work stuff."

Sarah said she'd make breakfast. Lizzie told her not to bother, she had to get to the office.

"Pregnant women *have* to eat breakfast," Sarah said. "It's so important for baby."

Ten minutes later the phone rang.

"What'd I do now?" It was Scanlon, drunk, and not too happy about being bothered.

"Henry, why weren't you in your motel room?"

"What are you, my mother? I went out for a walk. It's a free country."

She told him Lee was gone. She told him to go with the FBI, they would stay with him until Lee was caught.

Scanlon sobered up quickly. The fear she'd heard when they first met was back. "Oh, I know he's coming for me. I can't take this."

Lizzie promised the FBI would protect him, but he had to stay in his room. He said he would.

The moment she hung up, someone pounded on her door.

She was about to ask Sarah to open it but stopped herself.

It was Lee.

She whispered to Sarah to hide in the kitchen and call 911. Then she grabbed the softball bat and went to the door.

She imagined Lee was outside pounding on the door harder, about to break it down.

Lizzie whipped the door open and jumped back, bat cocked at her shoulder, ready to smash Lee to death.

Jack stood there, looking desperate. "You don't have call-waiting? I've been calling you for 20 minutes."

I'm pregnant, dumb shit.

She asked him what he was doing there.

"I just wanted to make sure you were okay."

He went to hug her. She stopped him, holding him off with the barrel of the bat.

Over his shoulder, she saw Sarah standing there, eyes wide.

"Did you tell him?" Sarah asked, the world's worst secret keeper.

"Tell me what?"

Lizzie fixed Sarah with a death stare.

"Jack already knows about Lee," Lizzie said, covering. "He was just leaving."

Jack said he'd feel better if he could stay with her until Jones got back.

Lizzie told him she'd feel better if he left.

Jack turned and walked back toward his car.

CHAPTER 61

Jones believed Taylor and Farley knew their client's intentions. He walked past the receptionist without breaking stride.

"He's in a conference!" Mrs. Taylor said.

Jones didn't knock.

Taylor sat at his desk, reviewing a file; Farley sat in front of him, reading a magazine; neither seemed particularly surprised to see Jones.

Taylor smiled. "Are we going to carpool to court this morning?"

"Where's Lee?"

"I presume he'll be in court this morning, as always," Taylor said. "Why? Has something happened that we should be aware of?"

"Cut the horse shit," Jones said. "Lee didn't show up for his drug test. You know that. You were there waiting for him."

Taylor shrugged. "I'm quite hopeful that we'll see him in court in just a few minutes," Taylor said, grabbing his coat. "Drive safely, Agent Jones."

Jones walked around the desk and put his face an inch from Taylor's. Farley stood up, debating whether to help his boss. He decided against it.

"Did you know your client had a gun at his house?"

"I certainly did not know," Taylor said. "Nor would I have condoned it."

"Did you or Farley ever think to ask Lee how many guns the family had at their home?"

Taylor became indignant. "Now, hold on. I was standing right there with you in court when the judge ordered Lee to turn over his guns.

As far as I know, he did. I don't search my own client's house to see if he's hiding something. Nor am I required to. If I had and found a gun, I had no obligation to tell you anyway. As a matter of—"

Jones wrapped his giant hand over Taylor's mouth.

Taylor's eyes grew wide.

"Is your client going after anybody we should know about?"

Taylor shook his head and looked to Farley, hoping for some backup.

"He's gone, Jonesy, that's my guess," Farley said. "That's why he took the cash. He's in Mexico by now."

Jones let go of Taylor's mouth.

Taylor shook his head at Farley. "What cash are you talking about, Donnie? Agent Jones here never said anything about any cash. Have you been holding back from me?"

Farley looked like a kid who had been caught doing something bad to the family dog.

Jones only had to take one step toward him.

"He called last night," Farley blurted. "He told me he was taking the cash and going to Mexico."

The lawyer's duty of loyalty and the attorney–client privilege applied. Neither Taylor nor Farley had an obligation to report their client was thinking of making a run for it.

Jones jabbed a thick finger in Taylor's chest. "People are going to know about this. I'm going to tell them the horse shit you pull. You won't get a break from an agent or prosecutor anywhere. You are in my doghouse, mister."

Taylor fired Farley the moment Jones left.

It wasn't personal. The whole point of Farley was to create trust and goodwill with law enforcement. Farley's value to Taylor was now zero. Taylor wouldn't have a hard time replacing him.

CHAPTER 62

BEFORE HE WENT ON THE RUN, THE FBI HAD NO BASIS TO LOOK AT Lee's computers. Once he did, the techs in D.C. had no trouble tracing Lee's past search history.

In the world of big data and interconnected databases, even a lousy police department like Blanton had access to an extraordinary amount of information.

Lee didn't even have to hack into anything.

The day Farley first called him and predicted he would need to find a lawyer, Lee pulled up the Blanton Record's Division database and found out Assistant U.S. Attorney Lizzie Scott signed a subpoena for his personnel file. Agent J.P. Jones served it.

Lizzie's home address and phone number weren't listed. The DMV wouldn't give it up without a hand-delivered subpoena or court order. The California State Bar website showed her birthdate. He started punching it into state and federal task force lists, but got nowhere until he found a U.C. Irvine Law School directory for first years. Lizzie's home address and phone number were listed. She'd forgotten that. It was so many years before she became a prosecutor.

After that, Lee seemed to lose interest in her.

The rest of his research was about fleeing. He checked travel sites, mapped out routes through Mexico, figured out how to hide money transfers to foreign accounts.

After reviewing all of it, a hastily convened meeting of FBI analysts and behaviorists in Quantico produced a rare consensus.

Based on computer evidence, demographic studies, and what they knew about Lee, they decided it was more likely than not that Lee was on the run, probably to Mexico.

They put his threat assessment as high—better safe than sorry—but bet that he'd kill himself before he tried to kill anyone else.

Once again, science let Lizzie down.

· · ·

LEE'S POLICE TRAINING MADE HIM GOOD AT STALKING. BUT IT wasn't that hard. Lizzie Scott had to be at work every day, which meant she had to leave work every day.

A week after he'd found out she signed the subpoena for his personnel records, he waited for her to leave work and followed her home.

When she wasn't at work, he checked out her place, seeing which windows could be easily popped open.

Then he fucked up. Stopping her on the road was stupid. Talking shit to Jones about seeing her was also dumb. He blamed the stress. He wasn't thinking clearly. The Marshals weren't exactly staking out her place, but they sent patrols. Santa Ana cops were doing drive-bys. He could see that by checking their radio traffic.

Her house was too hard a target. But he had options. You didn't have to be a genius to know she spent time in other places. Her fat-ass mom's house, the fucked up Convocation Hall parking lot every Sunday.

Then it occurred to him that he didn't have to know where she was going. Again, he just had to be there when she left her house to go there. All he needed was a clean ride, something that wouldn't come back to him. And he knew a great place to get a car.

· · ·

POOR VERN MOELLER.

Blanton wanted to fire him for screwing up the Rincon shooting investigation. The "Justice for Rincon" committee picketed City Manager Cooley's office, demanding that Moeller go.

That was fine with Moeller. He didn't want to be a cop anymore anyway.

But his lawyer Dickran Drooyan, wouldn't let him quit.

"You can't sue for wrongful termination unless they terminate you," Drooyan explained. "Just wait for them to do it."

They transferred Moeller to "jail duty." In reality, they had him cleaning toilets.

"Great," Drooyan said. "It's retaliation for you testifying against Lee. It'll help our case."

He worked a late shift (the only one they gave him, as if toilets could only be cleaned at 3:00 A.M.), then he drove home and fell asleep watching a replay of the Angels lose to Oakland.

At 9:00 A.M., his cell went off with a text. Al Jenkins wanted to see him. He called Drooyan. Did he have to go? The lawyer said yes. Don't give them an excuse to fire you.

Moeller dragged himself into a shower, ate some cold pizza, and stumbled to the car.

He was halfway down the block before he noticed Dwayne Lee sitting in the backseat.

"Holy shit!" Moeller said, jerking the wheel so he didn't ram a parked van. "You scared the shit out of me."

Lee looked bad. "Hey, Vern, how's it going?"

Moeller started to pull over.

"Keep driving, Vern."

Moeller stared at Dwayne through the rearview mirror. Dwayne looked like shit. "What's the deal, Dwayne? You got a plan or what?"

Dwayne nodded. "Drive to the impound lot, Vern."

There were 60 or so seized cars. Most had been towed on parking violations or failure to pay tickets. Lee chose a Trans Am, clean but for a dent in the hood.

"Let's go get the keys, Vern."

Moeller and Lee went to the pimply faced kid security guard. Moeller showed him his badge and said Lee was buying title to the car.

Lee filled out the forms, knowing exactly what each bullshit line required, and handed the kid $320 to cover all fines and tow costs. The kid handed him the key.

When they got to the car, Lee popped open the trunk of Moeller's car.

"Get in the trunk, Vern."

Moeller shook his head. "Please don't make me."

Lee stuck the barrel of the Glock in Moeller's throat and cocked the hammer.

Moeller scrambled into the trunk.

The pimply faced kid didn't even look up when the Trans Am left. It would be three hours before it dawned on him that the other car was still parked in the lot.

Lee noticed the Trans Am tank read near empty.

I can't buy a fucking break.

Lee bought gas.

Then he drove to a Big Five and waited in the parking lot until it opened at 10:00 A.M. Fifteen minutes later, he walked out of the store with four boxes of 9-mm bullets, a hundred rounds per box.

Then he headed toward Santa Ana.

CHAPTER 63

By 10:30 A.M., JONES WAS CONFIDENT EVERYTHING THAT COULD BE done had been done.

Scanlon was safe.

The FBI was looking for Moeller.

Every law enforcement agency in the state was looking for Lee.

Santa Ana cops were parked in front of Lizzie's house.

Judge Letts's chambers had been notified. Lee missed his drug test and was likely in the wind. But Lee wouldn't officially be a fugitive until his case was called at 11:00 A.M. and his failure to appear for sentencing was put on the record. Then bench warrants would be issued for UFAP—unlawful flight to avoid prosecution—the federal version of what the Brits call "doing a run."

Lizzie was dressed and headed out the door when Jones called.

"You're getting a police escort," he said.

"I don't want a police escort."

Jones said it wasn't her decision. The Justice Command Center in D.C. assigned all security calls to the senior FBI agent on the ground, which meant Jones.

"If Lee's going to Mexico, why do I need it?"

Because Jones didn't trust Farley, and he had no corroboration that Lee was actually *going* to Mexico. He had no ties there. And Jones had no faith in the thinkers back in D.C.

Lizzie promised she would drive slowly enough for the cops to keep up with her.

"That's all I ask," Jones said.

Sarah gave her a bag of homemade protein bars to take with her. "Baby needs protein."

Lizzie wanted to scream but didn't. "Just don't tell anybody about the baby. Please. Not until I'm ready. Okay?"

Sarah swore she wouldn't.

When Lizzie walked out of the door, Jack was still there, leaning against his car.

"I thought I told you to leave."

He grinned. "You meant the property? I thought you just meant your house."

She walked up and kissed him on the mouth. "We have to talk today, after court, okay?"

Jack was so thrown by the kiss, he could only nod.

She can't go to D.C. I won't let her go.

Lizzie pulled her car out of the driveway, giving the first Santa Ana squad car time to get in front of her. The second squad car trailed behind.

Jack followed.

There was no traffic that time of morning. Most days, Lizzie rolled out of her driveway and was pulling into the parking garage within 10 minutes, door to door.

Doing the speed limit felt like walking to work. But there wasn't much she could do, boxed in by cop cars like that.

Approaching the four-way intersection at North Bristol and 5th Street, she was tempted to blow past the lead car, but Jones would never forgive her. Plus, she didn't want to get anybody in an accident.

The lead cop car went through first.

Lizzie dutifully followed at a modest 25 mph.

She was thinking about what she would tell Jack about being pregnant, trying to imagine how he would take it . . .

That's when Lee smashed the Trans Am into her.

He timed it just right, catching Lizzie's car when it hit the middle of the intersection, t-boning it at the driver's door. The momentum of the crash carried both cars 30 yards down 5th Street.

Lizzie never saw or knew what hit her. The crash rocked her body to the side as the air bag exploded, stopping her momentum and hurling her back hard against the car's seat.

The lead Santa Ana squad car braked then threw it in reverse. The follow car veered off. Jack, two blocks behind, saw smoke and fire as a third car passed him.

Lee staggered out of the Trans Am toward Lizzie's car, the Glock in his hand, his face shredded bloody from flying glass.

Lizzie lay in the seat of her car, unconscious. The distance between Lee and Lizzie was a half-length of car, 10 feet at most. He lifted his arm and aimed at her head.

"Gun!" All four Santa Ana cops drew down on Lee. But none of them had a safe shot. Lee was too close to Lizzie.

Lee fired at the cops in front of him, pinning them in place, then emptied his clip at the cops behind him.

Lizzie choked and spat blood. She couldn't see anything because of the glass, the gasses from the air bag, the blood that flowed into her eyes.

She heard the metal snap as Lee clicked out the empty clip and jammed a fresh one home. He kept the cops down with more fire as he stumbled toward the driver's side window, smashed out from the crash.

Lizzie turned toward him, sensing his movement rather than seeing him, feeling the threat. She could hear him breathe, could feel his breath now hot in her face. Something bad, something terrible was about to happen.

Dear God, please, please...

BOOM.

She heard the shot rather than felt it. A wall of sound and pressure exploded against her, deafening her, blasting something hot, thick, and wet into her face.

Lee's head disappeared in a cloud of red mist.

Each cop looked at the others, knowing he hadn't fired the kill shot.

Jones fired it. He stood at the intersection of North Bristol and 5th, next to his Crown Vic, with his father's .38 still smoking in his hand.

Jack ran by him toward Lizzie.

Jones never told anyone that Jack was crying.

CHAPTER 64

LIZZIE HAD FACIAL BURNS AND CUTS, A BROKEN COLLARBONE, two broken ribs. She was lucky not to be blind, paralyzed, or dead.

Jones visited the hospital every day. Per FBI procedures, he was on administrative leave until the review board cleared him on the shooting.

"They're saying it was suicide by cop," Jones told her. "I just wish Lee hadn't made me take him out."

Mrs. Leonard visited, bringing along her own plastic surgeon to make sure Lizzie's stitches were done well. A host of Lizzie's fellow prosecutors also came, including Berg, who came by too often. Lizzie threatened to obtain a restraining order.

Jack came, too, twice. Both times, Lizzie was sleeping. She never saw him.

Jerk.

The Chief came, bringing a plate of homemade Italian wedding cookies and a dictionary of opera terms. He never mentioned the case or the crash or the job in D.C.

"I think I'm going to stick in Santa Ana, if that's okay with you, Chief," she said.

The Chief didn't seem terribly upset. He actually smiled at her.

Mom and Dad never left her side. They were always shy around "outside people." So, too, were the many Convocation members who came to hold prayer vigils, even though Lizzie wished they would stop.

But she drew the line at Elder Evans. "Do not let him come here."

"Oh, Lizzie, that's not right," Mom said. "It was Elder Evans's prayers that saved your life. And the precious life of the baby."

Lizzie was still pregnant.

Sarah was still unreliable.

"I had to tell Convocation what to pray for," Sarah said. "It was life and death."

As it turned out, this was one time where Lizzie was grateful Sarah couldn't keep a secret.

Because they learned about the pregnancy after the accident, the Convocation community never had time to raise moral qualms. They knew a miracle when they saw it.

Despite the horrible crash, the baby was still alive.

Thanks to Elder Evans.

. . .

DRIVING HOME FROM THE HOSPITAL AT AN AGONIZINGLY SLOW PACE, Sarah promised Lizzie that she would be out of her house as soon as Lizzie was well enough to look after herself. Until then, Sarah was going to nurse her back to health.

That night, Lizzie asked the question that had been on her mind for days. "Did you tell the people I work with that I'm pregnant?"

For a fleeting moment, Lizzie actually thought she saw The Look pass over Sarah's face.

"I didn't tell all of them," Sarah finally said. Tears welled in Sarah's eyes. "I just told Jack, so he could pray for you."

Of course you did.

Tears now streamed down Sarah's cheeks. "I told him when he came to visit you at the hospital the first time. Which was really nice of him."

"Go on. How did he react? What did he say?"

Sarah sniffed and wiped her tears. "Well . . . he seemed kind of shocked."

I bet.

The fact he never came to the hospital when she was awake told her all she needed to know. It was what she always suspected. She loved Jack. But she had no faith in him.

Sarah waited for Lizzie to yell at her. Instead, Lizzie kissed Sarah good night.

Lying in the dark, over her own objections, Lizzie did something she swore she would never do again.

She prayed.

She thanked God for saving her life and the life of her baby. It seemed ungracious not to.

She asked Him to send peace to the soul of Joe Rincon and comfort to his grandmother.

She asked Him to give strength to Lee's widow and kids. She asked these things, despite the fact she had no faith He would deliver or that He even existed.

I should really see a shrink.

Finally, as she fell asleep, she swore that she would not, under any circumstances, *ever* have anything more to do with Handsome Jack.

Aknowledgements

THIS BOOK COULD NOT HAVE BEEN WRITTEN WITHOUT THE
friendship and inspiration of my old colleagues at the United States
Attorney's Office for the Central District of California.